MY MISSING SISTER

DIANE SAXON

Boldwood

First published in Great Britain in 2025 by Boldwood Books Ltd as *Cuckoo in the Nest*. This edition published in 2026.

Cover Design by Head Design Ltd

Cover Images: iStock

A CIP catalogue record for this book is available from the British Library.

Paperback ISBN 978-1-83518-081-5

Large Print ISBN 978-1-83518-080-8

Hardback ISBN 978-1-83518-079-2

Ebook ISBN 978-1-83518-082-2

Kindle ISBN 978-1-83518-083-9

Audio CD ISBN 978-1-83518-074-7

MP3 CD ISBN 978-1-83518-075-4

Digital audio download ISBN 978-1-83518-078-5

This book is printed on certified sustainable paper. Boldwood Books is dedicated to putting sustainability at the heart of our business. For more information please visit https://www.boldwoodbooks.com/about-us/sustainability/

Boldwood Books Ltd, 23 Bowerdean Street, London, SW6 3TN

www.boldwoodbooks.com

Skye, my Startlewood Ice Queen.
06.01.2010–11.04.2025.
The inspiration for my DS Jenna Morgan series and the trigger for my
desire to murder.

1

PRESENT DAY – SUNDAY, 17 AUGUST 2025, 3.30 P.M. – ALEX

Why is it people assume everyone loves Prosecco?

I *hate* Prosecco!

I raise the narrow glass and plaster on a grin as I clink it against the other three.

It doesn't make the beautiful ring of expensive crystal; instead, it gives a weak clunk of cheap glass. That's the first thing that will need attention. I'm no snob, but I can't bear inferior products. I'd rather do without than suffer the humiliation. I've had enough of that in my life.

'Cheers!'

I tip my head back because it's the only way to take a swig from these stupid bloody glasses, especially if you have an actual nose.

'Congratulations.' Phoebe smiles up at me.

She's a short, plump woman with hair dyed a strange burgundy. It looks as though it was originally a deeper, richer colour but has slowly washed out, letting the original boring brown show through in streaks, heavier at the top where the roots have grown.

Her eyes also reflect a dull brown. As though she's not exactly overjoyed about me being here at all.

The feeling is mutual. This is the last place I want to be, but I don't have a choice. It seems, possibly, neither do they.

Her lips turn up at the edges in a fake smile. I can tell it's fake because it doesn't reach those lifeless eyes.

You'd think she'd put in a little more effort. Be grateful.

And that tall guy, Saul, the one with anxiety bleeding through the cracks of a confidence he's evidently holding on to by the skin of his teeth. Just in case I change my mind and the whole deal falls through. Not that I'm going to allow it to. According to the landlord, they need me more than I need to be here – they're desperate for my monetary contribution, otherwise they'd have to pay a third of rent and rates instead of a quarter. I noticed the term in the contract. It's put pressure on them. Made them rush to take someone in, which suited me just fine because little does the landlord know it's what I want. They may need the money, but I'm the one with a purpose.

With a gulp, I down the contents of the glass in one go, hoping my distaste for it doesn't show as I keep my gaze firmly on Saul. It's a guy thing.

His eyes seem to dart around the room. It's a telltale sign he's hiding something.

Gotcha!

Is he the weak link? Does he have secrets? Or is he keeping them for someone else? Exactly what, I'm not entirely sure.

Time will tell.

Before he starts to hop from foot to foot with discomfort, I take pity on him, give him a slow smile and move my attention to the last of the three.

Jill's chipped, nail-varnished, bitten-to-the-quick fingers squeeze the stem of her glass until I wonder how much more pressure it will take before the bowl separates from the stem and pops off. She's barely taken a sip, and it occurs to me, perhaps she's not keen on the overly pretentious drink either.

She's a tall, leggy blonde, her hair cut into a stylishly short, messy bob, thick fringe almost hiding those moss-green eyes as she peers at me through the curtain. If I'm not mistaken, there's a shy flirtatiousness in her expression I wasn't expecting.

To test the waters, I smile back, and her lips stretch upward in immediate response. One that makes my heart stutter and her cheeks flush.

Hmm.

My smile isn't so much pleasure as calculating. A thoughtfulness. Because this could be useful. An ally, if you like. Someone already in the camp. A friendly face.

Because the other two don't seem to be able to hide their hostility.

Considering it's my money saving their arses from being thrown out of their precious, wonderful house share. That's what the landlord implied, in any case. He was in a bit of a rush, said he might have to sell if they couldn't pay the full amount. Sounds like he might have been applying a bit of pressure. Blackmail, so to speak. It suited me.

A house share which was previously for four and is again now with the addition of me. Maybe they struggled with the cost.

Jill puts her glass down and snatches up the pen lying across the last page of the rental agreement. 'I think we pre-empted with our celebrations. Perhaps you should sign before we forget.' She waggles the pen at me, a small enticement. A flirtation again and I reach for it. Our fingers brush for one brief moment and Jill's eyes widen in surprise as though she felt the same electric shock I did. It's only static, hardly instant attraction, although there is no denying she's pretty.

She is not what I am here for.

Phoebe takes another swig of her drink and instantly tops her glass up, not bothering to offer the bottle to anyone else, her sullen gaze cruising over me. 'We thought you were a girl. Alex. The name, it's a girl's name. I just assumed—' She cuts herself off and tips her head back to take another gulp of the cheap Prosecco.

I raise my eyebrows. 'Is that a problem?' To be honest, no one has ever mistaken me for a girl. Alex is just one of those names. I never wrote Alexander. I rarely do.

She runs her tongue over her teeth and makes a smacking sound, her eyes meet mine and then slide away as she shrugs. 'Makes no difference.'

How come it feels as though it does? Maybe it's the disappointment lacing her voice.

She finishes off the rest of her drink, clicks the glass down onto the kitchen surface and wanders over to the window, her back to me. Have I just been dismissed?

I glance at the other two, puzzled. Jill looks uncomfortable, but there's a definite look of superiority on Saul's face.

I bow my head, take a moment before I scrawl my signature across the page and glance up just in time to catch the blaze of triumph in all three of their expressions as Phoebe turns as though she sensed the moment I made the last flourish of the pen. I gave myself a moment to disguise my own eagerness before I lifted my head. It was a deliberate move. I knew what I was looking for, but who knew it would be so blatant?

Evidently, my three months' deposit and this month's rent are desperately needed. If I had a fistful of cash, I swear they would snatch it from me.

My signature was only a technicality. After all, the transfer has already taken place, hence the celebration. Perhaps they'll be able to afford decent bloody glasses and a better-quality Prosecco now. Personally, I'd settle for a good long glass of Guinness. Just the one, mind you, as I have complete control over my drinking habits.

'Well,' I smile. 'Here's to great days ahead and a happy partnership.' I treat them to a wide grin, but only Jill responds with a weak smile as though she's become aware of the atmosphere and isn't sure how to respond.

'I guess I'd better unload my car.'

The term 'rat up a drainpipe' occurs to me as they quickly disperse, each of them mumbling under their breath about what job needs to be done, phone calls need to be made, a Teams meeting to join. Somehow, I don't think this lot are going to offer to lend a hand.

This is going to be interesting.

There seems to be a lot to hide here. There's certainly a lack of camaraderie. It makes me wonder if there is any kind of loyalty. How long it will take before one of them breaks.

Before the truth comes sliding out. Before I tease it out of them.

After all, that is what I am here for. Isn't it?

To find out what the hell has happened.

2

TWENTY-TWO YEARS AGO – SUMMER 2003 – ALEX

The summer sun has scorched the slide so much that the backs of my thighs stick and even my thin shorts can't protect my arse from burning as my flesh adheres to the scalding metal. I fling myself onto my back, lifting my legs high and fly down the slide, my bony spine grinding against the slippery surface. I skid off the end to land on the bright yellow spongy safety flooring which scrapes a layer of skin off the back of my legs.

A pain so intense, it feels like flames, licks at me, sending my nerve endings into convulsions.

I leap to my feet and rub my arse, my legs, almost crying with the agony, while my feet do a very unhappy jig across the hot ground.

Tinkling laughter catches my attention and I stare at the small girl in front of me. Eyes as blue as the summer sky fill her face until everything else fades, even the voices of surrounding children, until all I can hear is her laughter against a background shushing noise.

I should be angry. She's laughing at me. But, somehow, there's no meanness in her laughter as she takes a step towards me. I could shove her over and walk past. See how she feels when she hits the ground.

I narrow my eyes and give the busy playground a quick scan to see if anyone is watching.

I bet no one would notice.

Instead, my gaze returns to her little doll's face with its short button nose and rosebud mouth.

I get a squirrely feeling in my chest as I stare. The laughter drops from her face and she holds out something she'd had behind her back.

'Borrow this, if you like.'

She's holding out a bright yellow pad, like a seat cushion, but it's flatter and has what looks like a handle.

'It's very good and Mummy says it stops your bum from being hurt.'

Her voice is angelic, soft, with barely an accent to show she isn't from around here. I could have guessed that. The third eye is missing from her forehead. My dad always says that about the locals. He says they're as thick as the day is long. Which doesn't make sense to me, but he knows best. He's always telling me.

I take the pad, hesitate for a moment as our hands meet on the handle and give her a swift, wordless nod of thanks. Despite thighs throbbing with heat, I'm still willing to give it another go and I dash up the long set of steps, breathless as I reach the top of the slide. This time I whoosh down and fly off the bottom, landing feet first. With a whoop of laughter, I hold the pad out to the little girl and she grins just before she takes a dash to the steps.

Her legs are short and chubby, and I wonder how old she is as she takes one deep step at a time, her left leg leading, hauling herself up by the handrail, the yellow pad held loosely in the other hand, flapping around her knees as the gentle breeze catches it.

By the time she reaches the top, she stops behind three larger kids who've overtaken her on the steps, barging her out of the way. With a decided lack of temper, she blows out a breath so her fringe flutters away from her forehead while she waits her turn. She grins down at me and then shuffles onto the pad once the other kids have come down.

As she sits, the glint of the slide seems to take on another gleam, a softer, wetter look and I realise as I glance at the sniggering group of kids who barged past her that the last one deposited something. Maybe water, although it has an oily glow.

Little fuckers, as my dad would say.

I open my mouth to warn the girl, but it's too late and she shoots down the slide at breakneck speed.

'Noooo!'

The distress in a woman's voice behind me doesn't slow me down as I power towards the bottom of the slide, hold my arms wide and as the little girl launches off the end, eyes wide with terror, I take the full force of her body slamming into mine.

With a 'whoof', I wrap my arms around her and crash backwards onto the ground, not even acknowledging the pain as I lie with her cradled against my chest. Her face is nestled into my neck and for a moment I think she's crying, but when she raises her head her eyes are so wide they almost bug out of her face.

'You saved me,' she breathes, her little face filled with awe. I've never had anyone look at me like that in my life. Like I'm her hero.

'Nikki! Oh my God, Nikki.' The woman who screeched pulls the child from me, snatching her into her arms as she hunkers down next to me.

'I'm fine, Mummy.' Nikki's voice is strangled as though she's holding back tears that shock had held in abeyance. 'The big boy saved me.'

The woman turns her head, her eyes a mirror image of her daughter's. Her smile falters. 'Thank you so much. I wasn't close enough to get to her in time. That was so brave of you.'

I'm still flat out, disadvantaged, as I struggle to push up onto elbows that burn as though they've been set on fire. Despite being taught never to show pain, I can't help the whimper as I fall back down. My left hand cups my right elbow and slippery wetness fills it. As I draw it away, Nikki cries out at the sight of my blood-smeared hand.

I put on a brave face, but it's really hard.

'Yeah, the kids over there put something slippery on the slide.' I try to distract them.

'Oh, no!' The woman gives a peremptory glance at Nikki as she stands her on her feet, brushing at her T-shirt and shorts, and then crouches over me. 'This is not good.' She glances at me, giving me a quick all-over assessment. 'Where's your mum?'

I shake my head and consider whether to cry, like my dad tells me to if ever I need to get out of a situation. Unless that situation involves him, in which case, I get a hard slap if I even shed one tear. I'm too old to cry – ten, soon to be eleven – and too proud. One look at Nikki's face and I grit my teeth, determined to be brave for her sake. I don't want her to feel guilty. She's about the only person who's been kind to me in so long I can barely remember.

To avoid leaning on my elbows, I roll onto my knees and push myself to my feet, using hands which leave bloodied prints on the dirty yellow flooring.

'Oh, you poor child.' Nikki's mum takes hold of me by both arms to keep me still. Normally, this would be the red flag to run.

But I don't feel inclined to. She looks around. 'Is your mum some-where near?'

'Nah.' My voice is gruff and while I try not to sound ungrate-ful, the likelihood is, I'll get a thrashing far worse than this when my dad finds out. Not because I've hurt myself, but because I didn't knock the block off the boys who did it. Or he might wallop me for rushing to help Nikki. However he sees it, he'll call me a pussy and get me to put my fists in the air to defend myself.

But there's no defence from him. The loud crack of his palm against my cheeks as he dodges my fists is a regular sound. Apparently, it's not hitting if you don't make a fist.

'Who's looking after you?'

Her voice is so lovely. Refined, with the softest undertone of husky that makes you realise how safe this little girl, Nikki, is in her mum's care. My empty stomach rumbles. I bet she gets a proper dinner tonight.

I know I won't. Firstly, because Dad has gone out on the piss because he got his benefits payment today, and if I'm lucky, he might roll on by the town park and pick me up on his way to the bedsit we're currently placed in, otherwise, if he forgets, I'll have to find my own way back there. I'm not entirely sure of the address. They all blur into a haze after a while. Seven days here, ten days the next.

Some kids can't wait for the summer holidays. Me, I dread them. I like school. I'm good at spelling and maths. And besides, at school I get fed. Some days Dad will forget altogether as he sleeps off his hangover and there's never anything in the cupboards.

The woman is still staring at me and I remember she asked me a question.

'Oh, my dad. He's...' I nearly say buggered off but remember my manners just in time. 'He's had to go to the shops, so he left me here. Told me not to talk to anyone.' I give a weak smile as though he's a responsible adult.

From her narrowed eyes, I suspect Nikki's mum doesn't quite believe me.

'How old are you?' The question is casual, but I wonder whether I'm about to drop my dad in the shit. At what age can you abandon a kid? I mean, it's one thing for kids to be playing out around their own homes, but this is a public park, acres of it rolling through the middle of the town.

'Ten.' I puff my chest out. 'I'll be eleven soon, though.'

Nikki grins and there's a gap where two of her bottom front teeth are missing, incisors if I remember correctly. It gives her a cute look of a slightly manic fairy as her blonde curls bob around her cherubic, flushed face.

'I'm five!' she announces proudly and imitates my movement exactly, her skinny chest expanding, her shoulders back. 'Nearly six.'

Nikki's mum opens her mouth and I wonder if she is about to contradict her daughter, but she merely closes it again, her lips twisting as if to say, well – not for a while.

I get that look. She smiles and it's as though we just shared something. A small confidence.

After a moment, she sighs and digs into a huge handbag she'd dropped between her feet as she'd squatted next to the pair of us on the ground. She draws out a packet of wet wipes and hands one to Nikki and two to me. Obviously, I am the dirtier of the two of us. I was a bit scruffy anyway, even before the tumble. I scrub at my hands and then move to wipe the blood from my elbows, but she stops me.

'Ooh, ouch. Wait. I think we should take you to the first aid centre.' She points in the general direction and my muscles clench. Fear chases a chill down my spine, my dad's voice in my ear.

'Don't draw attention to yourself, do you hear, you little shit?'

I shake my head. 'I'm okay.' I attempt to wipe my elbows again with the now filthy wet wipes, but she stops me, taking them gently from my numb fingers and placing them in a small plastic bag, she's taken from her immense handbag, I assume for rubbish.

'Hold on. You can't do that, you'll get it infected.' She takes hold of me by the shoulders and turns me so she can inspect my elbows. The sting has died down, leaving a burning throb.

As she straightens, she holds both hands out, one to Nikki, the other to me.

'Come on. I'm not messing around. What did you say your name was?'

Clever of her, but I didn't.

Dad always tells me never to give my name. Not to strangers, not the cops, and certainly not to social workers. Schoolteachers only when I am in school. But there's something about her that makes me want to be honest.

'Alex,' I mumble, and against my better judgement, I take this lady's cool hand in my burning one and can't help smiling back at Nikki as she pokes her head around her mum's skirt and gives me a wide grin, showing more gum than teeth, which in turn makes me smile back at her. I don't know what it is about her, but she's so cute.

As we reach the first aid centre my muscles turn to liquid and I think I might just pee myself. Leaping in front of a flying little girl didn't faze me, but this? This is different. This is adults. Looking. Judging.

Dad says they'll take me away from him and lock me up so I

never see the light of day again if I complain about him. What he means is, if I tell the truth of how he neglects me. On occasion I've wondered if it isn't the better option.

The instinct to run is undermined by my muscle weakness and the pure fact that Nikki and her mum are staring at me, faces filled with – something. Concern? I don't know. Whatever it is, it makes my chest ache.

'Alex, sit down.' Nikki's mum's voice is gentle, not demanding, but persuasive and full of expectation.

I do as I'm told and within minutes, there's a young woman tending to me, cleaning up my wounds with some strong-smelling liquid that stings initially and then the hurt is taken away while I stare all the time into Nikki's beautiful eyes.

'What's your name?'

I turn my gaze to the stranger and my lips seal tight over my words. It's none of her business.

'Alex.' Nikki's mum places her hand on my shaggy, overgrown hair and she gives it an affectionate scrub. Like she knows me. Like she's familiar. 'He saved our Nikki from what could have been a very nasty accident, didn't you, Alex?'

The way she words it, there's no question I'm with her and as I glance up through my eyelashes at her, she gives me a conspiratorial smile and a wink.

I want to grin, but I lower my head and watch as the first aider finishes cleaning me up and then attaches a gigantic stretchy plaster to each elbow.

'You're such a brave boy. Would you like an apple?' The first aider gives an aside like we kids can't hear her. 'It used to be lollipops, but health and safety have put an end to that.'

'An apple a day keeps the doctor away,' Nikki sing-songs, and I grin at her.

My mouth waters. I'd devour an apple. I'd rather have fruit

than some stupid lollipop in any case. I haven't seen a piece of fruit in months. Maybe longer. Not in our house. Not since Mum...

'Yes, please.' I remember my manners. I'm not a heathen. Despite what my dad calls me. He's not the one who taught me those manners. My mum did. I've not forgotten.

I stand and wince as my thighs stick to the plastic seat.

'Oh, Alex.' Nikki's mum takes a gentle hold of me and looks at the back of my legs. 'You look like you've been burnt.'

'I stuck to the slide. It was so hot.' My voice is a low whisper, shame lacing the words. 'That's why Nikki gave me her cushion.'

'Aw, sweetheart.'

'We can put some of this on.' The first aider holds up a tube of something before she takes the lid off and squeezes it onto her fingertips. 'It's just an after-sun, but it'll take the heat out. There's no blistering, thank goodness. Now, Mum, when you get home maybe a cool bath will do Alex good.'

I open my mouth to deny I'm her son, but something makes me close it again. It's not doing any harm, and I can do without questions being asked – where is your mum? Oh, your dad's in charge today, is he? He needs to come and collect you. You'd better stay with us. We'll call social services, or – worse still – the police.

I can just imagine my dad's face when the police deliver me back to his door. Because he's not coming to get me. Certainly not from here.

So I keep my mouth closed. I don't miss the long look Nikki's mum gives me either, as she says nothing at all.

Instant relief floods over me as the young lady smooths the cooling lotion on and my eyes prickle like I'm about to cry.

But I don't want to. I don't want to look stupid in front of Nikki and these women.

My smile wobbles as I pull it into place and Nikki reaches for me, gently pushing my hair back from my face in an imitation of her mum earlier, her little plump hand smoothing across my overheated forehead and cheek, her skin smooth and cool. I almost want to take her into my arms and cuddle her, like a long-suffering teddy bear. God, this is killing me.

Instead, I take hold of her hand and link my fingers through hers. 'Shall we go and play? We can go on the swings.' My heart is full of hope.

I've got nothing else to do, no one else to play with. I want company.

The first aider closes her eyes briefly as though she can't believe I'm going back out to the war zone.

Nikki's mum straightens with a groan as her knees crick and grind. 'Thank you so much,' she says to the woman. 'I think we're probably done for today, Alex.'

I can't hide the disappointment as the smile slides from my face.

She tilts her head and meets my gaze. 'I think it's time for something to eat. What do you say?'

My mouth salivates at the thought of food. Any food. There's just one problem.

I give an awkward shrug and lean forward. 'I don't have any money. Dad forgot to give me any,' I mutter into her ear, ashamed to voice it, and she smiles that soft smile. It's not so much he forgot to, he wouldn't dream of giving me cash. The tight git. He has better things to spend it on than feeding me.

'It's okay. My treat for being such a hero, saving Nikki and getting yourself injured in the process.'

I nod. Is it more polite to decline or accept? I think I'd upset this nice lady if I said no, and besides, I'm absolutely ravenous. My stomach lets out a robust gurgle and Nikki's mum grins.

'Right, then. As long as it's okay with your dad. What do you think? Shall we ring him?'

I shake my head. 'He doesn't have a phone, but he won't be back for a while anyhow. He'd only just left.'

Which is a complete lie. I'd spent the entire morning at the library reading before I came out. At least there I could go into the loos and drink water from the taps when I was thirsty because Dad never left me with anything. Not food, drink or money. He never does these days.

'Okay, give me a minute; I'd better make sure someone takes a look at the slide.'

When Nikki's mum returns, we all thank the first aider for her help as she hands Nikki and me an apple each. My mouth waters as I crunch straight into mine. A great big bite of the shiny green apple. I screw up my face at the tartness and Nikki laughs as she hands hers to her mum who slides it easily into her big bag.

She leads the way to a restaurant, only a five-minute walk from the first aid building, so by the time we arrive, I've finished my apple and lob the core into a bin, swiping sticky fingers down my already filthy shorts.

I've seen this Italian restaurant before with its tables outside and the bright yellow striped canopy offering shade from the relentless heat of the sun, but I've never been before, even when Mum was around. We always just went to the library and then back home again to eat sandwiches made with thin bread and a single slice of ham.

As we slide into seats, a waitress approaches, high ponytail swinging wildly as she bounces on her toes and puts down some menus, a broad smile on her face. There are cushions on the chairs, and I wonder if that was the reason Nikki's mum chose this table as not all of them do. Considerate of my sore legs and bum.

She's a nice lady.

I like her.

She passes me the children's menu and I glance over at the one she has.

I can read all the words, even the really long ones. The teacher at my last school said I have a reading age of a fifteen-year-old. Dad says that's great, it means I don't need to go to school any more. I think he's joking, but I'm not sure. I'll find out in September when I should be starting Year Six.

Nikki's mum sees me staring and hands me the adult menu. 'I think you might have outgrown the children's menu. Did you say you were ten, Alex?'

'Tell nobody nothing, got it?'

My dad's voice echoes in my head, but it's too late. I've already told her more than I should, but the likelihood is, I'll never see these people again.

'Yes.' It's not a lie – I'll be eleven in another month, just when we return to school.

'Wow. I actually thought you were older. You have really good vocabulary.'

I stare at her.

I don't know how to respond. I'm big for my age, I know that. Teachers are always telling me I am. I pluck something out of the air.

'I can spell the word v-o-c-a-b-u-l-a-r-y.' I almost cringe as that's unbelievably simplistic. Any kid could spell that word.

'That's really impressive, Alex.'

I shrug. It really isn't. Maybe she's just trying to flatter me as I've not said anything particularly clever yet. Dad says it just sounds fucking precocious and to keep my gob shut when adults are around. And I know what precocious means too. It means being a little shit, according to Dad. But I think I can be a little more myself with this lady, not hide what I am.

'I see words and numbers in my head. Like pictures.' The words blurt from my mouth without thought and Nikki's eyes go round, while her mum's eyebrows lift into a look of surprise.

Mum said I'm really clever, but I don't mention my mum to this woman.

My mum taught me to read. When it was just me and her and my dad was out drinking, and she wanted to distract us both from the bruises on her cheeks and neck. I could read anything by the time I was eight. Sometimes, she'd close her eyes and let me read *Peter Rabbit* to her when she was just too exhausted to go on. When she was sprawled across my bed fast asleep, I'd sneak and get one of her books for adults. The ones she said weren't suitable for me. But I loved them.

We don't have books any more, but Dad drops me at the library not out of the goodness of his heart, but so he can go for a drink after a hard day. His hard day finishes at 3 p.m. because he told work he needed to be home for his son. Work is cash in hand, so he can still claim benefits. Mostly, I go at the weekend when he just wants to get rid of me, so I'm not under his feet.

Every day is hard according to him.

Not as hard as it was for Mum.

'Alex?'

I snap my head back up and catch the curiosity in Nikki's mum's eyes before she manages to veil it.

'I said are you ready to order? My treat.'

This woman, this stranger is going to let me order whatever I like from the menu.

I draw in a breath. I could take her for everything, like Dad would tell me to. But I can't. Why would you ever rip off someone who is being generous?

'A pepperoni pizza and a glass of milk, please.' I remember my manners and catch the quick rise of her eyebrows.

'Milk?'

'I like milk too.' Nikki smiles at me and the shock on her mum's face is comical. Like Nikki has never drunk milk in her life.

'O-kay.' Her mum draws the word out.

'It's very nutritious,' I reply, and watch the surprise lighten her features again.

I like this woman. She sort of entertains me. I feel no judgement, just something light-hearted, like she's actually enjoying talking to me and I'm not a burden.

The waitress returns and Nikki orders a glass of milk and a child's portion of ham and pineapple pizza, making me wonder why anyone would want pineapple on a pizza. Having said that, if I was hungry enough – and I have been – I'd give it a go.

Nikki's mum gives me the nod and I order my food and drink too, then she orders a Caesar salad, a side of fries and a glass of white wine.

Tension tightens my muscles, spreading so my shoulders start to swallow my neck.

I try not to look, but she's going to start drinking. And we all know what happens when adults drink.

I lower my chin and drop my hands under the table so she can't see my fingers shake. Perhaps I've made a mistake trusting these people. I'll eat and get out of here before she has too much. I don't need to witness this.

'Alex, is everything okay?'

The waitress arrives with our drinks in time to distract Nikki's mum and I force a smile as I pick up my glass of milk and down half of it in one go.

'Wow! You're thirsty!' Nikki laughs and takes a sip of her milk before putting it back down. Her heart-shaped face is so cute with its little milk moustache. She starts to wipe it off with the back of her hand until her mum gives a delicate cough and she picks up the white serviette with writing around the edges and dabs like a precious princess. My heart squeezes. I wish I had a little sister.

Her mum's eyes narrow as she contemplates me. 'I think you might be a bit dehydrated.' She looks at the waitress as the woman places her wine down in front of her, condensation frosting the glass and dripping onto the table. 'Could we have water for the table, too? Thank you.'

I eye the glass of white wine, and then drag my attention back to Nikki, who is tugging at my arm, asking a question.

'Which school do you go to?'

'Tell them nothing, lad. Hear me?'

I give an uncomfortable shrug. There is nothing to tell, really, except the truth. 'We've just moved into the area, so I don't know. Dad is trying to get me into school, but we don't know which one yet.'

'Oh.' Nikki's mum leans forward, her fingers on the stem of her glass to move it to one side without having to take that first desperate slug. 'I wonder if I can help. I'm a teacher at Nikki's school. We're local.'

A chill runs through my veins as the terror of what Dad will say hits me if he knows I'm speaking with someone in authority. He's right, I should have kept my big gob shut, it just invites questions if you engage. He's going to kill me.

My appetite dies.

In the silence, I realise she's observing me. Then she reaches out a hand and places it on mine. Her fingers are cool and soothing. 'Perhaps we'll leave it for now.' She glances over my shoulder. 'Our lunch is here.'

The fast rush of hunger nearly floors me. If I hadn't been sitting, I would have collapsed as the warm smell of garlic and pizza dough washes over me, weakening every muscle. I nod my thanks and scoop up one of the slices of pepperoni pizza as Nikki's plate is placed in front of her. I consider waiting, but the temptation is too much, and I raise the slice to my mouth, taking a huge bite.

The heat of the melted cheese isn't enough to stop me, and I groan with the sheer ecstasy of combined flavours.

Nikki's mum pauses with a forkful of chicken and lettuce halfway to her mouth and grins. She taps her chin and Nikki giggles.

I swipe unsteady fingers over my chin, and they come away smeared in grease and long, stretchy cheese. Nikki laughs again and I can't stop myself from laughing back. She's the sweetest thing and none of her laughter is cruel.

She takes a huge bite of her own pizza, her lips pulling back to expose little white teeth with that large gap at the bottom and closes her eyes in an imitation of me making muffled groans.

I barely notice as her mum picks up her wine and takes a sip, but something in the back of my mind registers when she places the glass back down and then pours water for all three of us.

She's not swigging her wine, desperate to get whatever that kick is my dad is forever searching for.

Nikki chatters away, telling us about her friends and how she can't wait to tell them about the boy who rescued her from smashing her face in.

Her mum's brows twitch as Nikki goes into detail about her near miss, an exaggeration of the actual events. By the time she's finished both her story and pizza, I realise her mum has pushed the portion of fries into the middle of the table and I'm happily helping myself without even acknowledging her generosity. I'd have had a hard backhander from Dad if I'd so much as dared to take some of his food. Mum always gave her food up for me, though. It had seemed so natural, I'd automatically moved back into family mode. Basically, it's not been that long since Mum—

The fry sticks in my throat for a moment as memories of Mum flood my mind and I find I can't swallow.

'Alex, are you all right?' The concern washing across Nikki's face brings me back to the present and I reach for the last of my milk to wash the glut of food away while I nod.

'Yeah, it just stuck there.'

She laughs and the moment of sadness rushes away as she belts me between the shoulders with a pudgy hand. I let out a laugh too and the tears that threatened dry up.

I don't know what makes me like this little girl so much, but there's a bond I know instinctively isn't going to be broken easily.

I pick up my napkin and imitate Nikki's mum, dabbing at my mouth instead of using the back of my hand which still has smeared yellow grease across it from earlier. I smudge that off too.

Just as I plop it on my empty plate, my attention is caught by a movement way beyond Nikki's head in the distance.

I stiffen.

It's him.

I don't even need to see all of him, I just know his overexaggerated swagger, shoulders flopping forward, arms swinging like a silverback gorilla as he pushes his way out of the automatic doors from the mall.

I'd recognise that walk anywhere.

The ball of grease in my stomach curdles and I swallow hard to keep it down as the waitress brings the bill and Nikki's mum pays her with a swift waft of her card over the top of the waitress's payment machine.

I'm too distracted even to consider this means she won't leave a tip on the table that I might have been able to swipe away without anyone noticing.

In the meantime, Dad is walking straight towards us. Probably on his way to look for me.

I slip from my chair and force a smile at Nikki and her mum. 'I need the loo.'

Panic is slicing through me. I don't want them to think I'm rude, but I do not need my dad seeing me with this kind woman and Nikki.

I can tell from his loose-limbed walk he's pissed out of his brain again and I can just imagine the abuse he's going to sling at these lovely people.

I edge my way around Nikki's mum so she blocks his view of me.

I lower my voice so he doesn't hear me, because I know the sound of his voice carries to my ears from miles away and perhaps the same is true of mine.

'Thanks for lunch. I really appreciate it.' I give her my best, confident smile because I know I'm going to slip away as soon as I've been to the loo, washed the greasy evidence off my hands and face and possibly climb out of the window. It won't be the first time I've had to do that, but normally because Dad can't afford to pay.

'It's my pleasure.'

There's a ripple of guilt and it compels me to rattle on. 'I need to get off now. Dad'll be expecting me home.'

Surprise flashes over her face and I realise I've made a mistake, of course. This woman is not stupid.

'I thought you said your dad was coming back for you?'

'I did. Then we have to go home. I bet he's looking for me.' I almost say he's going to give me a right bollocking but think better of it. I may not see Nikki and her mum again, but I still want them to think well of me.

'It would have been nice to have met him.' She squints as she looks up at me, her gaze conducting a slow perusal of my face.

My heart judders. Nikki and her mum meet my dad? You've got to be shitting me. I can't think of a worse scenario. He'd take one look at Nikki and a vile sneer would pull across his face that I would dare to associate with a girl. One so much younger than me. Another look at her mum, and he'd do that horrible, embarrassing assessment of her. And she'd know, because Nikki's mum is smart. I know she is.

'Maybe another time. I'd better get off.' Panic is a bird fluttering in my chest, trying to escape.

I automatically scrub a hand over Nikki's head and she leaps up, wrapping her arms tight around my waist and resting her head on my skinny chest. The panic in me stills for a brief moment until she lets me go.

'Bye, my hero.' She grins and steps back.

Nikki's mum smiles as she loops the strap of her open handbag over her shoulder, ready to get to her feet too and I consider how easy it would be to take her purple purse lying on top of everything inside. The way my dad taught me. Desperate times call for desperate measures, as he often tells me. And we are desperate.

Ever since Mum left.

Instead, I tuck my hands in my shorts pockets and bob my head, refusing to give in to the temptation to steal from this lady.

'Thanks again for the food. It was really kind of you. See you around.'

I slink off towards the toilets and stay in there for ages, taking my time going to the loo and then washing my hands. I don't want to come out and bump into Nikki and her mum again. I can't risk them meeting my dad and telling him what a hero I am. I know what he'd have to say, and partly it would involve him holding his hand out for a cash reward for my act of heroism.

The window is too narrow and small to squeeze through, so I bide my time and then sneak out again.

I scan the area and, in the distance, going into the mall are Nikki and her mum.

I take off in the opposite direction in pursuit of my dad, surprised he even came back for me.

3

PRESENT DAY – SUNDAY, 17
AUGUST 2025, 9.30 P.M. – ALEX

I cross my arms over my chest and stare out at the garden where my three new roomies are still sitting in front of their pretentious little firepit, which they don't need to have lit because (a), it's not dark, and (b), the temperature's not dropped below 28 degrees centigrade all day. We're having a frickin' heatwave. Even now, there's not a hint of a breeze in the air. Which is just as well, otherwise that firepit of theirs could quite easily set the whole neighbourhood alight if one of their sticks they've collected from the neighbouring woodland spits again.

Don't they know wood needs to be seasoned before it can be used? If it's still green it spits like hell, creating sparks. Even in a firepit. Especially in an open firepit. To my mind, they're too ignorant to buy the right stuff to go on it.

Or too broke.

It's not like they've used it to cook anything, which would have been sensible, practical. I might have joined them, but they seem to have been relentlessly drinking since around 4 p.m. this afternoon, not counting the bottle of Prosecco they consumed rather swiftly when I arrived. Would it be because I paid three months of rent in advance plus this month's share?

I sigh.

As far as I know, the money went straight to the landlord. But obviously it's eased the pressure for these three. Were they so desperate? That short of money, all three of them? Panic-stricken in case they had to pay the additional sum?

I don't know what I was expecting when I signed up for this. But this wasn't it. It's not like I'm about to get rich fast here, especially if they drink away the rent and then expect more. They won't get more from me.

This, for one thing, was not what I thought I'd be doing. Then again, I'm not here to make friends and influence people. I have a mission to accomplish. It's not official and I'm not being paid to do it. This is personal.

There's a burst of laughter and they all look my way as though they heard my thoughts.

I place my palm on the window and absorb its coolness, the heat of my hand causing a bloom of fog to trace its outline. If that lot weren't in the garden, I might have pressed my cheek against it too. But despite the lights behind me being off, it seems everyone can see me. As I just recently discovered after I unpacked my meagre belongings, there are no curtains, there's also no privacy whatsoever.

That was the other thing I never expected.

This is a three-bedroom house. Because there are four of us, it appears I've drawn the short straw and been allocated what surely was previously the dining room. I know I was the last to arrive, but this seems critically unfair.

The smell of stale cooking seeps through from the kitchen and I suspect it is always going to be the case as even with the doors closed, the smell will percolate through the ancient, old vents just above the skirting boards.

When I first walked into the room and opened the empty wardrobe, I wasn't sure, but I thought I smelled a familiar scent lingering on the air. Whether it was wishful thinking, my imagination or real, it's been swept away by the other, stronger smells.

I let my gaze cruise over the cheap white PVC-framed wide patio doors and wonder how many times someone has tried to break and enter through these. I don't *imagine* it's an easy task. I know it is. At the end of the day, there's a lot my dad taught me. Most of it bad and certainly none of it to boast about. Once in a while, that knowledge comes in handy.

On surveying the room, I can't believe no one had a set of double bedding to lend me. By the time I'd brought my stuff in, unpacked and chatted to the less than animated housemates for a couple of hours, which felt more like drawing teeth, it was apparently too late to visit one of the local shops.

Local isn't always best. Not when you have a car which gives you access to a twenty-four-hour supermarket.

I pick up my bunch of car keys which is now slightly heavier than before, with the addition of three extra keys. One for the front door, one for the rear door into the kitchen, right next to my patio doors, and the third for those patio doors themselves. They are apparently only accessible from the inside.

Of course, these are the type of doors you can simply lift off the sliders. If you know how.

And I do.

I slip out the front door, closing it with a soft snick behind me.

I don't let them know I'm going out. We're all grown-ups here, right? It's not like we're family. If I was polite, I could have asked them if anyone wants anything. But I don't feel we're quite that friendly. Not yet in any case. Not the way they eye me with suspicion. It makes me edgy. I'm the one who came here to extract information from them, but they're the ones who appear wary, as if I have something to hide. Which, admittedly, I do. I never thought I would be the one under suspicion, though.

One thing I did notice is there's not a lock on my bedroom door. There's a bolt on the inside, so once you're in, you're safe. But if you're out, how do you know who is snooping around in your space? Wouldn't you think previous tenants would have sorted security out with the landlord?

I need to fit a lock of some sort.

That is something I need to check if I'm allowed to do, because although I've not had time to read all the small print of the tenancy agreement, I think I noticed somewhere in there that we can't even put a nail in the wall to hang pictures, or drill holes to attach curtain rails.

There's a curtain rail already up, but it looks yellowed and ancient. I'll pick myself up a new one. I didn't measure, but you can get those expandable ones and I have a rough idea how long it needs to be. Estimating is something I'm pretty good at.

More important than the bedding, curtains are an essential item to my mind. I've got a sleeping bag in the boot of the car which I'd have managed with – let's face it, I'm used to it, I've used it on and off for the past eighteen months – but it's a bit rancid and sandy now.

What I want, more importantly, is privacy.

I do not need these people spying on me and just from the short time I spent with them sitting outside, when I could feel their eyes on me, I'm not happy. Wouldn't you think there would be curtains from previous tenants?

I park my car up, grab a trolley and stride through the long aisles of the supermarket until I reach the homeware aisle.

I can't help but smile as I look at a smart range of matching curtains, bedding and bath towels all neatly stacked. Who would have thought to match all of those? Nikki maybe, but not me. I've lived my life accepting what I'm given and thanking my lucky stars on the occasions when it's not hot pink, Barbie-themed bedding.

Not that I have any objection to Barbie, but when you're an eleven-year-old lad, it's not always the best image you can portray, even if you are desperate and grateful that it's clean at least.

It takes me a moment to select the entire set of clean-lined navy blue and white, and I take a guess at the curtain size. Although they are long, ceiling to floor, I suspect they won't be wide enough, so I choose a second pair and stack them in the trolley. I have a budget and I'm almost at the end of it. Not that I don't have any money, but most of it isn't in this country right now.

My stomach rumbles, reminding me I've had nothing to eat since a slice of toast at breakfast. Nobody offered me a sandwich or a share of their dinners. They all saw to themselves, barely talking as they shuffled around each other in the kitchen. The cupboards looked pretty empty, so I didn't like to ask. I've not been brought up to ask.

I race around the store, chucking in a couple of boxes of cereals, long-life milk, some tins of baked beans, soup and a few packs of own-brand flavoured rice. They're bound to have bread and some kind of spread back at the house, aren't they? Not entirely sure they would, I chuck in a loaf of thick white bread and some cheap butter.

I whack in a pack of four green apples.

An apple a day keeps the doctor away.

I smile as the saying dances through my mind.

By the time I've finished, my small borrowed car is stuffed

full, but there's a deep satisfaction that I'm getting myself sorted. I need that. A little stability just to keep me straight.

I cruise slowly down the road lit only by occasional street-lights. The deep navy of the sky forms a canopy overhead where stars hide in plain sight.

The house lights are all off as I park up in one of the two designated spaces and wonder where the others park their cars. If they have them.

There's a campervan parked on the road, and I wonder if it belongs to any of them. Old, classic dove blue and white. Bit rough, but one of those vehicles everyone seems to have an affection for. It occurs to me how much more I could have stacked in there if it belonged to me. As it is, my car is a hire car for the next three weeks. Unless I have to extend my time, of course. I'm hoping I will be done by then.

I fill my arms with bags and stride up the three long concrete steps to the front door. I jiggle my packages, leaning them against the door as I insert my key, turn, and – nothing!

It doesn't work.

What the hell?

I turn the key the other way, struggling to see in the dark porchway, but it's the right key. Isn't it?

I wonder if anyone noticed that I'd gone out because if so, wouldn't you think they'd leave the light on? I'm sure it was on when I sneaked out just over an hour ago.

I place everything on the ground, balancing the packages on top of each other and rummage for my phone so I can check with the torchlight if I have the right key. I try the other flat one, but it doesn't even fit. The third key is an old-fashioned round barrelled stem one which, if I remember rightly, they said was for the back door.

I pick all my shopping back up, trudge down the long side alley to the back gate and—

Shit!

It's locked.

'Guys!'

I haven't been gone so long, surely they're still in the back garden. The scent of woodsmoke trails over to greet me, which is all I get by way of a greeting.

I raise my voice slightly, hoping my new neighbours don't give me hell for disturbing everyone. Hardly an auspicious start. 'Guys! Could someone let me in?'

I'm met by silence, although I swear I hear a faint giggle.

Could it be my imagination?

I've almost lost the will to live as I trudge back to my car and dump the shopping back in the boot because it seems ridiculous to keep lugging it around. Locking the car, I head back and hammer on the front door.

I can scale the fence and take the patio doors off but it all seems a little melodramatic at this point, and in any case do I need them to know my skillset? It might just upset the whole applecart.

Stepping back from the porch, I look up at the windows. Every single one of them is in darkness.

This is so peculiar. Surely after I left, they didn't all immediately retire for the evening? I know what girls can be like, they have to do the whole make-up removal, cleanse, moisturise, teeth-brushing procedure. It's not like I haven't lived with women before.

Maybe Saul doesn't, but how weird is this? Every one of them in bed, fast asleep within an hour of me leaving the house?

No, this isn't coincidence, this is deliberate.

It feels like a set-up to me.

They've given me a key that doesn't work and bolted the back gate.

I don't think for one minute it's an oversight.

The bastards have locked me out.

4

___

TWENTY-TWO YEARS AGO – AUTUMN 2003 – ALEX

The worst thing about starting a new school is that moment when every single child swivels their head on their neck, craning to get a good look at you because they've all been together since nursery and you're a misfit.

I'm not actually a misfit, but in the last year, I've been to four different schools because my dad can't stay out of trouble. We're also on our eighth house. We started out by just sofa surfing as my uncle called it, until he threw us out because Dad drank all of his collection of whisky, filling the bottles up with cold tea to disguise the fact. Something my uncle found out the moment he'd poured himself two fingers after a long, hard day pushing paper. I never understood exactly what it meant, either the two fingers, which had a different meaning in our house, or pushing paper, which Dad often said sneeringly about his brother's job. Odd thing was, Uncle Alan was the one with the nice house, great car and a speedboat he kept on some dock somewhere we never had access to. Probably because he didn't trust Dad. He also had a long string of girlfriends with whom we were apparently cramping his style.

As weak tea sprayed from his lips that day, he turned a vibrant blotchy red, his bulbous nose bordering on purple.

'Jesus, Paul, I know you have your problems and I'm sorry about Lily leaving you, I truly am, but you can't just fucking drink all my whisky and not even have the decency to tell me! It's deceptive. Underhand.'

'I thought you wouldn't check, Alan. It was just sat there, going to waste.' Dad's voice took on that slight nasal whine I've heard before when he's trying to wrangle his way out of trouble. Especially with his brother.

Uncle Alan's mouth dropped open as he picked up two more bottles and sniffed the contents, already wise to the fact it was going to taste disgusting. But not the disgusting smell of whisky, which burns the nasal hairs from you, as I found out when I took a sniff, but the soft floral scent of weak tea.

'They were not going to waste. They're special. You're the one who wasted them by guzzling three whole bottles in under a week. That's just sheer fucking bad manners, man, with everything I've done for you.'

'You've done nothing for me,' Dad had raged. 'You won't even let me have a key to the front door!'

'If I gave you a key to the front door, I'd come back from work one day, and you'll have cleaned me out. Pawned everything you can pick up and burned everything you can't. As it is, you've managed to slug down my whisky, I assume in the middle of the night when I've gone to bed.' Uncle Alan had blown out a breath, shaking his head, disappointment in every line on his face. 'You can't be trusted.'

Dad's face had turned ugly. 'You've never given me the chance, you git.'

'You ungrateful bastard,' Uncle Alan countered with a low growl. 'Get out! Out of my house.'

'You fat shagger!'

Dad's rheumy eyes met mine as he put a hand on my shoulder, his thick fingers digging into the skin through my thin T-shirt. 'Let's go, buddy.'

'You can leave Alex, he's done nothing wrong.' Uncle Alan's tone dropped down to reasonable in an instant, which maybe Dad saw as a weakness.

'Where I go, the boy goes.'

'You've got nowhere, mate. Leave him with me until you find somewhere safe.'

Dad leaned into my uncle's face and snarled, 'He's better off with me than with a paedo, now fuck off.'

'No. You're the one who needs to fuck off, Paul,' Uncle Alan had replied, his face stiff with insult, but strangely absent of fear. Most men would have been bricking themselves in the same situation with my dad in their space.

So we did indeed fuck off.

Which is why we were in a one-room bedsit for a short while, with a Calor gas ring we kept hidden in Dad's backpack, so the mean fucking landlord didn't kick us out. How else are we supposed to heat our baked beans up, my dad wanted to know? But we still got kicked out.

I guess I should be grateful, because when Dad insisted he could make his own way, and keep his own son safe, he very nearly damned well killed me.

The sun is beating through the deep windows and my eyes flutter as tiredness overwhelms me.

'Alex?'

I jerk my head up and realise the whole class are looking at me again. It's nearly lunchtime and I am weak with hunger and desperation, knowing this meal may be the only one I get for the whole day.

Limbs that Mum had declared not so long ago were going to make a Premiership footballer out of me have now turned to string as my bones grow, the muscle thinning out with lack of sustenance.

My eyelids are heavy as I look at the teacher. 'Yes, sir?'

The man looks more resigned than disappointed. 'Nine times table, young man.'

I recite it, flying through the rhythmic pace as fast as I can, using the special finger technique my mum taught me, but almost not needing it any longer, it's just a habit.

Surprise lights the teacher's face.

'Well, thank you, Alex. I didn't quite mean for you to recite the entire times table, but I appreciate that you can. Perhaps next time you will listen to the question.'

I think I'm pretty good at reading people. I've had to become good for my own self-preservation. Although perhaps Mum taught me that skillset too before she left.

I am taken by surprise because despite the teacher's words his brow has wrinkled, and his mouth is twisted in a puzzled smile. He turns away, opens his mouth to address the classroom, and then closes it and looks at me once more.

'Alex, do you know your seven times table?'

'Yes, sir.'

As I recite it without hesitation, the numbers appearing in my head like the writing on a blackboard, he leans his bum on his desk and crosses his arms over his chest, his eyes narrowing and the quirky smile still on his face. I don't use the finger technique this time, it's the wrong table for that.

The whole class are staring at me as I finish.

I do know my times tables. Everyone should. I knew them by the time I was six.

Mum said I was a bright spark, but it's just the pictures in my head.

'Alex, what's thirteen times eight?'

As I rattle off the answer, the teacher pushes upright. 'Five times eleven times six?'

It takes me a second. I see the figures in my mind and the answer is there just waiting to be plucked out. I flush as the teacher gives a slow clap at my answer, and the rest of the class join in. I'm not sure they know why they are clapping and I'm pretty positive I failed to impress most of the lads, but the girls look animated.

I'm not sure if this is a good thing or not. Dad always says to keep my head down, don't get noticed, but there's a thrill coursing through me. A wobble of pride building in my tummy desperate to be released from the confines I've kept it in ever since Mum left. It just wants to break free.

She was always proud of me. Always telling me what a bright boy I was. Not like Dad, who says I'm thick as shit, but he doesn't know. How could he? He's never so much as read a book with me or helped with homework. Mum said it was in case it made him look bad. He said I got Mum's brains because he's still got his. He thought it was hilarious. Mum didn't, but she never said a word. Just the slight thinning of her lips gave away her annoyance. That was just before he belted her around the head for not laughing.

The dinner bell rings and I'm the first to my feet, my stomach roaring to let me know how much I need this food, because I can't actually remember the last proper meal I had. There was a can of beans and a slice of bread yesterday. It's not like Dad can't afford it, he won't. He'd rather spend it on the poison he's pouring down his throat, as his previous girlfriend said when we spent a couple of nights at hers. Truthfully, she seemed quite happy to guzzle it at the same rate until it was all gone and then the two of them argued after they'd consumed the last bottle of beer.

At least she seemed to have enough control to keep a roof over her head and hold a job down. She said he was a bad influence on her just before she chucked us out her door without even a look at me. I never existed as far as she was concerned. I was the sofa surfer and he got to share a double bed with her this time. At least we both got to have a couple of hot showers and wash our clothes before we were thrown out. I mean, who wants to look mank on their first day at a new school?

As it was, I was the one who went into the charity shop and found a second-hand uniform. The sleeves on the jumper are a bit short, my skinny wrists showing, but everything was clean and only cost a fiver for the whole lot including three shirts – the collars were a bit thin – and a pair of size seven shoes that were a bit big, but I could slip on two pairs of socks and I'll soon grow into them. The woman in the shop said she'd throw them in for free, seeing as they were a charity, because at the end of the day charity begins at home. I have no idea what she meant – my home has never been charitable – but I wasn't going to look a gift horse in the mouth.

God only knows where we'll sleep tonight. I think Dad said he still had the key to the one-bedroom flat we've used a few times. I'm not sure we're supposed to as Dad makes me sneak in, dead quiet. He says his name is on the list, but as this place is still unoccupied, we can use it for a while. I have no idea what list we're on, but when we get to the top of it, everything is going to be all right. That's what he tells me, every bloody day. In the meantime, this is heaven, even though there's no hot water and the leccy is off. It's not so bad this time of year, but I hope we're not going to still be here in the winter. I hope the council find him a place to stay that's more suitable. The trouble is, he told them to *stick it* not so long ago when they said we were on the list, just when he thought we were going to get all snuggly with his newest woman.

He says I'm to keep quiet so none of the social workers come around and take me off him. I've figured out he probably only wants to keep me because he gets some sort of payment if he has a kid. I can't imagine there's any other reason he wants me with him. He says I'm a liability. A stone around his neck. There are times I wish he would cut me free and I could find a nice, normal family to live with.

I'm at the door to the classroom when the teacher calls my name. I turn and he's beckoning with one finger for me to go to him.

My heart sinks. What now? I hope he's not going to question me. I hope I'm not in trouble. Worse still, has my dad done something and they've decided they no longer want me? Just like the long list of people he keeps pissing off.

'Alex, you seem to have a really good way with numbers.'

I'm not sure if he expects an answer, so I say nothing. *Keep your mouth shut, son, then you can't get in trouble.* Perhaps Dad should take a leaf out of his own book, because if he kept his gob shut, we might get to stay somewhere for more than a week.

The teacher's quiet sigh wafts across the top of my head and I look up at him.

There's something in his eyes that makes me uncomfortable. A poorly disguised sympathy, I feel. Does that mean he already knows about my dad? They all get to know sooner or later. Normally just before we move on.

'We have a special after-school club for kids who really like mathematics.' His voice is soft, persuasive. 'Talented kids, like you. Do you think you'd like to join us? It's on Tuesdays for an hour.'

I have no idea if my dad is going to let me, but I nod, still without saying a word. Sometimes it's easier just to agree.

He reaches his hand out and I flinch, before realising he was about to rest it on my shoulder, not belt me around the ear.

He drops his hand, but his eyes delve into my soul. A soul that cringes, curling up into a ball of mortification. Oh, yes. This man knows. Maybe not the how and why of things but certainly the what.

I don't want him to dive any deeper and at that moment my stomach leaps out a roaring rumble of hunger and breaks the spell which could have developed into an intimacy I don't want. I don't need this man's pity. I don't need his help. I just want to be left alone so no one knows the truth of my life.

His face suddenly creases into a smile as though he understands that too, and he nods. 'Off you go to lunch then. I hope we see you tomorrow. The club's straight after school and it's in this classroom.'

Terror clutches at my insides as I dash first to the bathroom before I pee myself. I scrub my hands and scrub and scrub but still the dirt doesn't seem to come off them.

There was something about him, his pity maybe, that made me feel like a grubby little stoat. I'm sure he didn't mean it, but I've learnt to avoid any sort of curiosity. Another hard lesson courtesy of my dear dad.

As I reach the dinner hall, excited voices reverberate around the high-ceiling room until it vibrates with energy. I don't know the process here as everyone is already seated.

Do I just...?

'Alex.'

I spin around and the maths teacher is behind me.

'Sir.'

He passes me, and with a casual glance swipes up a dinner

tray and hands it to me, taking up one of his own. 'I'm on play-ground duty.' He turns to the short lady behind the serving counter, with greying locks peeping out from beneath a white cap and a round face with cheeks flushed and shiny. 'Mrs Dancy, any chance of extras?'

She gives him a cheeky grin and piles his tray high. 'This isn't extras, this is a normal-sized meal for you.'

'Ha! Thank you.' He lifts his chin to indicate me. 'This is our new lad, Alex. He needs extra too, he's a growing lad.'

I don't object as she dollops mashed potatoes and minced meat on my plate. I think it's cottage pie but who knows? It's not exactly neat.

It looks nothing like my mum used to make and the peas aren't a fresh, bright green but a sort of dull sage. I know the word, as it was Mum's favourite colour. For clothes, not peas.

The mound of carrots she piles on is probably because no one else wanted them, but I'll take them. There isn't much I won't eat.

She then spoons a load of trifle into the other section on the tray and smiles as she persuades one more spoonful on. 'More than I gave Mr Shaw.'

Relieved she'd said his name because I couldn't remember being told it, I hold the now heavy tray and raise my chin, looking directly at her.

'Thank you, miss.'

Her smile widens, dimpling her ruddy, rounded cheeks.

'I do like good manners.'

'She'll remember you, lad. Extras every day if you play your cards right,' says Mr Shaw and I'm not entirely happy about it. I don't want to be remembered. Dad tells me not to attract attention.

There's not a lot I can do. As the saying goes, the die is already cast. That's what Dad says about his run of bad luck. I'm not sure

I'd classify what's happening to us as bad luck so much as bad choices my dad keeps making.

I look around for somewhere to sit but as usual in these schools all the tables are full with kids who already know each other. They have their cliques and no one makes it obvious that they want me in with theirs.

Mr Shaw walks past me to the far end of the hall where there's a taller table and chairs with adults seated talking quietly to each other. He's not noticed my dilemma and I really would prefer he didn't. It would be so embarrassing to be seen as teacher's pet if he tried to squeeze me in at a table with all my classmates. I don't need enforced friendships.

Lost in my own thoughts, I stare at the teacher's table.

I've never been in a school where the teachers eat with the kids. It's odd. Then again, this school isn't much like most of the ones I've been to before. Its old building is probably Victorian and all the walls are tiled in the halls. The rooms are huge, but there aren't as many pupils as I'm used to. Most places I've been able to disappear in the sea of faces.

'Alex! Alex!'

It's a cheerful, childlike voice and I scan the room, recognising it instantly.

The bright coils of Nikki's hair bounce around her face as she leaps from her small plastic chair and waves a hand in the air. 'Alex, over here.' Her brilliant blue eyes sparkle at me. Here, I feel somehow more exposed.

She grabs the vacated chair next to her and grins. At this point I could completely ignore her and turn to sit with some of the bigger kids because she's five years younger than me and what boy my age sits with a little kid? But for some reason I'm drawn by her complete disregard of anyone else's opinion.

I barely place my tray on the table, and she's on her feet,

wrapping her arms tight around my waist, her head tucked into my armpit, and she squeezes until I think my lungs are about to puke out of my mouth.

'This is Alex, he saved my life,' she announces theatrically to the surrounding girls, all agog with interest.

I know her tinkling laughter should bug me but God, she makes me feel so good.

So normal. I want to wrap one of her curls around my finger and give a little tug just to see her laugh.

I peel her arms from around me and slide into the chair next to hers, scanning the faces of the heavily girl-laden table. They're all grinning at me like loons. Most of them have a front tooth missing, but all of them have long, shiny hair of varying colours and shades.

It's like being surrounded by a flock of birds, all of them twittering at the same time and it seems to be attracting the attention of the kids on the surrounding tables.

To be honest I'm not worried. I should be, according to my dad, but he's not here and what he doesn't know can't harm him. That was a favourite saying of my mum's.

I'm too hungry to care though, so I start scooping potatoes into my mouth and just listen to their happy yammering around me as Nikki explains how I saved her life, embellishing the event so I sound more like a superhero. At least I didn't burst out of my clothes and turn green, or run into a phone box to pull on a pair of knickers over blue tights.

'And if Alex hadn't been there, I would have smashed my face in and Mummy would have had to take me to hospital. To A and B. And he burnt his legs and scratched his hands and there was blood gushing from his elbows.' She leaned forward in a conspiratorial manner. 'He never even cried.'

The girls all gasp, admiration staining their faces, and I can't help but grin. I don't correct Nikki on the A and B matter, but the words accident and emergency flash in my mind, just the way they did when Mum broke her wrist and we had to go to hospital on the bus.

It wasn't Mum who broke her wrist. She had her wrist broken for her.

I blink away the image and concentrate on my food.

This cottage pie is incredible. Who knew it would taste so good? Even those strange-looking peas taste okay and the over-cooked carrots fill a hole in my belly.

As I start in on the trifle, I'm aware of a strange hush.

I lift my head and the girls are all staring.

That's when I realise I'm eating like a rabid animal. Not stopping even to breathe.

I lower my spoon and sit back in my chair to give each one of them the benefit of my inquisitive stare, as though they are the rude ones, not me. Somehow I lost track of the conversation, but they don't seem to care much as they start wittering again as though nothing happened.

As I finish up, Nikki swaps her tray with mine, her untouched trifle still there and I realise she never started it the moment she noticed how ravenous I was.

Heat swarms up my neck and over my cheeks, but she makes nothing of it. She doesn't even mention the fact that she's swapped our trays and none of the girls surrounding us even appear to notice.

When I've finished, I sit back and just listen, my stomach swollen so the skin on it is stretched hard enough to play it like a drum and my chest swelling with something I can't quite describe, but it's a kind of comfort. A feeling I've not had in such a long time. That of belonging.

Movement catches my attention and a tall, beautiful woman

stands from the table where the staff are all seated. There's a half smile on her face I instantly recognise as she approaches.

She slides a hand onto my shoulder as I look up at her, sun filtering through the high window behind to form a soft halo surrounding her hair.

My empty heart fills with joy as I stare into the blue, blue eyes of Nikki's mum.

'Hello, Alex. I hoped we might see you again.'

5

There's no food!

What the hell type of house is this?

I bought cereals, bread and milk, enough to last a whole month, and here we are only four days later and everything I stacked in the cupboards and fridge freezer has gone.

I open the fridge and reach in.

'Don't touch my yoghurt.'

With a guilty spin, I face the short woman who seems to have appeared out of nowhere. Phoebe is running a brush through soaking wet hair so bright green droplets flick onto the cracked tiles of the kitchen floor. She's got a towel over her shoulder which appears to be tie-dyed green. I have a horrible suspicion I recognise it as one of my brand-new ones, but I say nothing.

'I wasn't going to. I don't like yoghurt.' Well, that's a lie as I'd eat anything, although truth be told, I'd have to be almost starving.

'Good! And don't touch anything else in there either.'

'Well, someone's had all my stuff. Milk, pizza, cereals and I'm bloody hungry. I've been at work all day.' Hangry is the term I would have used if I'd been speaking to Nikki, but it's not her and I'm not sure this little woman would get it. Also, I'm not exactly being truthful. I've not been at work. I've met up with a couple of guys from work I know and I've been dabbling, trying to find things out.

Her faded eyes spark with something like annoyance. 'Don't put it in there, then.' She shrugs. 'I put my name on everything, but it still goes missing from time to time. Thieving bastards. No respect. If you want to make sure your food doesn't go missing, hide it.'

'What?'

'Hide it.'

I spread my hands, palms up. 'That's so juvenile. We're not at uni.' My experience at uni was nothing like this as I was so much younger than the rest of them, but I'm not admitting to any of these that kind of information.

'Maybe so, but if you want to eat, you look after your own food. Keep it in your bedroom, or in your car.' Her tone is a little derogatory as she mentions my car, making me wonder whether or not she has one. She opens the fridge and takes out the lone yoghurt with her name taped to it. 'And don't take anyone else's or there'll be hell to pay.'

'Why doesn't it work when someone takes mine?'

'Because you never labelled your food, so it was fair game.'

'Did *you* take it?'

Without replying, she rips the top off the yoghurt and licks it before dropping it into the bin. She opens a drawer, rummages around, and when she can't find a teaspoon, she picks up a dessert spoon and barely manages to squeeze it into the pot.

As she shoves the spoon loaded with yoghurt into her mouth, my stomach gives a lurch. I'm not a fan of yoghurt, and particularly not peach. Worse though is the way she rolls her tongue behind her teeth as though sieving the yoghurt.

I turn away so she doesn't see my revulsion.

There is literally nothing in the fridge, unless the lump with a greenish hue is cheese. It's not even covered. I reach in and pincer it between thumb and forefinger and turn, ready to throw it into the bin.

'I wouldn't do that if I were you.'

I sigh and chuck it away anyhow. 'How bad can it be? Who wants to keep mouldy cheese?' I almost suggest maybe a previous resident left it there, but I don't want her to turn complete ice maiden on me and kick up any kind of suspicion that I might know something about a previous resident.

Phoebe raises one thin eyebrow and pouts. I can't take my gaze from the smudge of yoghurt at either side of her mouth. Can't she feel it? Why doesn't she lick it off, or wipe it away?

'You'll live to regret that. Jill is going to murder you.' She gives a bitter chuckle. 'Or at least, she'll send you a very strongly worded email.'

I frown at her, not grasping what she means.

'Sorry?'

'Jill—' Phoebe laughs, making a yoghurty gurgle in the back of her throat and I think I may just throw up. This woman is revolting. 'Jill doesn't like confrontation. But if you upset her, you'll know about it.' She takes a short-bladed sharp knife from the open drawer and points it at me like she's about to run me through and then laughs as she drops it back in the drawer with a clatter. 'You know what they say, the pen is mightier than the sword. Well, you'll receive a politely worded, passive-aggressive email.'

I don't let my curiosity get the better of me and merely shrug. 'She doesn't have my email address.'

'Oh, yes, she will have.'

Now I do have to ask. 'What do you mean?'

'We all have your email address. It's important we can contact you.'

'That's not right.' I can feel the heat of annoyance swarming over my skin. 'I haven't given any of you my email address.' I know that for a certainty. It's not written on any of the paperwork they saw. 'The only one who has it is the landlord.'

Phoebe swirls the last of the yoghurt out of the small tub and sucks it off the spoon with a loud smacking of her lips. I try not to cringe outwardly, but from the look of sour amusement on her face, she knows. It makes me wonder if it was all for show. Was she trying to get a rise out of me so she could make some comment about me being intolerant? I don't know.

She dumps the spoon in a bowl in the sink and it clatters to the bottom. Oily residue and a few clots of yoghurt float on top of what I assume is cold water left overnight. I hope one of the others is going to empty it because there's no way I'm sticking my hand in greasy cold water.

Except I might have to because from the rattle the spoon made, it sounds as though the entire contents of the cutlery drawer is in the bottom.

Phoebe makes her way to the kitchen door, flicking still-dripping wet hair over her shoulder as she turns to give me a cold stare. 'Just you wait and see. Jill will have your email address whether you want her to or not.'

She disappears through the door leaving a spatter of green hair dye up the cream walls and a green handprint emblazoned on the white doorframe.

What a dislikeable woman.

I've barely been here a week and already the atmosphere is getting to me. What is wrong with these people? They're supposed to be mature, level-headed professionals, and I barely know anything about them. Except I'm beginning to think Saul is a bit of a prick. This woman is peculiar, and I've barely even spoken with Jill despite our fairly positive start, or so I thought.

Maybe the fact I woke the entire household up the first night hasn't sat well with anyone but, come on! It wasn't my fault the landlord hadn't checked if the newly cut key fit or not and he had to come around the following day to bring me one that worked.

He's a funny old chap. Nothing like the person you think you know from the friendly communications we had prior to me signing the lease, I'd thought from the wording he was much younger than he turned out to be, but then I can hardly complain about him being disingenuous, when I haven't exactly been honest myself. In fact, there's very little truth in what I've told any of them so far.

Tall and skinny to the point of being a cadaver, sallow skin seemed to wrinkle over the landlord's cheekbones, so he resembled an elephant with flaccid skin, like he'd suddenly lost a pile of weight, and his frame no longer filled it out. Dark eyes were sunken into his face, and I suspect he missed nothing as they darted around the place, taking in every last move we made.

It's odd. From experience, I've never known a landlord take so much interest in their property. I've seen him lurking around several times, although we've had very little conversation, except for the first time when he looked me up and down and said, 'I thought you were a female.'

It made me wonder exactly what the relevance was whether I'm male or female. I'm still paying the rent, so why should it matter?

I'd asked then why they'd needed to get a new key cut; wasn't it returned by the previous housemate? None of them knew, let alone cared, including the landlord. She'd done a bunk, failed to pay her rent for three months, and then was gone. He'd seemed bitter about it. Like she'd run off with his money. But I know better. She'd paid her rent in full and simply left early.

I know better, because I know who that tenant was, and Nikki would never have cut loose and run leaving no word, she wasn't the sort. She'd have faced the music first, explained, returned the key and left with her head held high. Nikki is one of the most honest people I have ever known. Also, she wasn't short of money.

So what on earth did Nikki get herself involved in?

And what do this lot know about it?

6

PRESENT DAY – SATURDAY, 23 AUGUST 2025, 7 A.M. – ALEX

Alex, I know you won't get my messages until you arrive back in July with you being 'off grid', but on the off chance you get a signal and an info dump all in one go, I thought you'd want to hear from me.

I really hope you're not homesick. I know you made the right decision, but it doesn't make it any easier for Mum and me knowing you're all alone. Mum said to send her love, although why she can't send it herself, I don't know apart from the fact that she's decided, like you, to go off-piste, deserting me to take a thirty-five day, around-the-world cruise with her friend Bettina. She grabbed it last minute and said it was cheaper than staying at home. I would have gone with her, but there's no way I could afford to go. It's only cheaper if you've retired and got a great lump sum and a teacher's pension with no mortgage. Hehe. I certainly don't begrudge her any of it after all these years of teaching annoying kids – including the likes of you, teehee, and all the late-night marking too. She deserves it.

I wouldn't allow her to pay for me either even though she offered, and besides, I can't take thirty-five days off work. I've worked too hard to get where I am. Ten minutes off this job and they'll have forgotten who the hell I am. 'Go to the city, Nikki, get a great job in sales, Nikki, you'll love it, it's right up your street, Nikki.' Well, hell, it's not exactly turning out that way. I thought I'd be selling classy cars to the uber-rich, or high-end make-up into the likes of John Lewis, maybe even work for a fashion house, but no, the job I fell into out of university is selling medikits to the NHS. Once I make my name there, I can move on to bigger and better things. What tosh!

Anyhow, I digress. If I'd known Mum was going to bugger off and leave me for this long when she retired, I may well have lodged at home, although the travel is a bitch. I may still have considered it, but with her making it last minute, I'd already signed my rental agreement and paid a three-month deposit.

It's quite exciting really to have my independence. To be able to walk back from work, or stumble back from the pub without having to consider a two-hour drive, or that interminable train journey.

You know how much I love Mum, but it's time for us both to have our own space, especially now she's retired. She deserves some time just for her.

I moved into the house share today and I will say it does look like it might be fun sharing with these three. They seem quite the characters. Michelle is tall, beautiful and vivacious. She's the same age as me and sounds like a real party girl. Saul has all the moody blue characteristics I normally go for, so I must watch myself, although it may be Michelle and he are an item. Not sure yet. Will let you know.

The landlord came by to say hello and to be honest, he's a bit grim. I wouldn't want to meet him down a dark alley if you get what I mean. He seemed so friendly when I was talking to him to negotiate the contract, but in person he's all a bit stiff and formal as though he doesn't quite know how to integrate on a face-to-face basis.

I've not met Phoebe yet, but I'll let you know what I think when I do. The other two were a little closed mouthed about her. You know when you just sense something, but can't put your finger on it. I'm wondering if there's a bit of an atmosphere between them.

I'll soon find out.

We're having drinks later to celebrate my arrival. If there's any juicy gossip, I'll let you know.

I know you're not allowed to tell me anything about your top-secret mission but take care. Please be careful out there. Don't take any risks. Time drags without you. Take care, love you loads. Gobbles! x

I trace my finger over the word.

Gobbles.

My lips quirk up at the edges and my heart squeezes as memories rush in.

* * *

'Alex, Alex, come on. Mummy said you're to come home with us,' Nikki squeals as she rushes into the classroom.

I don't hesitate. With barely a backward glance, I throw my backpack over one shoulder and head for the door, knowing their house will be warm in the bitter February chill and I can almost taste the chilli con carne Nikki's mum will make. That or spaghetti bolognese. One of those meals she makes a lot of and freezes in portions because she's too busy to cook every night.

'Goodbye, sir.'

'See you tomorrow, Alex.' Mild relief passes over my teacher's face, I suspect because he has a family to get home to and hanging around waiting for my dad to pick me up is not in his job description. The after-school mathematics session finished almost an hour ago and the rest of the kids cleared off home straight away. Mr Shaw reckons I'm so far ahead with my maths that I could take my GCSE as soon as I go to senior school. He's looking into getting me a place for gifted children in the grammar school and is hoping for an answer anytime now. He says he thinks I'd qualify for a full bursary. I know what it means as I looked it up. It means I get to go to a private school for free.

Dad won't like it, I know, but Dad doesn't need to know yet. Mr Shaw said he'd find a way, when I hinted it wouldn't be easy.

I'm old enough to walk home on my own, if only we were within walking distance of the school, but the teachers know I don't live close by. I don't have any money for the bus and Dad had said he'd come by on his way home with some cash. He's been saying that a lot lately. He's full of false promises.

If he had any cash, he would have drunk it by now.

I know that. Nikki's mum knows that. Mr Shaw knows that.

In the past three months, all the teachers have slowly become aware of my 'domestic situation' as the social worker likes to refer to it. Dad had been keen to move on again, but social services said he couldn't move me this time. I was settled.

It was such a relief. I think Mr Shaw, who it turns out is the deputy head, and Nikki's mum had something to do with it.

Dad had to move us out of the modern one-bedroom flat because the bastard landlord didn't like him. He had something against him. Enough to have him moved on. So now we live in a big Victorian house that's just about to be condemned. Just the two of us while the social make some decisions. We shouldn't have had it, but they considered us a crisis.

It's much further away from the school, but I don't want to move schools. I love it here. I told them when they talked to me and they promised not to let on to my dad that's what I said. They tried to make it clear anything I say to them won't be passed on, but I don't know them. I don't trust them. They've given me no reason to and I am the one who has to live with Dad.

'Gobbles,' Mr Shaw calls out as I stride out the door to chase Nikki along the corridor to the staffroom where her mum will be waiting for me. She could have gone home an hour ago, but I know she's stayed, letting Nikki go to after-school club while she did her marking here just to keep a check on me. See if Dad picks me up. She doesn't want me walking home alone in the dark, very possibly to an empty house with no heating, lighting or food.

'Gobbles!' Nikki shouts over her shoulder to Mr Shaw.

A grin slides over my face.

We charge down the corridor, running, not walking because there is no one else left in the building but a handful of teachers and the cleaners. No one is going to stop us as we slide through the open swing doors into the staffroom.

'Nikki just said "gobbles" to Mr Shaw,' I blurt out, breathless laughter bursting from me.

Nikki's mum gives a wide smile as she casually runs her hand over the top of her daughter's head, then swoops up a briefcase and handbag as we all head for the exit door. 'Ah, gobbles to you too.'

Nikki giggles. 'When I was little—' like she isn't little now '— and first came to school, Mr Shaw used to always say "gobbles" every time I said goodbye. So I asked Mummy why he kept calling me gobbles.'

Her laughter rings out as she puts a hand over her mouth to smother the noise. 'And Mummy said – Mummy said, he's not saying gobbles, hun, he's saying God bless.'

The two curl over at the private joke they've just shared with me and I'm about to join in when the dark shape of my dad storms towards us from the shadows as we reach the main door.

Nikki's mum stumbles to a stop, her hand on Nikki's shoulder, her laughter choking on a sharp intake of breath.

'Mr Whittles. What good timing. We were just about to leave.'

Dad's face is bloated and flushed with anger. 'And take my boy with you?' It's a good guess, because I've been to their house before and he knows nothing about it. He never knew, because when Nikki's mum dropped me outside my house after we'd eaten, he wasn't back yet and the house was in darkness. That was 8.00 p.m. I asked her not to report it.

'No, no, of course not.' Nikki's mum's voice quivers with fear now and the lie she's told as she pushes Nikki behind her.

There's a moment when I think she's about to do the same with me, but her outstretched hand drops to her side. It's none of her business. She can't get involved.

'You better not. His fucking bitch of a mum left me, I'm not having another whore try to take my child.'

There's a shocked gasp from behind me and I'm not sure if it's Nikki or her mum. I cringe with embarrassment at his vileness. He was always like this with Mum, but he shouldn't speak to teachers like this. Especially not Nikki's mum. It's rude and disrespectful. So much so that my shoulders automatically curl in and my spine curves to make me less noticeable, I suppose.

Dad reaches forward and snatches for my wrist with his bear-paw hand, thick and hairy. I try not to cry out because I know Nikki's mum will step in to help, but I also know she'll 'get what's coming to her' as Dad called it whenever he thumped Mum.

I clench my teeth against the pain as he squeezes so hard he grinds my wrist bones until I think they're about to snap. It wouldn't be the first time he's broken a wrist, but it was Mum's back then.

Dragging me along behind him, the waft of whisky and week-old sweat follows us down the narrow school path edging the playground. 'Try to take my kid again, I'll report you to social services, ya slag,' he yells over his shoulder. 'Then see how it feels when *you* lose your job.'

My shoulders droop.

It means *he's* lost his job again. He's always bitter when he does. Like it's everyone else's fault but his own.

How hard can it be to keep a caretaking job? He just has to do as he's told. Keep his mouth shut. He can never keep his mouth shut. Especially as this newest boss was a woman.

A fucking bitch, above her station.

I glance behind us and Nikki and her mum are silhouetted in the main entrance of the school building. My chest feels tight as the soft sound of Nikki's crying reaches me and Dad stumbles through the school gate onto the dirt path leading us along a shortcut home through the woods, letting the darkness swallow us.

The urge to break free and run back to the light is almost too much, but if I do, I put Nikki and her mum at risk and I can't do that. It's the only thing that stops me.

My throat tightens at the thought of having to move school again. Just because of my dad's bad behaviour.

I'm better than that. I'm better than him.

Why should I have to suffer for his actions?

I stumble and he yanks hard at my arm so pain shoots into my shoulder and armpit and I whimper.

I whimper because I cannot cry out. I'm not allowed. Just as Mum was never allowed to make a noise.

My pain is not so much physical, but with each step away, my heart is ripped apart at the thought of being wrenched away from the only school I've been happy at since Mum left, and losing my new best friend.

7

PRESENT DAY – SIX WEEKS
EARLIER, 11.30 P.M. – NIKKI

The house is eerily silent when I arrive home after a couple of drinks with the girls after work. They wanted me to go on to a nightclub, but I wasn't in the mood. I kind of just want to be alone. I'm finding it really odd without Mum to speak with almost daily, even if it is only a quick WhatsApp chat.

I pause on the step. My ears strain for a noise, a sound of any sort.

I reach for the light switch and – nothing.

I blink at the darkness ahead of me. Bloody useless landlord. I'm sure Phoebe said she'd reported the light bulb. He never seems to fix anything and when he does, he creeps around like some strange little hobgoblin sneaking from one room to the next without knocking. It changed my attitude towards locks on doors. Luckily the only time he's caught me out, I was just taking my sweater over my head to get changed. The T-shirt underneath was hitched up but not showing anything of significance, just a little of my midriff.

By the time I tugged the sweater off my head, hair filled with static and standing on end, he was in the doorway, watching.

Dark eyes narrowed in quiet assessment. A quiver of discomfort had run down my spine. I'd not even heard him open my door.

As he stood there, I raised my chin. What would Alex advise me to do?

'While you're here, Mr Goody—' how is that name for irony? '—could you please fix a lock on the inside of my door? I'd be most grateful.' He could hardly say no, now could he? He actually had a screwdriver in his hand and yet I sensed a hesitation from him.

Creepy little guy. I can almost imagine him lurking in the darkened hallway waiting for me to come home. Although we have asked him only to call around between nine and five unless it's an urgent matter. It depends on what you classify as urgent. To be honest, I have very little to do with him as Phoebe seems more than happy to take over the position of mother hen. Well, as far as communication with the landlord is concerned, I'm happy for her to lead the way. I let her know if I need anything, or I've seen something that needs fixing, and she passes it on to him. In all fairness, he's quite quick about fixing things and he doesn't moan. I just don't like him. He makes me uncomfortable. It's his lurking I don't like.

I wonder whether it's him who has turned the electric off to do some job or other, although what he would be doing here at this time of night, I have no idea. Unless it's an emergency.

Still, I don't want to meet him coming the other way down the hallway. Or bump into him in my bedroom.

A light beading of sweat pops out on my top lip and I wipe it away as I hover on the doorstep.

'Hello. Is anyone home?'

My voice quavers and I want to kick myself. Really, why am I such a coward?

I wouldn't be like this if it was my own home. I'm used to

walking around in bare feet in the middle of the night, no lights on. Having said that, I've lived there all my life. Even though my dad died when I was eight months old, apparently he'd had life assurance which meant Mum and I were okay. Financially. I never really knew him, but what I do know is my mum never got over his death, never took up with another man, even though she's been on a few dates here and there. She was too much in love with him even to move house. I love our home.

But this place. It does something to me. Saps my confidence.

I draw in a breath and step inside, closing the door quietly behind me.

Perhaps they're all asleep.

It's not likely. It's one of my bugbears here. Bloody Saul seems to party continually. He's in marketing and all he does is socialise. Frequently here with a string of girls. I have no idea why his girlfriend puts up with him. I've met her a couple of times and she's really sweet.

Sadly, Saul is an arse. I think it took him all of forty-eight hours before he made a pass at me. Up until that point, I'd actually quite fancied him, then the realisation came that he's just a bit of an idiot. He thinks he's God's gift to women. And maybe he is, but not this woman.

The next man I find needs to be faithful and devoted. Not much to ask. Except I also need to love him back.

Sadly, there's a high bar to reach in my expectations.

I put one hesitant foot in front of the other as I work my way down the hallway, a vision of Alex popping into my head and I quickly dispel it. No, I am not going there. He's like a brother to me. Isn't he?

I tap my phone torch on. Darkness seems to press in even heavier on me, a threat to the thin beam of light guiding me through to my bedroom, narrowing in on it.

I open the door and reach around to switch on the light.

Nothing.

Dammit!

That's what's wrong here, why the silence is so dense. The power is off and even the quiet background buzz of electrical items like the fridge and definitely the washing machine and tumble dryer are absent.

I draw in a breath and try desperately not to panic.

None of the lights in the street were off, not that I noticed, and surely I would. Although there's no streetlight directly in front of this house, there's one not too far away. I don't want to go to the front door, or I might be tempted to step out and never come back, and also it's probably nearly the time the streetlights are turned off. Midnight until 5 a.m. in an experiment to save the council millions of pounds a year. I can think of more useful things, like maybe stop having all the boozy lunches we see them attending on a Friday lunchtime in the pub opposite the offices I work in. That would save a half day pay for all twenty of them once a week for a whole year, together with however much that boozy lunch costs us in their expenses. Maybe those extra four hours times twenty per month would stop the council from saying they are short-staffed. Maybe not.

My mind is rambling, trying to keep from thinking too deeply about the black-out.

I check the bolt on the inside of my bedroom door and then scan around, even looking under the bed just to check there's no one there, like I'm in a *Scream* movie.

I walk to the patio doors and stare out at the neighbour's house whose garden backs on to ours, and the two either side. One is in complete darkness except for the faint blue glow of what I assume is a computer.

The other one has a pale golden light in their top dormer window.

The third is lit up like a Christmas tree and I imagine all the people in there having a party from the faint bass vibrating through the hand I've placed on the window.

It makes me wish I was there with them instead of here, in this awful house.

We never seem to do anything together like that, like I imagined we would when I moved in five weeks ago. I thought this was going to be a blast sharing a house instead of being on my own in a lonely flat I could barely afford.

I thought I might get a cat as there's no clause in the contract excluding them, but of course, bloody Phoebe is allergic to anything with fur. Funny how she's not allergic to all the chemicals she puts on her hair, eyebrows and lashes.

Truth be told, I knew I'd made a mistake two days after moving in. This place is not for me, nor are the other housemates.

I look at the screen of my phone as I curl up on the bed and decide to send a voice note to Alex. I've already sent him half a dozen. All naggy ones about my housemates. I dread to think what he'll make of the notes, especially if he doesn't receive them until he gets back in the country. One long information dump which he'll probably delete without listening to.

'Hey, Alex. I know you can't reply but God, I just needed to speak to someone, or rather at someone and you drew the short straw. Hehe. That's only because Mum is still away. It'll make me feel better if nothing else. I've just returned to the house share, I can't call it home. It's the furthest I could ever feel from home. I'm a bit spooked.

'The electric is out and there's no one else here. I don't have a clue where the fuse box is so I'm going to have to go and investigate because I can't sit here in the cold and the dark hoping someone else might come back. I can hear you laughing at me now while you're probably holed up in a tent somewhere without heating, lighting or running water, so sorry to be such a whiner. Just talking at you makes me feel safer, though, so you're coming with me.

'I've unbolted the door to my bedroom and I'm stepping back out into the hallway. I feel like you're with me, so it's given me a little more confidence. I don't know where to start, but there's no way I'm going down that cellar on my own. Oh God. I'm sorry. How thoughtless of me.

'I do go down there when I need to use the washing machine and tumble dryer but I make sure it's during the day. The kitchen isn't big enough to house them apparently as the boiler can't be down there because of the flue, and it's a ginormous thing, not wall mounted, but taking up an entire corner of this piddling little kitchen. Still, it kicks off heat and it's nice to lean against in the morning when I'm having a quiet cup of tea.

'I know I'm rambling here, anyway, there's nothing in the hallway so I'm having a quick look around the kitchen. I'm not exactly sure what I'm looking for. At home it's a neat little white box you pull up the lid of. Mum showed me how once when I was staying alone in the house one weekend after you'd left for the Army, when we'd just lost Bruce. Poor Bruce, he was such a lovely boy. I miss having a dog. Perhaps Mum will get another one once she's settled down after her extended holiday.

'In this place it's probably from World War II as the landlord is too tight to replace it, so really I'm looking for something off white or even yellowing. Nothing. I can't see anything at all even resembling it. Nothing in the living room either.

'I'm going to have to go now as this is running my battery down and without somewhere to charge it, I'll be without a light too if I'm not careful. Don't worry about me, hehe, I'll survive. You know the boogey man isn't coming to get me.'

I press the off button and continue back into the hallway, regretting some of the things I just blurted out to Alex. Will it upset him?

I puff out a breath, wondering if I can delete my last message before he listens to it. I'll have to look later when I'm back in my bedroom. I'm bound to be able to. I just never have before, but it wasn't the most delicate of me and a hot flush steals up my neck as I remember my words.

I push it to one side for now as there's something more pressing to deal with and that's getting the power back on in this nightmare of a house.

Now there's not even the sound of my own hushed voice, nothing but silence and the thrum of distant music from that house accompanies me.

'Cheeses, Alex. I wish you were with me,' I whisper to myself.

I shine the light over the cellar door and baulk at the thought of going down there.

I've never been comfortable with cellars. For good reason.

I try to do my clothes washing and bedding on a Saturday morning when everyone is in the house, so I'm not on my own down there in the cellar. It might sound cowardly from a fully grown woman, but I can't help it. It gives me the shivers.

The only issue is you have to sneak in in between everyone else bagging the same time.

Instead of opening the door to the cellar, I'm a coward and I turn and creep up the stairs to the first floor instead, one step at a time, testing each one for a squeak or a creak.

By the time I reach the top, I am breathless.

I lean on the doorframe outside Saul's bedroom while I scan the beam of the torchlight across the wall and over the ceiling, making the house even spookier than before as shadows chase the light in hot pursuit.

There's nothing.

This is a strange house, extended out the back which is my bedroom. A cheap little extension with a flat roof and nasty patio doors that stick if you try to slide them open and let in a horrible draught mainly from the top so I can't even plug it.

Saul's door is ajar, and I give it a gentle nudge with the toe of boots I should have removed before coming upstairs. Another one of the rules as apparently the landlord will charge for unsightly marks and stains on carpets.

Still, no one will know I've been up here – there's no one home, otherwise they would have responded when I called out. Wouldn't they?

I don't step inside but simply glide the beam of light over the room like a hot knife through butter, slicing away the night.

No one is here. Unless he's under the bed and why would he be there?

I almost chuckle at the thought of Saul being frightened of the dark.

Then I consider he might be hiding in it.

The hairs on the back of my neck prickle and I back out of Saul's room as quick as I can, trying to shake off the feeling someone is watching me.

I don't shut his door entirely in case he's the type of person who notices these things. I don't know about Saul. Cocky though he is and seemingly shallow, I wouldn't put it past him to be a bit more wily than I give him credit for.

I move along the hallway to the next bedroom.

'Phoebe?' I give a gentle knock and listen for some indication of sound before I turn the handle on Phoebe's door and poke my head around, keeping the light down low in case she's asleep in bed, but she's not. Her bed is perfectly well made and empty.

Fear crawls up my spine and I back out of her bedroom, quietly snicking the door closed.

My breathing is the only noise now other than the thud of music down the street which is more of a vibration through the soles of my feet and into my chest like a heartbeat as I move further away from it.

My heart pounds out of rhythm and I lean against the wall for a moment, gathering my nerve to look in the next room. Do I need to? Or am I just snooping?

Whatever the answer, I reach for the doorhandle and pause.

There's a soft thud from within.

I hold my breath, each beat of my heart a number I count while I wait to hear another noise.

Nothing.

'Michelle?'

I give a gentle knock, but there's no further noise, no sound.

I turn the handle and ease the door open, drawing in a sharp gasp.

Torchlight flickers with the tremble of my hand as I pan it over the figure in the bed. The room is bereft of sound, as though it's been sucked away into a bottomless pit.

On silent feet, I tiptoe to the side of the bed.

'Michelle?'

There's no response. She's lying on her front, head turned towards me and one arm flopped out of bed, her fingers seemingly reaching for a phone on the carpet beneath them and I wonder if it was the sound of the phone dropping that I heard.

I reach out a hand and touch her shoulder. The warmth of her body reassures me she's not dead, but when I bring my ear to her lips, her breathing is so shallow she must be in a deep sleep.

Maybe she's had too much to drink. I can't remember her mentioning she was going out tonight, but then I'm not sure I let her know I was either.

I tuck her arm beneath the covers and pull them over her shoulder before I come to my feet, backing out of her bedroom as quietly as I can, guilt snaking through me as my intrusion into her space feels wrong.

Now I know someone else is in the house, it feels less threatening, even though she is zonked.

There is no sound as I sneak back down the stairs and then loiter for a moment outside the cellar door.

I really hate cellars.

I check my phone for battery life and it's getting low.

Perhaps I should have woken Michelle, made her come with me, but it wouldn't be fair.

I hope she has just over-imbibed a little and not taken drugs. To my knowledge, she's not a drug taker, but it was a little odd how comatose she was. Whatever, she was breathing, comfortable and safe if not exactly responsive. Perhaps I'll have a word with her tomorrow. For now, I'll leave her to sleep it off.

I'm not so sure about Saul and his endless line of women. Is *he* on drugs? Does he sell them to these women?

The idea makes me shiver as I give the cellar door a gentle push, watching it swing in on itself so my beam of light loses its effectiveness as it reaches the bottom of the long, steep stairs and is swallowed up.

My stomach hitches and I contemplate whether I'm brave enough to go down there, or if I should just go to bed and leave it for someone else to deal with.

I can't do that. My own conscience won't allow me to ignore this and let someone else walk in in the dark. I'm not so bothered about Saul, but Phoebe might be scared.

I lower myself one step at a time into this dark dungeon, my hand fisted around the banister rail in case I fall headfirst into this pit.

The steady tap, tap, tap is louder down here. The noise everyone reassures me is the pipes heating up, or cooling down, whichever. I'm convinced that's not the cause.

I reach the bottom and stand for a long moment, unsure if I can do this.

Panning the light over everything, the washing machine, tumble dryer, both of which appear to be full of clothes, then raking it around the top of the walls. I'm about to give up, when...

There!

There it is.

I draw in a long breath, determined now I'm here that I'm going to fix this thing.

I step under it and reach up.

The ceilings down here are pretty low so it's not difficult to get hold of the yellowing electric box.

I yank at the front cover, but it doesn't pull up like the one at home, so I walk my fingers around to the top and give it a firm pull. The lid swings down and clangs against the wall so I almost pee myself at the loud noise piercing the silence.

My heart is pounding and I notice the tap, tap, tapping has stopped, almost in response to the clatter of the metal lid against the wall.

Heat smothers me as terror starts to clammer for attention.

I shine the light into the electric box, not quite sure what I'm looking for. I try to remember what Mum told me to do.

If one of the red switches is down, flick it up.

But they are all down.

Does that mean I need to flick all of them up?

I reach in and push the first switch. It's far stiffer than I was expecting and I grunt as I push harder. My finger slips off and the sharp snap of my fingernail sends pain shooting through the tip of my finger into the palm of my hand. Cheeses!

I grit my teeth and try again, this time using my thumb.

The switch flicks up and a soft hum starts.

Did I do it? Has it worked?

I flick the next switch and the next and now I have the hang of it, it doesn't seem so difficult. It just needed a little brute force and a lot of determination.

Quite proud of myself, I look around the cellar and the quiet hum I hear now seems to be coming from the washing machine and tumble dryer, their lights flickering for a moment before they steady, indicating they are on standby.

I breathe out a sigh of relief as I close the small cabinet, grease and dust from years of it not being cleaned layering my fingertips.

Still in darkness except for those figures glowing from the white goods and my torchlight, I turn and make my way back to the stairs.

From memory there's no light switch down here, so I need to make it to the top of the stairs to turn the light on. I should have thought of that before I embarked on my mission to save my world.

I am halfway up the stairs when a soft scraping noise comes from behind me and I freeze.

I don't want to turn around. I don't want to see what's behind me.

There was no one down here a moment ago. Was there? Or did I miss something lurking in the shadows?

'Who's there?' I demand, my voice just above a squeaky warble.

The air goes heavy as though the whole cellar is holding its breath. Then I hear a shuffle, a soft movement.

I gasp, terror coursing through me as I race the rest of the way to the top of the stairs, the torchlight bouncing wildly off the walls in my haste to escape whatever is down here with me in the dark. Panic is choking the life from me and I let out a sob as I reach blindly for the door.

Just as my fingertips scrabble for the handle, the door flies open, brilliant light flooding through until a dark shadow blots it all out.

8

PRESENT DAY – SIX WEEKS
EARLIER, 11.50 P.M. – NIKKI

I lurch forward, tripping over the top step before I launch into the hallway, my hands hitting the floor so hard that vibrations tremble through to my elbows. My phone skids along the wooden flooring of the hall and smacks into the opposite wall. My knees crack against the cold floor, sending a wash of nausea to cramp my stomach.

I lower my head to the floor, relief weakening every muscle.

'What the fuck are you playing at?'

I look all the way up at the dark figure towering over me and let out a bark of hysterical laughter as he reaches above my head to turn on the cellar light.

'Saul. Where have you been?'

I don't know if the relief is evident in my voice but at least it's not the creepy landlord. I blink rapidly, trying my best to get rid of the tears blurring my vision.

His expression closes. 'What do you mean, where have I been?'

I push myself up, my muscles aching.

I scramble to my feet. He doesn't offer a helping hand, nor

does he step back to give me room. He smells of fresh air and alcohol.

'I came back and no one was here, except Michelle, who is out cold. The electricity was off.' I pull the cellar door shut behind me and switch off the light Saul just switched on, unable to stop the shudder at the thought of being down there in the dark with whatever else is lurking around. It didn't sound small to me, but then again, I was terrified and that could easily have exaggerated my fear of the unknown.

'I just turned the power back on again. It looks like everything had tripped.'

Saul leans against the wall, his arms crossed over a chest I think I'm supposed to be impressed with, but I've seen bigger and better.

'It's not the only thing that tripped,' he manages to sneer through what I think he believes is a sexy look. I'm not falling for it.

I move past him and reach down to pick up my phone. The screen is cracked diagonally from corner to corner. I sigh and slip it into my pocket, reluctant to let Saul see.

He just has such an irritating demeanour which makes me think he won't be able to resist some snarky remark.

I place my hand against my heart and puff out a breath. Should I ask Saul to go into the cellar and check? See what was behind me? He looks as though he's happy to prop up the wall all night.

I move away from the door, pointing at it. 'Do you want to have a look down there? I thought I heard something.'

'Like what?' He pushes away from the wall, his arms dropping to his sides, his eyes widening.

'Maybe a rat.'

His nose wrinkles and he steps back. 'No chance. I'm not

going down there if there's a rat running loose. Leave the door closed and we'll get the weasel to check in the morning.'

'The weasel?'

'You know, the landlord.'

'I didn't know you called him that.'

'We do.'

Who does he mean by 'we'?

I don't know why we're loitering in the hallway. With one last glance at the cellar door, I walk towards the kitchen and Saul follows. I could do with taking a drink to bed, but I was hoping he might go to his room and leave me in peace.

'Why didn't you turn the light on down there?' he asks as I turn my back to him and reach for the kettle.

'Because the electric was off when I walked in.' Frustration edges my comment as I half fill the kettle. Enough for the two of us. Phoebe keeps going on about not wasting electricity, but honestly, I think she uses more than anyone with all the laundry she does. Maybe that's what tripped the power.

'No.' He edges up to the sink and leans against the countertop. 'When you turned the electric back on, why did you come up the stairs in the dark?'

I flick the switch on the kettle and move away; he's getting too close and I'm not comfortable with that. Not comfortable with him. It's a tight space and his bulk makes it smaller. 'Do you mean to tell me there's a switch down there?'

'Yep.'

How was I supposed to know? Why would you ever turn the light off when you're down there or not turn it on from the hallway before you go down? It doesn't make sense to me, but then this is an old building. Everything is a bit odd.

Saul follows me across the room and as I open a cupboard, he reaches above me for a mug, his body pressing against mine.

I freeze mid-stretch as something hard presses against my backside. Could that be his phone? But he's just placed his phone on the countertop and I realise from the heat of it through my clothes that it's his erection he's pushing against me. My mind freezes, unable to think of my next move.

'Hey, what's going on?'

Saul moves away from me without so much as a guilty start, and I find I can just about breathe again as I turn to face Phoebe.

'Oh, hi. I never heard you come in.' I'm lightheaded as I lean against the bench and assume my face is devoid of all colour as weakness seeps through every muscle. I can't imagine what would have happened if I'd been alone in the dark with Saul. Did he think I enjoyed that? Would he have taken no for an answer? I've known men like him before.

Phoebe's face is poker-face straight. 'Evidently.'

Saul throws one of Phoebe's teabags into his mug. 'You want one?'

'Nice of you to ask.'

She squeezes in between us, reaching up for her mug, with her name emblazoned on it so no one can be mistaken.

I edge out of the way and let them jostle for space, making their own cups of tea, taking the water I've just boiled. I get the impression that Phoebe wanted to manoeuvre me out of the way. Does she have a thing for Saul? It never occurred to me before.

They both move away to nab milk from the fridge and of course Phoebe lets Saul have some of hers. I've never known him buy milk. Never seen anything in the fridge with his name on it.

A thought comes to me.

I skim a quick gaze over Phoebe. 'Where did you come from?'

She looks up, a puzzled look flickering over her face. 'Me?'

'Yeah.' I keep my attention on her and she shrugs.

'Why?'

'Because when I came in fifteen minutes ago, there was no one here, apart from Sleeping Beauty upstairs.'

Phoebe raises a dyed purple eyebrow. 'Sleeping Beauty?'

'Michelle. She's fast asleep.' I tilt my head to listen and hear no movement from overhead. Perhaps I'll check on her again, now the others are here. Right now, I'm wondering where Phoebe was lurking all the while I wandered the house looking for the fuse box. I watch her closely as I continue.

'The electric was off and now, within moments of me turning it back on, both of you turn up out of nowhere.'

Phoebe squints at me and then lets out an indelicate snort. 'What are you trying to say? That we've been here all the time, sneaking around in the dark, trying to put the willies up you?'

I think of the noise down in the cellar.

'Were you in the cellar behind me?'

'What?' She splutters out a laugh and looks to Saul for support. 'Were we in the cellar together in the dark?'

His laughter is just as cruel as hers.

I didn't mean both of them, but whereas Saul's smell was of fresh air and alcohol when he first walked in, hers is of garlic and food.

I turn away, unsure of myself. Taking on one at a time is bad enough, but they tend to gang up when they're together, making you look foolish.

Am I foolish? Am I imagining it?

I'd not filled the kettle enough, so now I'm going to have to put more water in.

I try not to show my annoyance, but these two are the most inconsiderate people on the planet. I could make something of it, but quite honestly, my knees are still weak from sneaking around in the dark with an overactive imagination, and I don't think I can cope with any kind of confrontation right now. It's not worth the effort and I feel Phoebe is always willing to go to war, especially if Saul has her back. He just stirs trouble up for fun. I don't trust him. Come to think of it, I don't trust her.

While I wait for the kettle to boil again, I shake a sachet of hot chocolate into my mug. I don't want coffee this late – it will keep me awake all night – and I don't fancy tea. I always feel it's a morning drink. Something Mum, Alex and I would have while we sat at the dining table having breakfast together. For so many years that was our habit.

Until I ruined everything.

9

TWELVE YEARS AGO – JULY 2013 – NIKKI

Alex is home from the Army on leave and I can't believe how hot he is. I mean he's supposed to be my brother, right? But we're not related. No familial connection there at all. I mean I do know my biology and I know although we treat him as family, our blood is not the same.

That still doesn't stop me feeling a little guilty at the lustful thoughts I've been having about him, especially since he's been away. Not so much out of sight, out of mind, more absence makes the heart grow fonder.

Originally, when Mummy fostered Alex, it was supposed to be short term until things were sorted and his family took him in. I didn't really know much about the events leading up to him coming to live with us back then, all I was told at the age of five was his mummy had died and his dad was a bad man who went to prison. Then it seemed his wider family didn't want him. I felt sad for him when I found out. I love Alex. He's my hero. He always has been. That's why Mummy liked him so much. Because he saved me. More than once.

Mummy fostered Alex until he was eighteen. She'd asked a

number of times over the years if he wanted her to adopt him so he'd have the same name as us, but he always said he was comfortable with how things were. He wanted to keep his own name. I think she was a little insulted, but she never pressed the matter. She's been as much a mum to him as she has to me. In fact, it's an in-joke that she loves him more. I know she doesn't really, but from the day we first met he's had a special place in both our hearts.

Alex will never know how devastated Mum was when he chose to be fast-tracked to university, having taken his A levels early. I think she'd have liked to have kept him at home longer, but he was ready to fly.

He is a whizz at chemistry and an absolute mathematical genius. Quite literally, even Mummy couldn't keep up with him and she's a bright cookie herself. Always knows more than anyone else. Except Alex.

He's not a nerd, nor is he cocky like some of the boys in my class. He never was. I think that's his attraction. Well, there's a lot more attractive about him than just his personality these days. If you get my meaning.

'Corrr, Nikki. Is that your bruvver?'

I turn to Charlotte and smile. 'Yes.'

'Fuck me, but he's hot. Can you introduce me?'

I flinch a little at her language. I don't really like it but loads of them say that word at school. Worse is the C-word so many of the boys call the girls. It makes me cringe. It's not a word Mummy ever uses and I notice Alex doesn't use bad language at home. Not often, in any case, and certainly not since he grew up. Mummy said he had a real potty mouth when he first arrived with us, but she smoothed out his rough edges, making him into a man we are all proud of.

Charlotte has met Alex but that was before he joined the

Army, who recruited him while he was at university, and our hormones hadn't kicked in then.

There's something about the uniform that makes my heart flip as we watch him saunter from the car he's just unfolded himself out of, a huge Army holdall dangling from one hand as though it weighs nothing. It doesn't weigh nothing. It will have at least half a dozen books in and all his dirty washing which he never allows Mummy to do for him, insisting she's not his slave. I think it comes from his childhood when his dad bullied his mum.

He's grown now.

Each time he comes home his shoulders seem broader, his arms more muscular.

My stomach does a funny little flip.

He's not overly tall now I've sprouted. I was five foot six inches last time I was measured, and the top of my head comes to his chin, so he's probably five foot eleven or so. Maybe six foot. Mum reckoned he would have been taller if he'd been fed better as a child.

His hair is cut so short around the back and sides you can almost see his scalp through it, but it's so thick it still holds on to that floppiness over the forehead he's always had.

He glances up at our bedroom window as though he senses us watching and for some stupid reason we both duck down, giggling.

Why didn't I just act cool and wave back like I would normally? Charlotte's hormonal stupidity has rubbed off and made me go daft.

To cover up my temporary insanity, I bounce off the bed and make for the door, leaving her behind as I charge down the stairs to greet him. He drops the bag on the hall floor and I launch myself from three steps up into his arms the way I have ever since he left a few years ago. It's almost a nod to the memory of him saving me from the slide accident.

He lets out a slight 'whoof' of surprise but is grinning as he swings me around in a circle.

We've not seen him for four months and it feels like a lifetime.

'We weren't expecting you until tomorrow.'

He lowers me to my feet but we still hold on to each other.

'I can go, if you want me to.' He thumbs over his shoulder and the deep dimple in his left cheek winks in.

I laugh. 'Don't. Mum would kill me if her favourite child left home without saying hello.'

'Where is she?' He raises his head, looking towards the kitchen where she's often to be found.

'She'll be back shortly, she had a meeting with the head.'

I loop my arm through his and we make our way to the kitchen so I can put the kettle on. He always likes a cup of coffee. Black, two sugars.

I turn and Charlotte is hovering in the doorway.

'Alex, this is Charlotte. You remember my friend from school, don't you?'

He turns and if he hasn't melted Charlotte's knickers with his smile I'd be surprised. She sort of wilts against the doorframe, a hand coming up to push her hair behind one ear. 'Hi, Alex.' Her voice whispers from lips she's just licked and embarrassment curdles in my stomach. Can she make it any more obvious?

Alex does not help the situation and burns her cheeks with his charm.

'Of course I remember Charlotte. How could I forget? Although you have grown since I last saw you.' He gives a slightly lewd wink, making me cringe even though I know he's only joking.

It was probably about a year ago since he last saw her,

but he is right, Charlotte's boobs have definitely grown, unlike mine. I still have a flat chest. I'm a bit of a late developer. Although I do know Charlotte wears a padded bra as well to emphasise her boobs. Mummy won't let me. She says the time will come soon enough to be an adult without pushing it and to enjoy childhood for as long as I can. I'm not sure I understand what she means. I can't wait to grow up.

Maybe when I do, Alex will marry me.

Charlotte gives a little girly giggle, a bright blush staining her cheeks. 'We're going out tonight, that's why I'm here. I'm sleeping over.'

Alex looks at me. I can see the question in his eyes. Was Charlotte going to use his bedroom tonight as we weren't expecting him back?

'Charlotte's sharing my room. She always does when she sleeps over.' I don't know why, but there's a part of me wants to reassure Alex that his room belongs to him. It always has. We wouldn't ever let someone else use it without his permission. He's family.

His eyes are on mine as he gives a faint smile as though he knows I'm reassuring him and appreciates it.

'Where are you going?'

Neither of us speak for a moment because we've told our mums we're going to the school disco. It's only a partial lie as we *are* going there. We're just not going in, not staying.

My mummy is not stupid. She absolutely knows teenagers cannot be trusted, which is one of the reasons she claims to prefer teaching junior school. It's also the reason we are actually going to the disco to check in first as Mummy knows people who know people.

She sounds like the mafia, and to be honest, I think she may have connections because she seems to know exactly what I'm doing at any given time of the day and where I am.

The where I am is not so hard to figure out as I have the Find My Friends app on my phone so she can stalk me whenever she wants. That was the deal if I was to have a phone. Fair enough. However, what we discovered, Charlotte and I, is if you turn your phone off when you're in a particular place, Find My Friends registers you are still there until you turn your phone back on again. Clever stuff all teenagers should know.

I realise Alex is staring at me.

'Sorry?'

'I said, where are the pair of you going?'

'Oh, uh, the school disco. I thought I said.' But the high pitch of my voice is a dead giveaway and there's a rush of heat up my neck, spreading across my chest.

'You want to try again?'

'No, that's where we're going. Honest.'

Only my voice warbles on the last word and Alex's right eyebrow slowly rises into his hairline. I recognise that look. It means he's on to me. This is a man who learnt every trick in the book when he was a boy.

'Right.' He gives a slow nod, his gaze not shifting from mine.

I start to shuffle from foot to foot, uncomfortable in the wake of his quiet observation. He's my big brother, for goodness' sake. The flush races up my neck and blooms in my cheeks in a way I know won't be attractive. It'll turn all blotchy against my pale and pasty skin.

He holds the silence for so long I almost want to punch him in the arm. Then his face relaxes. 'Would you like a lift?'

Charlotte's mouth drops open. 'Oh, yeah!' she breathes, her voice full of hope and unrequited love.

'No!'

We look at each other, me shaking my head, Charlotte nodding hers.

'It's okay, we were going to get the bus.' The words blurt from my mouth and then I realise his suggestion could be the ideal situation. If Alex drops us off at the school, then he is witness to us going into the disco if any questions are asked. Whereas, in reality, we're going to the pub down the road a way where a local band is playing a gig. The lead singer, Brad, is Charlotte's absolute heartthrob, although I am beginning to suspect anyone in trousers may qualify for that dubious position since her breasts grew.

'Actually, Alex, yeah. A lift would be good if we're not putting you out.'

'No problem, Mum said I can borrow her car while I'm home, so I thought I'd do the rounds, call on a few friends. I'll drop you off first and then you can let me know when you're done and I can pick you up.'

I know he knows something is hinky, but I'm not admitting to it. Charlotte and I may just have to leave the gig early in that case as the school disco finishes at 10 p.m. while the gig goes on until 11 p.m. We were going to make the bus an excuse. It broke down, or we ran and just missed it and had to wait for the next one. Having said that, Mum has never let me get the bus home, but I am grown up, now. We were banking on that argument.

'Cool.' I nod. He might not remember, because basically, he was such a bright spark he never really hung around enough to go to school discos. By the time he was my age, he'd shipped himself off to university, with Mummy's help of course, and had a chaperone because everyone else was so much older than him. That must have been some kind of hell. I bet he never got up to anything exciting at my age. Not that I've had the opportunity either, yet. That's what we're hoping for tonight. Fun, excitement.

'Ten o'clock usually, isn't it?' he asks and debunks my idea that he might be in any way ignorant to the ways of the world. Alex is not. He is my saviour, my protector and I guess I can't have it all ways.

'Maybe pick us up at half ten,' Charlotte interjects. 'That way we don't have to rush out and can have a chat to our mates.' She flutters her eyelashes and it's cringingly awkward. But Alex doesn't respond as though he's not even noticed her flirting with him. Thank God!

I tug on her sleeve and try to break the spell he seems to have over her. 'We'll go and get ready. We have to leave in an hour.'

Charlotte and I rush upstairs and she flops onto my bed, giggling. 'He's so fucking gorgeous.'

'I thought you liked Brad?'

'Yeah, well. Your brother is so much more – sexy. And dangerous. Don't you think he gives off an air of sexy menace?' She rolls around in peals of laughter and I don't get it. I mean, I love him as a sister, but it's awkward because I can also see what she means. I choose to ignore her. She doesn't need encouragement.

'Come on, let's get ready.'

The front door closes downstairs and Mummy's voice drifts up. 'Hi, girls, I'm home.'

Then there's a high-pitched screech which shatters the air and has Charlotte leaping off the bed and on her feet as she looks around wildly for a place to hide. I'm sure if it was a beast running up the stairs, she would sacrifice me to it.

I put my hand over my mouth.

As it is, it's my brother.

He's probably hidden behind the doorway and then leapt out in front of my mum. It's not like he hasn't done it before.

Delighted laughter soon breaks through, drifting upstairs.

'Calm down,' I tell Charlotte. 'It's Alex giving Mummy a fright. It's a boy thing. He does it every time. He's the master of menace.'

10

TWELVE YEARS AGO – JULY 2013 – NIKKI

I don't know what I expected, but it wasn't this. The music is literally hammering off the walls and I want to press my hands against my ears, but it won't make any difference because the beat of it is pulsing from inside me. My heart throbs against the inside of my chest as though it's about to bounce out. I'm not entirely sure I like this feeling.

Charlotte is right in front of the small makeshift stage, her arms around some guy who hit on her the moment we walked in the room. He's bought her alcohol which has made me cross with her. The deal was we'd stick to soft drinks because this is our first time and we want to get the lie of the land so we can come regularly. We were also supposed to stick together. It seems everything we agreed on went out the window the moment we walked in, and I'm feeling insecure and lonely.

She's bouncing up and down in front of Brad, the lead singer, her face flushed, thick chestnut hair flipping around her shoulders. She looks so beautiful as coloured lights pass over, illuminating her smooth skin, her radiant smile.

I think we might be in trouble if she doesn't slow down on the

Bacardi and Cokes. I know she drinks at home – her mum allows her the odd one – but I don't. Mummy isn't really a drinker and she's very cautious in front of Alex, with his dad being an alcoholic.

An alco-frolic as I once used to call it, even though I didn't actually understand what it meant. It made Alex chuckle. There's nothing I wouldn't do to make Alex laugh. He was a sad boy for such a long time and the only person who could make him laugh was me. Now, he just thinks I'm a clown because I've dumbed myself down for him. Not that he would approve if he knew. He's always encouraged me to use my brain, even if his is so much faster than mine, he slowed down for me, helped me understand my homework, not just do it.

I'm pretty sure I've aced my GCSEs.

I know lots of the girls who will think it's because Mummy is a teacher, but the truth is, it's Alex's patience with me. We'd sit at the dining room table, all three of us, while Mummy did her marking, Alex would help me with my homework and then do his. Sometimes late into the night. His was never-ending, but I think it was self-inflicted. As he tells me, nothing worthwhile in life comes without hard work. He's the antithesis of his dad. I had to look the word up, of course.

Mummy says he's got an old man's attitude and a young man's brain.

'Hey.'

I turn as someone nudges me in the ribs.

Tall with a streak of blond through his dusky brown hair, the guy staring into my eyes looks a little intense for my liking.

'Hi.' I give him a weak smile and turn away to watch Charlotte.

'Is she with you?' he shouts in my ear, and I nod without turning.

'Bit of a slut, isn't she?'

My mouth drops open and I whip around.

He grins. 'Any chance you're like your friend?'

I lean forward as though to whisper in his ear.

'Fuck off!' I yell, loud enough to burst his eardrums.

He rears back and for one moment, I think he's about to hit me.

Someone wraps their arm around my waist and I'm imprisoned. 'Mate, fuck off, would you? She's obviously not your type.'

The blond streak guy slinks off, but my heart is still racing as I turn to the guy beside me. He's not much taller than me in my heels, but he has a sturdy, square jawline. His steady grey eyes inspect my face. 'Are you okay?'

I nod. 'I'm fine, thanks.'

'I was watching you from over there. You looked lonely.'

'I'm not. I'm just watching my friend, making sure she's okay.'

'Are you a lesbian?' I'm pretty sure he's said it as if it's an insult. I'm not insulted; I have plenty of friends who are lesbians and it doesn't matter to any of us. Funny how lads seem turned on by it, though.

'No. Just friends.'

There's a part of me regrets saying no, but actually he's really good-looking and it might be nice to have someone to talk to, not that talking is easy in here with the music blasting out. The band aren't even much good. Charlotte said they were going to be brilliant.

What can you expect though? We're hardly in the centre of London. This is the wilds of Shropshire, for goodness' sake, anyone worth their salt would have moved away long before they reached their thirties if they were any good.

'Can I buy you a drink?'

I nod because he seems harmless enough and he did get rid of the other freak.

'Coke, please.'

'Just Coke?' He runs a quick assessing look over me. 'You driving?'

I nod again, turning to face the bar just in case he catches the flush rising in my cheeks. I'm not even old enough to hold a provisional licence, not for a car in any case, and there's no way Mummy would allow me to ride a motorbike, so I'm not allowed to apply for a licence until I'm ready to start driving lessons. After all, according to Mum, why would I need ID?

He leans forward, close enough so his chest is touching my shoulder as he grabs the barman's attention with a crook of his finger that impresses me.

Instead of a bottle of Coke, a thin brown stream of it comes from a tap into a pint glass. I never drink pints – for one thing, my stomach would explode with so much fizzy stuff inside, and for another, those glasses are huge and heavy.

He takes the glass from the barman and hands it to me and then accepts a glass of something amber, giving the barman a nod so I get the impression they know each other.

'Thanks.' I sip at my drink and there's something odd about it. Is it because it's not a bottle of Coca Cola, but the cheap alternative that comes from a tap and is mainly water and sugar?

It's not bad, but it's certainly not wonderful.

Charlotte is still bopping, her head flung back as she laughs up at the tall guy with her.

'She's having fun.'

'What?' I can barely hear the lad.

'Your friend. She's having fun with my brother.'

'Your brother?'

'Yes.'

I gulp down some of my Coke and decide the quicker I drink it, the sooner I can go and persuade Charlotte we need to go home. It's coming up to quarter past ten and we agreed Alex should pick us up at half past at the school. We've got to get there yet.

A fine sweat breaks out across the back of my neck. This is not going how I planned. In fact, I feel miserable.

I nod towards the pair who are wrapped in each other's arms. 'We need to go soon. I'll have to go and get her.'

'She's okay. She's safe with Steve.'

'What?'

'I said she's safe.' He's yelling in my ear so my whole head vibrates.

'Okay.' I nod while I take another slug of my drink and then put the almost empty glass down on the bar, indicating the loos which are right next to the exit into the beer garden. 'I've just got to go…'

My voice drifts away. I turn and make my way through the crowds of people who must have poured in during the last hour. The atmosphere is thick with cheap aftershave and sweat.

I don't want to spoil Charlotte's fun, but we made a mistake. We misjudged the type of people who would be interested in this band and it's predominantly men of a certain age. Not teenagers like us, but quite a bit older. They've all rushed in now as the ticket price doubles after 10.30 p.m. I'm not sure they've come to see the group, more just another drinking place staying open late. It doesn't feel safe to me. We're out of our depth.

I sit on the loo in the cubicle with shiny black tiles and dim lights with my head swimming and my knees weak.

'Shit.'

My fingers fumble with the lock on the door and I do a little sideways step as I move over to the sinks.

I've never been drunk before. I've never really had anything to drink, but I'm pretty sure this is what it feels like and I don't think I like it. I think there was something more than just Coke in my glass.

An older woman walks in as I trip on by and she tuts as though I've done something to offend her. A giggle bursts from my lips as the room goes hazy. Rather than head for the bar, I stumble through the door into the beer garden, snatching in gasps of air thick and heavy with the scent of honeysuckle sprawling over the walled garden. Pretty golden fairy lights twinkle and blur in front of my eyes as I try to find somewhere to sit, just for a moment. But the place is heaving, both outside and in. The bass of the music vibrates through the soles of my feet.

My head is spinning and I just want somewhere quiet to sit for a moment before I go back in and run the gauntlet through the crowd to drag Charlotte away.

I stumble along the side alley leading to a gate to take me outside into the car park at the front of the pub where I stand staring up at the stars on this cloudless night.

'There you are.'

The voice makes me jump and I turn, recognising the man in front of me as the one who bought me the drink. A drink, through my fuzzy brain, I suspect he spiked with alcohol. Silly me. I should giggle, but suddenly I feel I don't want to.

'I wondered where you'd got to.' He takes my arm and guides me down the edge of the car park past several cars until we reach the end of the surrounding wall which drops down to form a small shelf I sink onto with barely any encouragement from him.

He leans in and I think he's going to kiss me. Suddenly, I don't want to be kissed. I don't want any of this. I'm not in control and I don't like it. There's a flutter of panic in my chest, but I don't seem to have the strength to do anything about it.

'No, my head is fuzzy.' I raise my hand to ward him off, stop him from doing whatever it is he intends but he takes it in his, pressing it against the front of his trousers. I try to pull away but he forces it back until my fingers brush the hardness beneath the material.

He groans, his head tilting upwards as he closes his eyes. 'Oh,' he growls, ecstasy trembling through his voice. 'That's good. But you can do better than that.'

His hand grasps my wrist so hard I think it might snap as I wriggle my fingers to try and break loose, but it only seems to inflame the situation.

With his free hand he reaches for his zip and starts to tug it down.

My head clears a little as panic sets in and I try to jerk free.

'No, no. I don't want to.'

I try to come to my feet, but he slams a hand on my shoulder then twists his fingers through my hair until I lower myself back down, never letting go of my wrist for a moment.

'Come on, slag. You know you want it.' He gives a sharp jerk and I cry out. 'Why else would you be here, blagging drinks out of men?'

'Stop. Please, stop.'

For some reason all the advice girls are given in this type of situation slips away in the light of the pain he's inflicting. The bones in my wrist creak and fire burns through my scalp.

'Don't. Let me go!'

I can't manoeuvre to give me any room so I can stamp my heel into his foot as his legs are wedged between my knees. He's yanking my hair, pulling my face closer to his crotch.

'Come on, bitch.'

'You'd better let her go right now if you want to live another day. Another minute,' comes a voice full of gravel.

The guy in front of me freezes. His grip loosens but he doesn't let go.

'Fuck off, mate. It's none of your business. She's with me.'

'Well, see, that's where you're wrong. It's every bit my business.'

The guy straightens, reluctantly loosening his grip.

I gasp for breath. Shock sends waves of tremors through me as I look through eyes blurred with tears past this man to Alex.

His face is chiselled with fury as he glances first at me, then at the man standing over me.

'She never said she had a boyfriend.' He untangles his hand from my hair and I wince as he pulls at a lock stuck to his sweaty fingers.

Alex's eyes narrow. 'Did you even ask her?'

The guy shrugs, a sly smile slipping over his face. 'Hey, she was ready and willing. I bet you know what she's like. A proper little goer.'

Alex's gaze slides to my face as he does a quick recon. Either this guy is stupid or I know Alex well enough to feel the fury vibrating from him.

Alex steps in closer. 'Did you even stop long enough to ask her age?'

'Her age?'

'Yeah, dickhead. She's not even sixteen. So, not only were you about to force a young girl into having nonconsensual sex with you, but you were about to commit rape of an underage child, which would make you a paedo.' His voice vibrates with conviction.

'Jesus Christ.' The man steps back from me as though I'm a hot coal he's only just realised he's juggling. His legs smack into the wing of a car and he jolts to a stop. 'How do you know?' There's definitely a grey pallor to his skin.

Alex lets out an over-exaggerated sigh as he digs in his jeans pocket and rattles out a bunch of keys, holding them out to me. 'Nikki, go wait in the car while I explain to this moron the reason I know your age is because you're my sister.'

There's a burgeoning warmth of pride stirring in my stomach, but I know I need to concentrate.

'What about Charlotte? I need to get her.' My words are a little slurred even in my own mind.

Alex does a slow turn, his brown eyes darkened in the orange glow of light from the streetlamp harden. 'I'll deal with Charlotte. You get in the car. And lock it.' His voice is low. I know he's angry but I'm pretty sure it's not directed solely at me.

Despite the heat of the July night, I'm shaking by the time I spot Alex walking towards Mummy's car where I'm slumped down in the front passenger seat, Charlotte wrapped around him like an octopus. She is definitely three sheets to the wind whereas I've had a few moments and a terrible experience to sober me up and make me think I may never drink again.

Alex opens the back door and Charlotte flops in, waving her hands in the air. She yells, 'Go, go, go!' like we're a gangster mob and the police are chasing us.

There's a moment when I think Alex may drag her back out and leave her on the side of the road as he tries to fix the seatbelt around her while she giggles with drunken delight, her hands roaming over his back in frenetic encouragement.

I leap out of the car and open the opposite door. 'Charlotte.' I tap her – maybe a little bit hard – and grab her attention. She sobers for a moment, looking at me through squinty eyes. 'Sit up,' I demand and she does as she's told. I whip the seatbelt around her and do something akin to a baton exchange with Alex and he slams the seatbelt into the holder.

'Right.'

We both slam the car doors at the same time and leap into the front seats with a sigh.

I glance across at Alex as we both plug our seatbelts in. He's vibrating with fury and it occurs to me he could be angry because Charlotte and I are drunk. He's seen enough drunkenness in his lifetime. Although his dad was a nasty drunk by all accounts and we're both a bit sloppy and useless.

'I'm sorry.'

'It's not me you should be apologising to. Jesus, if anything had happened to you, what the hell would Mum do? Do you actually appreciate how much danger you were in there?'

'But – I didn't do anything wrong, Alex. It wasn't my fault.'

He rests his hands on the steering wheel and stares straight ahead into the dark. I can't take my eyes off the grazing across his knuckles which I'm pretty sure is fresh. Did he just beat the other guy up? There's a fear he might get into trouble for this.

'Nikki, just because society thinks young women should be safe to go out and do as they like, it doesn't mean to say there aren't predators out there who also think they know better and are just waiting for the opportunity. It's society's obligation to protect you, but you also need to take steps to look after yourself. That guy—' He stabs his thumb in the direction of the wall. 'He was a monster just waiting for his prey to come along and it happened to be you.'

'I wasn't drinking.' My mouth is dry as I glance in the back of the car at Charlotte, who is now snoring loudly, her mouth open, her chin on her chest. There's a thin strand of drool dripping onto her new top.

'You got spiked.' It's not a question.

'He bought me a drink. It was only supposed to be Coke, but I think there was something else in it.'

Alex closes his eyes and lets out a sigh. 'Remember when

Mum taught you not to accept sweeties from strangers?' He looks sideways at me. I nod. Tears are pricking at the back of my eyes. I feel stupid. Ignorant. Naïve.

'Yeah, well. Same theory.'

'He was horrible.'

'Yeah, Nikki. There are horrible men out there.'

With his reference specifically to men, I wonder if he is thinking of his own dad, a nasty alcoholic by all accounts who Alex never speaks about, but Mum has occasionally mentioned in passing, sometimes just to smooth the way when she's needed to explain why Alex might want his own space, time to chill on his own without me demanding attention the whole time and I realise what emotional predicament he's going through too.

'I'm sorry, Alex.' And I am. The incident may not have been my fault – far from it – but I put myself in this position by being dishonest with Alex and with Mum, not only that but involving Alex in my deception.

'How did you know where we were?' My voice is thick with tears.

He lets out a derisive snort. 'I knew you were lying the moment you opened your mouth. When you weren't at the school in time for the pick-up, I followed my nose to the nearest gig.'

'You told him I was underage. That's not true. I am sixteen.'

'So sue me.'

He puts the car in gear and starts to drive and I feel a terrible sense something between us has changed. Broken.

11

This lot are bloody weird.

For one thing, nobody seems to want to talk about past tenants. Why is that?

I've had a little prod, asked who used the room before me, but none of them seemed to take an interest. I'm pretty sure it was Phoebe who said the previous tenant had a brief stay as they didn't pay their rent and moved on.

But the previous tenant would have been Nikki, wouldn't it? She would never renege on her rent. For one thing, she's not hard up. She's been doing really well for herself according to her mum, Julia.

Or had there been another housemate in the meantime? That would have been a mere few weeks. We barely even knew Nikki had gone. Surely they can't have had someone in the meantime.

And where did the last set of curtains in my room disappear to? Did the last brief tenant take them when they left? I can't imagine Nikki making do without curtains. So where did hers go? Nikki's mum has had nothing back, which is why the police believe Nikki up and left of her own accord. There were no clothes, no bedding, no make-up. Nothing. It was as though she just took off.

It's bizarre.

This whole place is bizarre.

I thought Saul and I would get along well, being almost the same age. You know, brothers in arms, best bros, all of that crap. I don't know why I should have thought it, I came in here with the preconceived idea he wasn't to be trusted and maybe he felt those vibes. But we are living in each other's spaces, you'd think we'd at least get along.

I've never had an issue with the lads I've been working my mission with. With them, you have each other's back. It's that or be killed. Same as when I was in the Army. You like some people, you don't like others, but you learn to trust them with your life.

Saul's only conversation is reserved for when the girls are around and it's boastful and boring. He reminds me too much of my dad. A brilliant mind dulled with alcohol and egoism. I only hope Saul doesn't break the way my dad did.

He's not my business though.

What *is* my business is finding out what happened to Nikki, but before that, there's someone else no one talks about, but Nikki mentioned her in one of her voicenotes.

'Hi, Alex, it's me. I hope you're keeping out of the midday sun, you know what it does to mad dogs and Englishmen. I can't wait until you get home. I really could do with seeing you.' Her voice loses its cheerful momentum for an instant before she continues quietly. 'I really wish you were here. There's a strangeness about this place which is giving me the heebie jeebies. As soon as you get home, you need to come and stay, although you'll have to bring your sleeping bag and a blow-up bed. Come and see what you think of these housemates of mine.

'Saul is a bit of a knob if I'm honest. I don't know what he did to upset Michelle, but she's gone. I mean literally packed up and did a moonlight flit, taking almost everything with her, except her bedding which, apparently, she told Phoebe she could have. Phoebe could never afford something of that quality, she's always scratting around taking people's leftovers, and I don't just mean food. I could tell you some right tales about things going missing. I swear she has kleptomania, but if you dare to touch anything belonging to her, she turns into a rottweiler.

'Funny thing is Phoebe's always envied Michelle her bedding, she really admired it when Michelle first bought it, so it seems strange that she claims without any evidence it belongs to her now. Not that I would necessarily want it, but how do we know Michelle left it for her? And when? Michelle made it pretty clear she didn't like Phoebe, so why give her this bedding when she knew I liked it too? And we were friends. Or at least I thought we were, we certainly got along much better than Phoebe and Michelle did. I know it sounds petty, and seriously I didn't need the bedding, but really? Giving it to Phoebe? Why would she?

'The bedding was of course some gorgeous, exclusive designer stuff which Michelle managed to get for free because she's an influencer. I don't know who she influenced. Although I followed her under her "stage" name as she called it, I never really had much time for that kind of thing. I think I'm more cerebral than to allow myself to be influenced by a nobody. I don't mean to sound bitchy, but I don't understand. How can anyone consider themselves influencers by getting a few freebies and advertising them? Does nobody use their own ideas and thoughts? I think Mummy brought us up to use our own minds. Well, certainly you've used yours to good effect, but I'm starting to wonder if I've put mine to best use.

'Isn't it odd? You think you're getting to know someone, and they take off, just like that. Nothing said. No forward contact. I sent her a message, but I think she's blocked me because I can't see her profile on Insta and TikTok any more, so maybe she didn't want any reminders of her past time here. Essentially, we were only house sharing for a few weeks. Strangely though, I felt we'd sort of bonded. Us against the other two. It's the reason I can't understand her giving anything to Phoebe. We'd chat for hours in my room while she wasn't influencing anyone and I was having a break from work, which is crazy right now. I always feel like I'm having to prove myself there. That's a whole different bugbear though.

'I don't want to bore you whining about stuff, but I've not seen Mum in three weeks now and it's blummin' odd too. I realise how much I really miss her, how much I offload on to her. She's sent a few messages, but you know what she's like. It's brief. She refused to pay for the ship's Wi-Fi because she said it cost almost as much as her holiday, and now she only sends a message when they pull into port, provided the signal is good enough and she's not about to be charged on her roaming contract. Considering she doesn't know where it covers, it doesn't help. For the first seven days, they were at sea, so I heard absolutely nothing. Not sure if you've heard? Knowing her, she'll have telephoned you every day. Snort. Her favourite son.

'The strangest thing here though is, I know it's an old house, but the past couple of nights I've heard this incessant tapping which is driving me insane! The others say it's probably the pipes heating up, but the heating is off in the middle of the night. So could they be cooling down? I've contacted the landlord, which Phoebe and Saul were not happy about. Phoebe was miffed because she's designated herself the official landlord/tenant mediator, and I now feel I've put her nose out of joint.

'Saul said he's a grubby old guy who sneaks into the house when no one else is around and snoops in their private stuff.

Personally, I'm not sure Saul doesn't already. I think he's a bit of a sex fiend. There are some very odd noises coming from his room at night. Well, even in the days sometimes, if I'm working from home. I prefer not to. It doesn't have the best atmosphere.

'I've been offered Michelle's room now she's gone, but I think I prefer where I am, all things considered about Saul's sex life, because he would be my direct neighbour and the walls are thin. At least this way, he's above the kitchen and not my room.

'I never thought about it when I signed my contract, but now Michelle is gone and there are only three of us, we have to bridge the gap in the rent and the bloody utilities, which I barely use, but I've never known anyone use a washing machine and tumble dryer the amount Phoebe does. She must be racking up the electric bill daily.

'I've decided to look for somewhere else. This place is just a bit freaky and after being at uni where everyone mucked in and was friendly, I was hoping for more that kind of vibe, but it's not. It's all a bit vicious. Sorry to burden you with it, but I know you enjoy my bitching anyway. Can't wait to see you when you get back. Take care, love you loads. Gobbles!'

She's right. It's an odd atmosphere. A tension you can't quite put your finger on, but also, I think this is the voicemail that made the police decide not to pursue looking for her too hard – ultimately, she said she wanted to leave, that she didn't like it here. According to them, this also indicates she wasn't happy in her present job. The case is open but as they pointed out, in the UK, a person is reported missing every ninety seconds. Almost 400,000 reports of missing people are made every year, out of which 180,000 people are actually missing, the rest turn up within hours, at most days of taking off. It's a hell of a statistic to contend with. It's not that they aren't taking Julia's desperate pleas seriously – they've taken her DNA and so on, but in their eyes,

Nikki has good reason to have taken herself off for a while. They are wrong, but I can see it from their point of view. I also know Nikki too well and absolutely know she would not take herself off, despite her protestations about these people.

Saul is peculiar. A jack the lad who never seems to want to grow up. I can deal with him, but I can see what Nikki means from a female point of view, he is a bit of a hog.

Jill, I would say, is stranger than the other two. I can only assume she arrived after Michelle left as Nikki never mentioned her at all. She has to be a recent addition, yet no one talked about it. She's out all sorts of hours, so I presume she works shifts. I don't even want to contemplate what she does, but after a closer look, the girl is stick thin. It makes me wonder if she's on drugs.

I know it's none of my business, but everything kind of is at the moment. I need to find out all I can about these strangers in my midst.

Jill, tall and undeniably beautiful, with fabulous nails I suspect are false, letting her down by being bitten and bloodied around the edges. I know I'm a man, but I also recognise dyed hair when I see it, and her make-up is just a little on the thick side of heavy. It makes me wonder if she's one of these influencers too. She's never said, never offered for me to follow her on TikTok or any of the other social media. I mean, she'd have to actually talk to me to do that.

Every time I come in, she scuttles off. I have no idea what she thinks I am, but she doesn't act the same with Saul and Phoebe. On the contrary, she's often in the garden laughing and having a drink with them. The moment I step outside she's like smoke whipping up a chimney.

Then there's those bizarre emails she sends.

Dear Housemates, it has come to my attention that the washing machine and tumble dryer appear to be in constant use from around 6 p.m.–11 p.m. every weekday evening and most of the day on Saturdays and Sundays. I can honestly say I have no idea who could possibly have that much washing for one thing, but also whoever is utilising these white goods to such an extent please consider how much this is costing us. That is all of us! Divided by four as per our contract. I will not be paying the full quarter of the electric bill but will offer a reasonable amount towards my own usage which is considerably less.

The other matter is from this weekend, I will require the washer and dryer from 2 p.m. until 4 p.m. every Saturday and I suggest we have a scheduled timetable for each of us so this awkwardness does not arise again.

I have stuck a schedule to the cellar wall for everyone's convenience.

Hugs

Jill

She has a point. Why she doesn't feel confident enough to verbalise it in person, I don't know, but each to their own and I am quite thankful for that. At least it means if we have a schedule, I can sling my washing in when it's convenient for me and not 11 p.m. when everyone has gone to bed.

Phoebe's instant reply was:

Thanks, Jill. I do hope the schedule you've stuck up doesn't leave marks on the wall as the landlord will deduct from your deposit. I'll advise him who is responsible.

Hugs

Phoebe

Wholly passive-aggressive. Or possibly even outright aggressive. In the light of Phoebe's neglect, I'm surprised she even has the gall to mention leaving marks on walls.

The next email tickled me even more. I mean, not the idea, but the whole self-possessed judgementalism.

Dear Housemates, I realise we are all obligated to keep our own rooms clean, but it has come to my attention that I am the sole person who appears to clean the shared spaces.

This is not fair and unless everyone wants to pay me at the same rate as a cleaner, or someone wants to employ a cleaner to do their bit, then I suggest we all take it in turns to do this job. I would suggest once a week is sufficient, unless like Saul you have continual visitors and make more mess than anyone else, in which case please clean up after yourselves at the time. Of particular note is the amount of cutlery dumped in cold, greasy water in the sink. This has got to stop. Every morning, I come down to this and I am the one cleaning all the cutlery for you to use again. Please wash this at the time of use. We do not have a dishwasher!

As far as the rest of the cleaning is concerned, I am happy to take the fourth week of next month, seeing as I have already done my quota of cleaning, and some, for this month.

I have stuck a schedule on the side of the fridge for everyone's convenience. No marks will be left as the fridge is easy wipe.

Hugs

Jill

Again, Jill is right.

When I first arrived a few weeks ago, the place was immaculate. You couldn't have found a fingerprint if you were working for Scenes of Crime.

Since then, there has been a rapid deterioration, and I'm not going to claim I am entirely blameless, but I agree with Jill, Saul makes the most mess with the constant flow of friends he has through the door.

Women, predominantly.

His response:

> Fuck off, Jill.
> Hugs
> Saul

It's not my business to get between them, but I don't see there was any need for his response. Apart from anything – I know my dad wasn't always right – but he taught me never to put anything in writing that could incriminate you.

I never have.

I never will.

12

TWENTY-ONE YEARS AGO
– FEBRUARY 2004 – ALEX

I sit bolt upright in bed, the last vestiges of my dream yanked from me by a noise so strange, yet familiar enough to make my heart race like the beat of an ancient drum.

'Mum?' The word whispers from my lips.

Despite having no curtains, the room is doused in the heavy black ink of the darkest time of night, when clouds cover the moon and stars, and dawn is still not seeping into the horizon.

I slip from beneath thin covers and my school coat, which is layered on top for extra warmth, and creep towards the closed bedroom door. My hand slips on the round brass doorhandle as I try to turn it. I wipe the sweat from my palm and try again. It's not heat that makes me sweat; on the contrary, it's freezing cold in this big, draughty old house. No, it's fear coating my skin with a slick film.

Night-time noises are not normally something that would get me out of bed. My dad is noisy and recklessly clumsy when he's drunk, and he's drunk most of the time these days. More than ever before.

It's become worse lately. The short days and cold nights have kept us cloistered together with this half term creeping by like an eternity.

Nikki and her mum are on holiday somewhere in Spain. It was booked long before they met me, and as Nikki's mum is a teacher, she has to take a break when she can. Apparently, summer holidays are a no-go as it's so expensive.

Nikki wanted me to go with them, but her mum said Dad would never give permission, and besides, I didn't have a passport, and she couldn't change their holiday to accommodate me. Otherwise, she would have loved to. I believe her. There's something about Nikki's mum. I feel protected. She's the one who sent for social services the moment Dad had ripped me away from her at school that day.

They'd turned up on the doorstep a couple of hours later when he was flat out, sleeping the drink off. They took me away for the night and put me with temporary fosterers. Nikki's mum said she would have had me if she'd known they were going to send me to strangers.

She says if it happens again, she'll be prepared.

I don't quite know what she means, but I am grateful for anything she can do.

We're back to school tomorrow and I'm excited to show Mr Shaw the work I've done on my maths. I have a few questions, but I managed to complete the set of GCSE books he gave me. I know I should have offered to pay for them, but there's no way Dad is going to throw away good money on books for me when he can throw it in the form of drink down his throat. He's progressed to vodka because it's stronger and he can get pissed quicker and cheaper. There's not a day goes by now he's not drunk as a skunk. It was bad enough when Mum first left, but at least he had a job back then. Now he's unemployed, there is nothing for him to do but drink all day.

He's no longer a responsible adult, as they tell me he needs to be. But what am I supposed to do about it? They're the adults. He's my dad. Do they expect me to grass on him?

Instead, I've spent most of the time in my bedroom while he's asleep and I slip out of the back door the moment I hear him stir. I've got no money, so I can't go far, but there's a small community library not far away. It's warm and there are books I'm happy to read even if the choice isn't vast. I often sit in the corner by the window with a pile of kids' books so the librarian can't see I'm reading Wilbur Smith and Ian Rankin. I might love numbers, but you've got to feed the imagination too. Right?

I'm not currently in the library and right now, I wonder what the hell he's up to. Since the last social services visit where the guy read him the riot act – and let's face it, Dad has no respect for women, so this time they sent a man – he's toed the line. At least, he's pretended to. He's told me to keep my gob shut no matter what they try and tempt me with. I'm not allowed to admit that I know he drinks and in all fairness, most of his boozing happens once I've gone up to bed, although there's a bottle of vodka underneath the kitchen sink he believes I don't know about. It's pretty obvious – I've never known him make so many cups of tea. But I can still smell the booze on his breath.

Thanks to Mrs Fletcher, I got to stay at school even though he made some horrible accusations against the teachers there. Predominantly, Mrs Fletcher – Nikki's mum. She was having none of it and told social services I was special. Me. Special. Who knew? She thinks I have potential and she let them know I'd thrive in their school as they already know my home situation. It's all about control, she said, reducing the chances of me going down the wrong path. Seems they agreed with her as I'm still there. Or I will be once half term finishes.

My toes curl against the worn-out stair carpet as I creep down in faded pyjamas too short in the leg, each step creaking loud enough to be a gunshot.

I hesitate at the bottom.

The house is silent again. No hint of the sounds I'd heard earlier.

Is Dad down here?

Is someone breaking in? Not that anyone would want to break into this house with its shabby old settee and mismatched armchair, not to mention grubby windows you can barely see through.

I pause again to listen. There's nothing.

I swear it was a woman's voice, shrill. Like Mum's used to be whenever her and Dad got into a fight. Until he silenced her with a fist, or a boot.

A chilly draught sneaks in from around the front doorframe, sending a shiver down my spine and pebbling my skin in goosebumps.

I pause for a moment and then I hear it.

An intake of breath.

A soft sob.

I press a hand over my mouth, cover it with my other hand, desperate to keep quiet, so whoever it is doesn't even hear me breathe.

Like I can hear them breathing.

Heavy and stilted.

As though they're trying to stifle the sound.

I reach the door to the sitting room and hesitate, terror skittering through my veins like a bird, trapped and tormented by a cat.

I slide my hands from my mouth, take in a deep breath and step into the room.

My jaw drops.

'Dad.' That one word escapes my throat, gnarled and tortured.

He turns his head.

Eyes shot through with thin spider veins stare at me unseeing. Tears streak down bristled cheeks to drip off the end of his chin.

My frantic gaze takes in the scene in front of me.

The woman on the floor who my dad is crouched over is still. Roots show through the dyed black hair fanning out around a small pale face. One I don't recognise from the constant flow of women who traipse through. There are two regulars. None of them ever talk to me. They're here for an hour or more and then gone.

Rough women. None of them like my mum. She was delicate and beautiful, her hair a shiny brown like tempered chocolate, her eyes soft hazelnut.

This woman falls between the two types. Despite the colour growing out, her hair is lush and shiny, her facial features more delicate than the coarse faces of the other women he's had around lately. There's make-up, but not slathered on like one of the women he sees from time to time.

I'm a man, with a man's needs, Alex. You've gotta understand.

I don't understand. There's something even at the age of eleven I understand to be sleazy, wrong. There's a taste of dirt in the air each time one of them leaves as though they've tainted the atmosphere with their presence. The heavy scent of perfume clings to the settee, mixed with another smell I don't recognise, although I do know it's associated with their lurid visits.

Is this woman the same? I can't detect her bitter scent.

Thick black eyelashes rest on her high cheekbones.

Dad leans back as I bend closer to inspect the deep bruising forming a bright red necklace around her throat.

He's choked her.

It was always a favourite tactic of his with Mum. Just a thumb in the soft, fleshy dip of her neck. It stopped her from screaming. Eventually.

It might just have stopped this woman permanently.

I straighten. My chest feels as though someone is sitting on it.

Dad's eyes are filled with tears. Not of remorse, but fear that he's at last pushed so hard that he's toppled over the edge of a steep cliff he keeps teetering on the edge of.

His eyelashes are black spikes, the blue of his irises almost iridescent against their bloodshot background.

His lips quiver, pulling into a downward arc. 'I think I've killed her.'

My heart pounds so loud in my ears, I can barely hear his voice above the frantic rhythm.

'Alex, son, what are we going to do?'

We?

What are *we* going to do?

I have never been a part of Dad's team. He's never wanted me on his side. I'm just an encumbrance. The pain in his arse who just gets in the way of him living his life. That's what he tells me on a regular basis. The same thing he told my mum before she left. I wish she'd taken me with her. I'll never understand why she didn't.

'We need to call the police,' I murmur in the bleak hollowness of the room.

Horror fills his momentary flaccid skin to make it taut and stretched. 'Police? We can't call the police, you thick shit!' Anger rolls out of him, barrelling over the distress of a moment ago.

He leaps to his feet and for one mad moment, I think he's going to choke the life out of me too. Leave me alongside this woman for dead.

'Are you stupid?' he screams in my face, so close droplets of spittle pepper my skin. I don't move. I've learnt the best way is not to move. Just stand still and wait for the tide to roll over both him and me.

'I'm not going to prison. What do you think would happen to you if I get sent down? Huh? Do you think anyone will give a fuck? No, we're not calling the fucking pigs. You have to help me so I don't go to prison and you don't get taken into care, because believe me, there are worse things in life than living with your old dad. So help me, you little fuck!' His eyes are bulging and the waft of alcohol washes over me as he grabs me by both shoulders, pushing his face into mine so somehow I will listen. I will understand his predicament. His eyes are wild and panicked. 'We can put her in the cellar, then move house, like we did when...'

Three loud bangs come from the dividing wall to the house next door and we freeze.

He's woken up old Tim next door and that takes some doing as the old git is deaf as a post. Or so Dad says.

The house shudders under whatever tool he's used to hammer on the wall.

Dad shoves me away and strides over to the wall, takes off his boot and hammers back. 'Fuck off, you old git!'

I bend at the waist and stare down at the motionless woman while I catch my breath.

A numbness steals over me.

My face is frozen, my mind blank.

Old Tim bashes the wall again and Dad screams back at him, spittle flying from his lips. He's completely off his head.

This isn't helping. He's just attracting attention. Tim is yowling about calling the police. This is the very last thing we need, having the pigs arrive. It's one thing to call the police yourself and report an incident, it's something completely different having them turn up, hammering the door down, as you've been reported by the neighbour.

Even I agree with Dad. He's right in one way. I don't want to go into care. I know what it was like for just one night in a stranger's house. It's scary. I lay curled in a tight ball all night with my eyes open, waiting for someone to burst through the door and beat the living shit out of me. I don't want that again. It was scarier than living with Dad. On the other hand, maybe Dad deserves to go to prison. Maybe...

Hysteria throttles Dad's voice but he continues to yell, his face a dull puce edged with a green hue. 'Fuck off, you old bastard!'

Without warning, the woman shoots bolt upright, almost smashing her face into mine, eyes wide with terror as she drags in a great gulp of air, scraping it past the obstruction in her throat.

I spring backwards with a cry as my heart leaps into my mouth and I whack, arse first, onto the threadbare carpet.

Her hand flies to her neck, clutching at it as she pulls in more air, her narrow chest expanding while her lungs fill.

I scramble to my knees by her side and she throws herself into my arms, sobbing. Sobbing so hard I can barely hold the skinny weight of her.

I look up and Dad is motionless where he stands by the dirty old fireplace I'd filled with wood I gather each day and lit earlier in the evening. It doesn't last long, but the heat it brings for that short time is welcome. It's nothing but ashes now.

Even if it burst into flames in front of my eyes, nothing could warm me through now.

Ice trails its sluggish way through my veins as the woman holds on to me and I stare at my dad.

He slowly lowers his arm, his fingers slackening as the shoe drops.

13

I pick up my phone and dial Julia, dreading the hope I'll hear in her voice as she answers.

'Hello?'

'Julia.'

There's a moment's silence. 'No word then?' She must have heard it in that one word. Her voice is frail, as though everything she ever lived for is gone.

'No. I'm sorry.' I cast a glance around the virtually barren room I live in and my hope almost dies too. 'There's nothing. No trace of her. Not a single indication she was even here. She seemed to leave in a hurry according to this lot.'

'Have you spoken with the landlord?' I shake my head and realise she can't see me so I tap the video on the WhatsApp call now we have the initial bad news over with.

Julia has aged. Her beautiful, sleek hair shot through with silver silk strands looks a little unkempt, the dark smudges under her eyes tell of her lack of sleep.

My heart squeezes in my chest. There's nothing I can do here, I am sure. I'm failing her, but I don't know how to make it better.

'Hey. Good to see you.'

She raises her hand to her hair to smooth it down which indicates she's fully aware she's not washed it as often as usual. I'd love to ask her how the holiday went but it all seems too futile and distant now. The sole subject of our conversation is Nikki.

'Have you heard anything from the police?'

Julia shakes her head, her eyes deep in their sockets, no longer the brilliant blue reminding me of Nikki, but a watered-down version. 'They really don't seem to think it's terribly serious. They're looking into it and have taken DNA, listened to her voice notes you sent them. They tell me so many people go missing, but normally turn up again within a few weeks. She's young, she's free, she's single and I was—' Her voice breaks on the next words. 'I was away, not there for her, so she decided to take off. She wasn't happy with the house share. They didn't even report her missing, they just assumed she'd left. With no word. Surely that's not right? And then, she wasn't happy at work either.' There's a quiet snuffle and Julia wipes at her eyes with a white tissue. 'I didn't know. She never told me. The police seem to be under the impression it's not abnormal, but it is for her, Alex, isn't it? She's never done anything bad in her life. She's always told me everything, hasn't she?'

Except, it seems, she never mentioned she wasn't really happy at work. Maybe she thought her mum deserved to retire and take her holiday without worrying. Maybe she'd have told her when she came back. We may never know.

I don't know if she catches my hesitation in replying, but she stops talking.

'She *has* always told me the truth, hasn't she?'

I draw in a breath. She has. Except that one time when she decided to go to a gig at the local pub instead of going to the school disco. The time she was sexually assaulted, almost raped by the guy I then stalked for the next two weeks while I was on annual leave and then gave one of my mates in CID a tip-off when I spotted him setting up another young woman. His DNA was already in the database and it seemed he'd got away with that type of move all the previous summer. He went down for seven years. But no. I never told Nikki or Julia. What was the point?

'Yeah, Julia. There's nothing you need to worry about.'

Only there had been another time. After all, what child tells their parents everything? What parent truly wants to know the real down and dirty? Because everyone has something they want to hide. Don't they? Nikki certainly did. To my knowledge it was the only other time.

When Nikki had finished her finals at university and she moved into my Army quarters while she looked for a job. We never told Julia any of what transpired from that visit.

I say my goodbyes to Julia and close my eyes, with the feeling I get every time I think of Nikki the last time I saw her. The last time we could bear to look at each other.

Nikki had been living in my quarters for six months while I was seconded so the moment I walked through the door into my accommodation, I was bowled over by the scent of her. No longer the little girl I loved, she was now the woman I was in love with. Not something I was ever going to tell her or anyone else. It's not something I'm proud of. It was, after all, quite unexpected. What a hideous situation to be in.

I assumed when she was a teenager, it was just a crush and as I'd joined the Army, it wasn't much of an effort to avoid her without anyone catching on.

Only now, she was living in my house, driving me crazy with her mere presence. The smell of her hovering on the air. She was supposed to have gone by the time I arrived back. Mum had arranged it all, of course, because neither Nikki nor I had been comfortable in each other's presence for some time. Not that Julia knew, she just thought we were terrible at organising things.

Four nights into my return and I walked in on her crying.

It was the first time I realised something happens to your heart when the love of your life is upset. There's a fist squeezing it until every drop of blood drips out before your eyes.

I never want to feel that again. Not that I have any control over it.

'Nikki?' I'd said.

She looked up at me from where she'd hunched over on the settee and I saw she was holding something in long, elegant fingers.

'Nikki, what's wrong?' I sank to my knees in front of her and that's when I saw it. The pregnancy test. I'd seen these before, only the ones I've looked at have all been negative. One clear blue line. This one had a definite two striping across the pen-like plastic and my stomach lurched.

Her blue eyes sparkled like Ceylon sapphire as she stared into my eyes. 'I'm pregnant.'

I nodded once and said nothing. What could I say?

'Don't tell Mum.'

I shook my head. 'It's not my place to tell her. You need to, though.'

She flung the pregnancy test to one side. 'Alex, what am I supposed to do? I can't be pregnant. I have a life to lead and I've not even started. I'm not able to support a baby yet, I won't even get maternity leave. What the hell am I supposed to do?'

'Who's the father?'

She looked at me aghast, as though that was last thing on her mind. And apparently, it was.

'I don't know.'

'Liar.' My voice was a low whisper.

She stared at me, the wash of tears dashed away by a rush of anger.

'You weren't here. You don't know!'

I reared my head back as though she'd slapped me. What the hell did she mean?

'Who is he?'

She gave my shoulder a bump with the heel of her hand and I toppled backwards onto my arse.

'It's none of your business and besides, that's not the point in any case. I don't want you to go and beat up your best friend, I want your help in deciding what to do.'

My best friend.

My best friend?

I drew in a breath and instead of getting up, I pulled my knees up to my chest and looked her dead in the eye. 'He's married.'

'What?'

'Iain. My best friend. He's married.'

Her mouth dropped open and she stared at me a long moment before tears filled her eyes and my heart shattered. I've never been able to bear her tears. They crucify me.

'Married? He never told me he was married.'

She slumped back on my sofa, her body seeming to hollow out in the middle. 'I never knew.'

'Yeah. Lisa is his wife's name. She's about ready to drop.' I nodded in the direction of Nikki's flat stomach to drive home my point.

'She's expecting?'

'Any day now.'

Fury burned in my stomach. At her, yes. How stupid could she be? How gullible? But more at him. My so-called best friend having an affair with my sister, because that's who I introduced her as when he came around the first day she arrived, just before

I left for my secondment. What I didn't say to her was, 'This is my best friend Iain, and he's married so please don't have sex with him.'

Instead, I'd asked if he'd keep an eye on her.

It appears he took me at my word.

The bastard.

I rolled to my feet and paced away across the room until I stood in front of the windows which looked out onto a small grass patch I'd called my garden.

'You're going to have to tell Mum.'

'No! I can't, Alex. She'll hate me.'

I turned to face her. 'Your mum would never hate you in a million years.' She might be disappointed, but that's a whole different matter. I know for a fact that Julia could never hate her own daughter. Nikki had no idea what the hate of a parent is really like.

She leaped up from the settee and came to me, buried her face in my neck and wrapped her arms around my waist. 'Alex, I don't want to think about it tonight. Don't make me think about it, just hold me, please.'

Although it almost killed me, I did exactly as she asked and let her burrow into me, holding on tight like I'd never let her go.

But there's always a time to let go.

Two days later, Nikki was doubled over as I returned home from work. Tears streaked her face and I cradled her in my arms, rocked her to give her any comfort I could.

My sweet girl. It's not her fault. She's just a little too trusting.

'Alex.' She raised her hand and cupped my cheek. 'There's no baby. It's gone.'

Shock had rippled through me. 'You terminated your pregnancy?' I couldn't believe she would act so rashly, that she'd make a decision before talking it through with me, with her mum, who, to my knowledge, she still hadn't told.

She looked as stunned as I felt though, and pulled back to look up at me. 'No, no. I hadn't made a decision. I'd not thought it through.' She blew out a breath. 'The choice was taken from me. I started my period this morning.'

I'm not sure which one of us was mortified the most.

Now, I close my eyes and pinch the bridge of my nose between my thumb and forefinger. I feel bad for Julia, because like most parents, there are certain things their children don't want them to know, but it's not my business to disillusion her. She doesn't want to know her daughter didn't always tell the whole truth.

14

TWENTY-ONE YEARS AGO – MARCH 2004 – ALEX

It's been a whole week since that strange woman leaped out of my arms and raced for the door, leaving behind my dad and me in a fog of confusion.

He tried to cover things up between us, saying it was just a joke, they were having a bit of fun, he didn't mean it, but I'm not stupid. I know what he did. And that was no fun. Certainly, the woman didn't think so, nor did he as he screamed hysterically, pounding on the dividing wall. We're just lucky the police weren't on the front doorstep hammering on the door. I reckon it was only because of the deadly silence following the gunshot sound of her slamming the door.

My heart raced as I slunk off to bed with Dad's words ringing in my ear.

'It won't happen again. I didn't mean it. I promise, kid. This is the end for me.'

It's happened before. I've no doubt it will happen again. It's our way of life.

I'm so exhausted, I'm slumped over the school dinner table, automatically shovelling food into my mouth with little interest.

'Cheeses!'

I lift my head up as Nikki places her dinner tray on the table and flops into the chair beside me in the school dining hall, puffing out a loud, dramatic breath as she crosses her arms over her skinny little chest.

Normally I would pull one of her pigtails, or rub the top of her head, but today I'm not in the mood. I'm distracted. I've not had a single opportunity to do what I want to do this week as that woman coming back to life seems to have jolted Dad into instant sobriety.

He's not drunk a drop since and I'm stumped.

By Tuesday, he'd got himself a job on a farm shovelling shit, but someone has to shovel it. Strange how this man who claims how hard it is to find employment suddenly managed to when he gave it some effort.

At least he gets paid in cash daily and he said if he does okay, they're going to teach him to milk cows and he'll get paid a lot more because you have to know how to attach the equipment to their udders.

Makes my tummy all queasy thinking about it.

He bought me a term-time bus pass on Wednesday so I can get myself home, just in case he has to work over and social services find out I'm loitering around the school. I might as well be at home alone where they are less likely to see a red flag waving. At the end of the day, it's cash in hand and he can't have his cake and eat it. Whatever the hell he means by that.

There was even food in the house last night. Admittedly, it was the supermarket's own-brand pasta, mushroom soup and a reduced-price roast chicken that had gone cold, but it tasted pretty damned good when I threw it all together and heated it up under the watchful eye of my dad.

We're not out of the woods entirely. The reason I make dinner is because the tremors in his hands are so fierce he'd end up cutting or scalding himself. He says he's going cold turkey, but I know it's chicken we're having.

He daren't pick up a sharp knife, but at least he can shovel shit.

The farmer even dropped off a whole load of proper logs for the fire last night and Dad didn't even have to walk home. We soon got them stacked by the fire and all I had to do was rummage around for kindling in the wooded area behind our house. I never realised wood isn't supposed to spit and spark the way it's been doing all the time I've been bringing it home. Dad says that's because you're supposed to let it season which I had to look up. It means don't use green wood. Now I understand, in the future I'll know to find the older stuff, not branches that have just fallen. Because there will be a time when I need this knowledge. Knowledge is power.

It's the first time heat has managed to seep all the way through to my bones and I'm pathetically grateful.

I was grateful for the milk and Weetabix this morning too. It filled my stomach and the energy that kicked in stayed with me until lunchtime, although when it drained out of me, it seemed to go in a manic rush, leaving me weak. Now I need my strength, when I'm being pestered by this little monkey, who I am really starting to like, even when she is a pain.

'Cheeses!' Nikki says again up close in my face while she grins.

I sigh.

She wants my attention, but it's elsewhere at the moment because I need to formulate a plan. Perhaps if I just deal with her, she will leave me in peace.

'What's up?'

She jumps up and walks around behind me so she can

whisper in my ear. Loud enough for the whole table to hear, but she's trying to be discreet.

'Mr Folkestone told me I have to buck up my ideas if I expect to leave school with anything other than air for a head.'

I crank my neck around to look at Nikki. 'Are you saying Mr Folkestone called you an airhead?'

Nikki does a dramatic roll of her eyes up to the ceiling and I do wonder if Mr Folkestone has a point.

'Yes. Cheeses!'

My lips twitch. 'Where did you hear that word?'

'What word?'

'Cheeses.'

'Well, Mr Folkestone, of course!'

'Mr Folkestone is really old—'

'Older than my Grandad Fletcher,' she interrupts.

'—and he shouldn't be saying things like that. Not in front of kids.'

'Like what?'

'Well, calling you an airhead and saying—'

'Cheeses!'

Nikki evidently likes the word. She's used it enough times in the past five minutes.

'I don't think your mum will like you saying it.'

She leans in closer and lowers her voice. 'Why not? Mr Folkestone uses it all the time in class. Cheeses this, and cheeses that.'

I stare at her for a long moment considering whether or not to tell her. If I don't, she's liable to say it in front of one of the other teachers and get into trouble. With the school and her mum. What the hell.

'He's saying, Jesus, Nikki, Jesus.'

Her big blue eyes go round and googly until I think they're about to pop out of her head as she flops back into the seat next to me. 'You mean the little baby Jesus?' she breathes back with a dramatic whisper that emphasises the cute lisp she has.

No flies on her.

'Yes.'

'He's saying Jesus?'

'Yes!' I clench my jaw because I need some thinking time of my own, but I don't want Nikki getting into trouble because she comes out with that word in class. I remember the first time I said 'fuck'. I wasn't even five. They sent for my mum. She was horrified.

I shudder.

When she told Dad he couldn't say it in front of me, he punched her in the mouth and shouted it so the whole house shook.

Maybe it's a different classification of word, but not for some parents and teachers who don't want it to come out of the mouth of a five-year-old, especially when they are both mother and teacher.

'Look, don't say it again, okay?' I smooth her hair down and then snaffle some fries from her dinner tray. She doesn't object, she has an appetite like a bird, but then her mum feeds her a full cooked meal at night too, so she's hardly going to miss six fries. 'Some adults say rude words kids shouldn't repeat.' That's what my mum told me back then. Not that I took much fucking notice.

Nikki crams a handful of fries in her mouth and speaks around them. 'It's my birthday next week. Mum said I can have a party on Friday after school and invite who I want.' She pauses to swallow. 'Will you come?'

Dad hates Nikki's mum. She's not too keen on him, and that's an understatement. He says she's an interfering bitch. She's not. I love Nikki's mum. Sometimes in the dead of night when I lie awake, I think other than having my own back, I wish Nikki's mum was mine.

Social services say Dad's to stay away from her and not cause trouble. It means I can't go to their house, either. Social services wouldn't want me to know where they live, just in case I tell my dad. I'm not likely to, but then what if he gets me in a headlock? It scares me to think he might go around to their house and choke Nikki's mum like he did the other woman. Like he did to my mum on a regular basis.

I'm quiet for a long moment while Nikki pushes more fries into her mouth and chews, looking at me with quiet expectation.

'Don't know if I'm allowed to come to your house.'

She leans into me, whispers in my ear. 'Cheeses.' And then giggles.

I smile. My gaze wanders across the room to her mum, who is watching us.

Nikki tugs at my arm, her face in mine as she waggles a bunch of fries at me. 'It's okay.' She rubs my arm in a comforting gesture. 'It's at Making Donalds.'

I don't correct her, it's cute.

She leans in to whisper. 'Just don't tell him whose party you're going to. Mum says she can give you a lift there and back home afterwards.'

'I don't need a lift home, I have a bus pass.' I say it in a sort of superior way because Nikki's too young to get on a bus without an adult. Then again, something else occurs to me.

I frown as I think it through. I could just tell Dad I've been invited to a McDonald's party. I'm not sure he's interested enough in my life to ask whose party it is. He'll assume it's one of the lads in class. Basically, why would anyone think a five-year-old would invite an eleven-year-old to her party?

I didn't have a party when I turned eleven. Dad never even

noticed it was my birthday. He was dead drunk on the sofa and I had to make my own tea that night, which was an out-of-date Pot Noodle with a yellow reduced sticker on it from the local corner shop. Twenty-seven pence, which was all I could dredge up from the coins down the back of the sofa cushion. To be honest, it was a treat. So was the silence in the house when I curled up with a book and read.

Nikki nudges me to bring me back to the here and now.

I nod. 'Yeah, okay then. I'd like to.'

She lets out a whoop as the fries flop around in her fist.

I grab her wrist and bite the fries from her fingers, and she hoots with laughter, throwing back her head so everyone turns in our direction. It may not be considered healthy for me to be with someone so much younger. Perhaps I should be out playing football with the boys in my year, which I will in a few minutes, but I like spending part of my lunchtime with Nikki.

We have a strange sort of bond.

She makes me feel seen.

I always wanted a little sister, and I consider Nikki is mine.

Also, she's just planted a little seed in my head which has already started to germinate. I hadn't anticipated hanging on until next week, but I've waited this long. It can wait a little longer.

I just need to put my plans in place, because I have a sick feeling in the pit of my stomach that I know what Dad has done.

15

The initial impression I get when I first walk through the front door into absolute darkness is that no one is home or, unusually for a Friday night, they could be in bed early. They're not really early to bed people though, certainly not at the weekend, so maybe they're out partying.

It's not my business. I barely know these people, despite my best endeavours to become their friend. They're not interested. To be honest, neither am I. I'm not here to befriend anyone, I just want to know what the hell happened to Nikki. Because the police have come up with a dead end. They seem to believe she's an adult, possibly sloped off with a boyfriend she thinks her mum won't approve of and she will turn up of her own free will. That is not Nikki's character, and I know someone here has to have a clue as to her whereabouts.

It's not that the police aren't taking it seriously, they've done what they can. Who knew there were so many missing people in the UK? One every ninety seconds. According to Julia, they've been to her house and taken DNA evidence in case a missing person's body turns up fitting her description, which I shudder to think about and know in my heart this is not the same as before. Apparently if someone doesn't want to be found, they won't be found. There's nothing to indicate Nikki is a vulnerable adult according to the police. However, she's not used her phone since the last message to Julia, which doesn't make sense in light of her voice notes to me.

> Mum. I'm taking a few days away. I'll see you soon.

And the email to her work, resigning with immediate effect.

It's not normal behaviour from Nikki. A few days is long gone now, and she is still missing. She's not used her phone or cash cards since. As far as Julia knows, Nikki didn't have a credit card.

I pause for a moment in the hallway, pulling myself back from thoughts of Nikki and Julia.

I was under the impression all of my housemates worked, but Saul is still at university. He's doing his second Master's in Publicity and boredom. Snore.

The two fingers of whisky I had in the pub on the way home sits nicely warming my stomach, mixed in with the steak and chips I treated myself to. I'm a cautious drinker, ever wary that at any point, alcohol can tip a person over from an occasional social drinker to a high-functioning alcoholic, to a homeless pisshead. I know. I witnessed it with my own father, although I would go so far as to say I think he may have missed out on the occasional social drinker stage.

I don't get the opportunity to drink so much in any case. My job entails applying yourself mind and soul, and a whole lot of sobriety. Add into that some of the places I'm sent to don't have alcohol and where very possibly it's an illegal offence punishable by death.

When I was fast-tracked to university at sixteen, I was too young to drink and the older students never wanted to get involved with a kid who had a chaperone, making sure I did my homework and was in bed by 10 p.m. It suited me. I'm not exactly a recluse, but I'd classify myself as a loner. I'm selective with my friends. Even my family.

Just as well, the type of jobs I take on.

Off the radar, exceptionally high paid, nil tax in the UK as long as I'm not resident here for more than forty-six days per year. Or the 183-day rule as it's called.

I know I signed a six-month bloody contract with the landlord here, but what was I supposed to do? It was the minimum contract he would let me have. Robbing bastard. But in some ways I do see his point, as his lodgers don't seem to stay long. I thought it was only Nikki, but it appears not. There's some mystery surrounding each one of them and I don't like to prod too much, as they might become suspicious.

This means though, since I first entered the country, completely oblivious to everything, I now have thirty days left to find Nikki. So far, I've not got a clue as to her whereabouts.

I reach for the doorhandle to my room and hesitate.

I move closer, hold my breath and listen.

Muffled noises come from within, and I try to fathom what the hell is in there. Has someone let a cat in? Is it rats?

I twist the handle, fling open the door and slam the light on.

'What in fuck's name are you doing?'

Of the two people in my bed, one of them flings themselves under the covers while the other grasps hold of them, pulling them up under his chin.

'Saul. What the fuck?' Confusion hits me.

He lowers the cover and gives a lopsided grin. 'Hey, bro, I wasn't expecting you back so early.'

Almost speechless, I stare at the writhing ball of a figure under my quilt and hope she's not carrying on where they left off when I interrupted them.

I squint at Saul, holding my hands wide, and shrugging my shoulders. 'What are you doing in my bed?'

He doesn't seem in much of a hurry to get out. 'My bedding was dirty, pal. I didn't think you'd mind.'

Fury steams through me until I think white puffs of smoke might just explode from my ears.

I storm over to the bed and for the first time, there's a flicker of something akin to fear burning in Saul's eyes.

As I rip the cover off him, the diminutive woman unfurls and shoots from the room, straight black hair flying out behind her, squealing obscenities which could possibly be Taiwanese or Mandarin. I don't consider myself a linguist, but I have learnt some of the basic language, I just don't know the dialects, which are rich and varied.

'What did she say? Was that even English?' Stark naked, Saul seems to have little interest in following her. Ignorant git.

'I think she said, go fuck yourself, but not in my bed.'

I grab him by his naked arm, and he really isn't as muscular as he appears fully dressed. I push him out my door stark naked, slam it, and throw the bolt across. That's it! Landlord or not, I will be putting a lock on the outside of my door tomorrow. I'm not having this dirty git having sex in my bed. It makes me wonder how many times he's been in my room and what the hell else he's done in here.

I stare at the bedding.

I'm not really fastidious. I mean, let's face it, I grew up being moved around from pillar to post for eighteen months, through every kind of slum you could imagine. But I don't think I ever had to sleep in bedding with someone else's bodily fluid smeared over it.

Screwing up my nose, I strip the bed and scoop everything up in my arms.

As I throw open my door, there's a small naked woman tiptoeing along the hallway towards me. At a guess, she's been hiding out in my fucking bathroom. It is *my* bathroom, I pay extra to have sole use of it because I am the only one downstairs. The others share the upstairs bathroom. I'm going to slap a lock on that too.

She is diminutive. Saul is no gentlemen, as I already know, but it looks like he has simply deserted her, buggered off to his own bedroom, leaving her to her own devices.

Somehow his callousness stirs pity inside my heart as she freezes, terror streaking across her beautiful, delicate face.

I drop the bedding on the floor and reach inside my bedroom, snagging a hoodie off the back of the door.

I hold it out to her, trying to look solely at her face and not do that thing I'm desperate to do which is scan her up and down. I mean, it's pretty damned hard when there's a beautiful naked woman standing in front of you.

She makes a peculiar squeaking noise as she accepts it, pulling it quickly over her head. The hem hits her around mid-calf and I give her a smile. I'm not what I would classify 'big', but I am six foot two, which is probably a good foot or so taller than this woman.

She bobs a little and mutters, 'Thank you, thank you,' in such a small voice.

I bow my own head. '*Wǒ de róngxìng.*' I may be making a right tit out of myself, but I think it's the way to say 'my pleasure'. I may have the wrong dialect, wrong actual language, but I feel sorry for her and just because I want to kick the living shit out of Saul doesn't mean to say I need to take it out on her. When you get right down to it, she's not the one to blame. Just as all those women Dad brought home weren't to blame either.

Not having a clue where her clothes are, I point to my hoodie. 'Just leave it in there.' I indicate the kitchen next door to my room and she nods her understanding and takes off in that direction.

Which leads me to wonder whether there are bodily fluids all over the kitchen surfaces where they obviously stripped in the first place. I'm going to have to sterilise the room and remember for the future every time Saul brings a female home to disinfect.

He really is a scabby excuse for a human being.

Pulling the bedroom door shut behind me, I scoop up the bedding and set off along the hallway and down the cellar stairs where there's a washing machine and tumble dryer and the dimmest light you could imagine.

I try to ignore the tight squeeze in my chest as I reach the room at the bottom but my breathing has started to come in quick, hard snatches. I thought I had this under control; after all I have been down here a few times now, but maybe the kick of anger and adrenaline has set my nerves on edge, sensitising them to my surroundings.

If the landlord expects he's saving energy with this bulb, he's sadly mistaken. Then again, he may be saving money as the light fitting is so old, he'd have to change the whole unit when the last old light bulb blows.

The washing machine is on full spin and the dryer is doing a lazy tumble of what looks like a month's worth of green towels.

The sound crushes in on me, reminding me of a time when nothing but white noise filled my head and horror consumed me.

My knees go to liquid, and I lower myself onto a short-legged stool and watch, hypnotised by the rhythmic motion of both machines.

My chest tightens as the walls close in around me and the memories I've blocked for twenty-odd years come rushing back like a dam bursting to haunt me.

16

TWENTY-ONE YEARS AGO – MARCH 2004 – ALEX

I've got a belly full of Coke, fries and burger, not to mention the dozen or so leftover chicken nuggets Nikki's friends couldn't manage to finish off. They're only five- and six-year-olds after all, and I'm eleven. I've a big appetite which I think comes from being deprived of food.

I didn't scoff them all, but Nikki's mum packaged them up and pushed them into my backpack, together with a slice of cake so enormous it'll last the whole weekend. I might even share it with Dad.

'You're a growing lad. I know you won't waste anything.'

'What about you?' I turn my face up to her.

She laughs and pats her flat stomach. 'I don't need anything to encourage the weight to go on here.'

I think she's being kind. She always is. Nikki brings an extra banana or apple in her bag for me and I know her mum has sent it. There's no fuss made about it, and I would never ask. They're so generous. I love them for it.

For a moment she looks a little uncomfortable and then casts a quick glance around the manic kids to make sure no one is watching, before she slips something out of her big shopping bag into my backpack.

'I hope you don't mind, but I thought you could do with these.'

I peer inside and a hot flush steals over my skin.

Has she noticed I'm not as clean as the other kids? I know I'm not. Part of it is to do with the icy water we have in the pipes in this latest house we've moved into. According to Dad, the reason we keep being moved is because all the landlords are wankers. I'm beginning to suspect not all of them are. The problem lies more with him than them.

The boiler has been out of order for months, apparently the landlord should be fixing it any time soon. Just in time for summer, my dad says. In the meantime, I have to boil a kettle and fill the sink so I can give myself a quick wash before my bollocks freeze.

The other reason I might be a bit whiffy, according to the biology teacher, is some of us have hormones. When they kick in, we get spotty faces and greasy hair. That's something to look forward to. There are other things as well happening just to the boys that I don't even want to think about. At least we don't bleed to death every month for the rest of our useful lives.

Inside the small bag are two toothbrushes, a tube of toothpaste, a box of Dove soap, a bottle of shampoo and conditioner combined, and a small roll-on deodorant. Personally, I prefer a spray, but beggars can't be choosers.

I think some of those hormones might already be finding me as I sometimes smell under armpits that have started to sprout an occasional fine hair. One of the teachers said I was big for my age. I am. I'm the tallest of all the boys. One of the girls is the same height as me and she already has greasy hair and a spotty face. I think she also has boobs, because she's started to get a bit wobbly there when she runs.

I suddenly become aware of Nikki's mum studying me.

I force myself to look up at her. 'Thank you.'

'You're growing,' she replies. 'I'm not sure your dad is the most observant of his own personal hygiene, and I wouldn't want you to go without because he's not given it a thought.'

I touch the bag and offer up a smile so she can see I'm not insulted. I kind of am, but then I'm so grateful too, so I go with the grateful and force that smile a little wider.

I've noticed the rapid deterioration of my dad's teeth recently. He might have started brushing them again, but I think it's too late. He's done a lot of damage. They are yellowed and decaying and he broke one off when he went on his last bender, which is what he calls them, when he bit into something called a scratching, which from what he said is pig fat. Made me feel sick, both the idea of chewing on hard pig fat and a rotten tooth snapping off, but he barely noticed, just spat it out.

He stinks a bit too, but he says it's because he's been shovelling pig shit now as well. Pig shit smells different from cow shit because they eat different food. He has a cold shower every night when he gets home, but we've no shower gel or soap left.

I can pop this in there now. I only hope he doesn't ask where I got it from as he's never going to stop hating Nikki's mum, ever since she called the social workers on him.

Perhaps I can just use it a few times before I sneak it in there and say I found it in the bathroom in McDonald's. I wonder if he'd believe me.

My toothbrush at home is old and worn with some of the bristles falling out each time I use it now, and I've barely a half-squeeze left of the toothpaste on the side of our sink. Maybe now

Dad is working, we'll get ourselves sorted a bit. Mum used to be so diligent about these things.

Nikki's mum turns and tries to gather up the children so their parents can pick them up safely. When all's said and done, she's their schoolteacher as well, so she has to take extra care.

I tug at her cardigan sleeve and indicate I'm off. The bus stop is only over the road, and there's no way she could know the bus I'm going to catch is travelling to the other side of town from where I live.

'Are you sure, Alex? If you hang on twenty minutes, I'll see you across the road and onto the bus.' Worry crosses her pretty face. She knows I can't accept a lift from her. If anyone spotted us, Dad would go apeshit and knowing him, he'd report her to his social worker and then she'd be in trouble too. As she says, we try to avoid conflict at all costs and it really isn't worth the aggro, or the risk of her job.

'Nah, I'm okay. If I wait for you, I'll miss the next bus. It'll be here soon.'

The last thing I need is her coming across the road and seeing where my bus is headed, which is precisely the opposite direction to home.

I hitch my backpack on and make my way to the crossing, looking both ways just in case a car comes racing around the bend. When I reach the bus stop, I turn and raise a hand to Nikki's mum, who is peering through the McDonald's window. I hope I've got this right. I'm quite good with buses. Dad and I have been catching them on and off for the past year when he can afford it as he was banned from driving. He tells me it was because some idiot pulled out in front of him, but I saw the letter. He was over the limit, whatever that means. I think it was because he'd been drinking. He was lucky they didn't send him to prison, but apparently it was something to do with the fact they took into consideration his wife had left him with a young son to look after. It makes me wonder if it's the sole reason he keeps me with him, so he can play the pity card any time he gets caught doing something wrong. Terrible excuse, if you ask me, and all the more reason he should be acting responsibly. But no one ever does ask me. Except Nikki's mum. Mrs Fletcher.

A cold wind gathers speed as it tears downhill towards me. I zip my jacket up to my neck and punch cold hands into shallow pockets as I stare across the road at McDonald's where the kids are all warm and cosy and every one of them will be picked up by their parents. Parents who love them. Only one of my parents loved me. One would have been enough, only now she's not here, I have no one.

Tears fill my eyes and I convince myself it's another side effect of the blasting wind as I swipe them off my cheek, stamping my feet to keep warm.

As the bus turns up, I flick my pass at the driver and hope he doesn't look too closely. Most of them don't bother, but once in a while you get one who wants to read the entire pass, small print and all. But this guy is running late and there's a sudden surge of teenagers behind me who've obviously run in a gang from McDonald's, their laughter and high voices fill the bus as I take a seat near the front, so I can get off when I recognise where I am, whereas they charge to the back seats where they think the driver can't see them.

I don't look back as the bus pulls away. I'm sure Nikki's mum will still be watching, worried.

It's nice that someone at least worries about me.

Luckily the buses all come around on a one-way loop so unless she could see its destination, there's no chance she'd realise I wasn't going home.

My left leg starts to bounce uncontrollably as I watch for the stop I need to get off at. Rain streaks down the bus windows and the teenagers have steamed up the insides with their heat and laughter.

I hit the stop button and swing out of my seat, making my way to the driver's side and hang on to the rail.

As he pulls the bus up, the doors stick for a moment before a loud whooshing noise tears them open, and hesitating, I realise my mistake.

This isn't it. I've chosen the wrong stop. I don't want to get off here. I take a step back.

My cheeks heat up and I glance at the driver as he stares ahead.

The bus stop is empty, no one to save me by at least getting on here.

Words choke in my throat, but I manage to get them out. 'I— I made a mistake.'

The driver stares at me, doors wide open so the cold wind throws itself onboard.

'You pressed the bell.'

'I know, I...'

'If you press the bell, you have to get off.'

'But I made a mistake.' Panic quivers through me.

'Too true you did.' He jerks his chin up. 'Now get off and stop wasting my time. I'm sick to death of you kids.'

I don't know if he thought I was with the bunch of wild teenagers, but if I get off here, I don't know where I am.

I back away from the door. Fear making me speechless.

A hefty hand lands on my shoulder, and I whip my head around to stare into faded denim eyes.

'Alex, isn't it?'

I nod, recognition coming slowly. After all, why would I know this old lady? But I'm sure I do.

The woman turns her body, small step by small step, her shoulders and neck unmoving as though they have been welded together, her body stooped.

'He's with me, young man,' she addresses the driver, who is not young in my definition, but maybe it is all about perspective. She points a gnarled finger at him. 'He won't be getting off here, he made a small mistake. He's a neighbour of mine and he'll be getting off in another four stops from here.'

She turns away from him, taking small unsteady steps until she reaches the chairs for people with disabilities and sits heavily, grunting out as her backside hits the seat. 'Young Alex, come and sit here, you can look after me.' As I scootch onto the seat next to her, the driver closes the doors, and she points her bent finger at him again, raising a warbled voice so the whole bus falls silent. 'Kindness doesn't cost anything, you know. Just because you're having a bad day, there was no need to be rude.'

He grumbles under his breath, but the bus pulls away from the kerb and she sits back in her seat, letting out a long sigh. 'Nice to see you, Alex. How's your mum? I've not seen her in such a long time. Is she keeping well?'

I don't really know what to say to her, but I remember now, she was the lady Mum used to occasionally take to the supermarket when we had a car. When I had a mum.

'She left us,' I mumble.

My head is bowed, but she reaches out a hand, placing it on top of mine so I look at her. Apparently, there is nothing wrong with her hearing.

'Oh, son, I wondered why I'd not seen her. I've not seen you or your dad around either.'

'We had to move away.'

'When did that happen?' I assume she means the disappearance of my mum, although both events took place relatively quickly.

'Last year. Christmas time.'

She takes my hand and wraps both of her cold ones around it, concern etches deep lines around her pale eyes. 'I'm so sorry. Your mum was always good to me. I hope she comes back soon.'

I slide my hand from inside hers and nod. 'I don't think there's a chance. We've not heard from her since.'

The old lady shuffles around on her bottom so she can face me without turning her neck. Her eyes are large and round, sunken into deep sockets, but I see the concern. 'That's unusual, isn't it? You're her pride and joy, she always spoke so highly of you. She adores you. I can't imagine her leaving you behind.'

Neither can I. I shrug.

'Has your dad been to the police?'

A number of times, but I don't think it's been regarding my mum. I don't really know. He doesn't talk about her. Not since Boxing Day when she apparently walked out of our lives, leaving the front door wide open in the early hours and never coming back.

I nod. I have so many questions right now, but I don't feel she's the one who can answer them, so I'll keep quiet, just until I scope things out.

Dad told me Mum couldn't live with us any more and just went. Deserted us.

Her little suitcase was missing and some of her clothes, but she'd left her phone and purse in the handbag she normally used, which worried me at the time when I found it underneath the settee.

I kept asking Dad, what if she needs us? How is she supposed to contact us without her phone and money? What if she doesn't know how to get a hold of us now we've moved?

Eventually, he told me she'd cleared the bank account out and taken all our money, so we were never going to hear from her again. She didn't love us. Neither of us, not just him. She couldn't, could she? Not if she just left the two of us to our own devices and took all the money we had in the world.

Only now, it makes me wonder how she took the money out of the bank without the card she normally uses, as that was also in her purse.

My chest squeezes tight so I can barely breathe, and there's a slow, slithering panic in my tummy where all the chewed-up McDonald's is sloshing around, stewing in Coke.

The bus pulls up to our stop and I grab the old lady's shopping bags and help her down the step until she seems steadier on her feet. It seems the least I can do to repay her generosity. We're barely off the bus when the bus driver shuts the automatic doors, almost catching the woman's coat before he drives off at speed, or as fast as a bus can go, evidently making his point. I wonder if it made him feel any better or will he carry that anger for the rest of the day, until he gets home. Just like Dad does. Will he batter his wife with his fists until he feels better?

The old lady doesn't appear concerned as she starts to totter off down the road towards her house, leaving me with her bags, evidently believing I'm going to carry them all the way to her door.

I don't object. Truthfully, I don't mind. She helped me, I can spare her a few moments and my strong arms.

'Where are you off to now then, if you don't live around here?'

I shrug as I try to decide which way she's going to go, because whichever way, I need to go in the opposite direction. I can't let her know what I'm about to do. 'Just calling in on an old mate. Dad's picking me up later.' I think I should reassure her, as she's probably the type to double check.

'Oh, who would that be, then?'

My brain races to think of one of the boys from the school I attended when I lived here as there have been so many since, but I manage to pull out a name. 'Kyle.'

'Kyle? Oh, I thought they'd moved to Devon.'

Ice trickles through my veins as I stare into her astute eyes, knowing her brain hasn't been affected by senility.

'Yeah, they're visiting relatives which is why I thought I'd come and see him.'

'Oh—'

Before she can ask any further questions, I change the subject.

'Didn't you have a son who moved away?'

Clearly quite happy to be distracted, her face creases into deep crevices as she smiles. 'Oh, yes. He lives in Australia. Moved out there ten years ago now. He's coming home to visit in the summer with his wife and my two grandsons. I can't wait to see them, although what it will be like all of us sharing my tiny little house, I don't know. I might be glad to see the back of them.' She chuckles and it's evident she doesn't really care about the lack of space, she'd just love them to be with her.

She opens a small metal gate and we're soon at her front door.

'They've asked me if I want to go and live with them in Australia,' she says, quite proudly, her bowed shoulders straightening slightly.

My mind isn't fully on her as I know I need to get away before it gets so late that Dad will query where I've been. He knows I was going to the party, but he'll also know roughly what time it would finish.

It's not as though I can rely on him rolling in drunk and not even knowing what day it is, never mind the time. He seems a lot more astute lately. His temper isn't as quick, but his tongue is just as sharp and his fists just as hard.

I must have made some sort of encouraging noise, as the old girl is prattling on about living in Australia. Or not.

'I think I'm too old.'

I shake my head. She is. She's ancient. But it would be rude of me to say anything.

'You should go. Maybe have a holiday first, see if you like it there. It can be very hot, I've heard.' I think I learned it from a television programme.

'Yes, that's one of my concerns. But, more importantly, I'd be leaving my friends behind and what if I travel all that way and find I don't make any new friends?'

My heart gives a thud. I know exactly how she feels. You reach a certain age and everyone has already found their friends. It's difficult to muscle in on a new group of them. The boys at my school aren't so bad, but you can tell they've been together since birth. I'm more of a hanger-on than a leader.

'Oh, Alex.' She puts her hand on my arm just as I lower the heavy bags onto the front doorstep. 'That was insensitive of me. You must miss your old friends too.'

I nod.

'Although you're so young and you have so much time to make new ones.'

I open my mouth to tell her about Nikki and her mum as she struggles to poke her key in the door, her crooked fingers fumbling.

I take the key gently from her, poke it in the lock and turn it, swing open the door and move the bags inside.

'Can I get you a drink, Alex?' Her voice warbles with hope, making me realise that despite her so-called friends, she is lonely, but I can't do this. I haven't got time.

She's so nice, though, I don't want to let her down.

'Maybe another time, Mrs...?'

'Jean, love. You can call me Jean.'

'Jean, maybe next time, but if I don't go and see Kyle now, I might miss him.'

Her face falls and disappointment is written in her eyes.

'Okay, love. You take care of yourself and if you ever want anything, just knock on my door.'

Little did we know, I'd be doing it sooner than either of us expected.

17

PRESENT DAY – SATURDAY, 13
SEPTEMBER 2025, 5.45 P.M. – ALEX

This is bizarre!

I turn in a circle, taking everything in.

There's no evidence anyone ever lived here.

The place is immaculate.

I puff out a breath. What the hell is going on?

There's a bed with a mattress which looks vaguely grubby, and that's it.

'What are you doing in here?'

I spin to face Saul, my heart giving a sharp knock. I hope the shock doesn't show on my face.

'I came to talk to Jill.'

'She's not here, mate. She moved out this morning.'

I frown. I only saw her last night, admittedly through my window in the garden with the firepit flames casting golden shadows over her face, making her blonde highlights glow burnished orange in the light. But still.

'She never mentioned.'

'Yeah. She told us last night. Well, that's what Phoebe said. I'd had a bit too much to drink, can't remember a thing. My head is like a bucket.'

'I thought we had to give a month's notice?'

'Ordinarily, yeah. She just left a month early and the deposit covers it, I should imagine.'

Strange, as I had to pay three months' deposit. There seems to be a different rule for each of us.

'Did it cover the clean, too?'

'The clean?'

I open my arms wide and turn to indicate the pristine room.

'Nah, it's okay. The landlord sent someone around.'

'Wow, at such short notice? Did he also send someone to move the chest of drawers?'

'The...?'

'Chest of drawers. There was a chest of drawers in here.' I point to the blank space under the small window where I know for sure there was a chest of drawers.

'She must have taken it with her.'

'Hmm.' I feel like asking how she managed to. Did she hire a van, because I'm pretty sure someone mentioned she didn't drive. Did she have help? Did her dad or someone come and fetch her? Because I have a million questions I need to ask.

The very questions I want to ask about Nikki. Because Nikki very definitely didn't have assistance moving. And although her mum has reported her missing and the police have conducted investigations, there appears to be a foggy recollection of when Nikki actually went off radar. Sometime while her mum was at sea. Sometime after she stopped sending voice notes to me. That leaves roughly a ten-day window for her to have disappeared. And someone here has to know. According to Julia, when the police asked the landlord he had no recollection of the last time he'd seen her. He said, why would he? She's only a tenant and he wasn't her dad. She simply took her stuff and went. Both Saul and Phoebe said they couldn't remember the last time they saw her, that she kept to herself. Now I've got to know them, I don't find that part so surprising.

Saul shrugs. 'Mate, all I know is Jill moved out while we were at work and shit.' Pretty sure, as it's a Saturday, Saul was less likely to have been at work, and more likely to be down the local having a few drinks. 'You know what she's like. She doesn't like confrontation.'

If that's so, why would she have told you and Phoebe last night and not emailed the three of us as she usually does?

I decide to keep my thoughts to myself and take a different tack.

'Strange how many girls seem to do a flit from this place.'

'What do you mean?'

'Well, the reason I got my room was because there was an urgent vacancy.'

'I guess it's just the way rentals go, don't you think?'

'Eh, I don't know.' I skim another look over the room. 'Seems to me this was done in an almighty rush. And yet—' I wash my hand over the room, highlighting the cleanliness. The emptiness. Even the curtains have bloody gone. What is it with curtains?

I turn. Look him dead in the eye. 'Do you think someone upset her?'

His eyes go wide. 'Upset her? What makes you think she was unhappy?'

'Because she rushed off without telling anyone.'

'I told you, she told—'

'I know what you said.' I interrupt him and walk towards the door, giving Saul a heavy-handed pat on his shoulder. 'But do you know what? I call bullshit.'

His heavy forehead screws up into deep wrinkles and I get a

little stab of satisfaction that this guy will probably be bald in another five years' time.

'Why would you say that?'

I don't really want to show my cards yet, but there's something about this situation that makes me edgy.

I tug at my bottom lip with my forefinger and thumb, cast one last glance at the room and walk out, murmuring to the man following close on my heels, 'Because I don't trust you.'

18

TWENTY-ONE YEARS AGO – MARCH 2004 – ALEX

I check my watch. I've been waiting for twenty minutes, and the fine drizzle has managed to seep through the waterproof barrier of my second-hand jacket where my backpack straps lie to send an icy trickle down the inside of my coat sleeves.

Since I've been standing here, staring at the house, I've not seen any sign of movement. There's no one home, I'm absolutely convinced.

I have no idea who lives there now, if it's a family or a young couple. I don't know. What I do know is if I don't move soon, I'm going to freeze to death. The longer I leave it, the more likely someone is to come home from work. It's getting on for six o'clock now.

I push away from where I thought I'd be sheltered under a tree, but the gnarled old branches spiking into the sky are bereft of leaves, allowing the persistent drip, drip, drip to fall on me.

The road is quiet and reasonably empty of people with an occasional car passing. I can't see anyone watching me as I slip down the side of my old house to the back garden. The gate is rickety – it was bad enough when we lived here, but it's older now and more fragile, as though it's been well-used.

I push through and head for the back door, hoping they've left it open. Dad frequently did, Mum was always on his case. Funny how his habit for doing that kind of thing seems to have evaporated since she left us. It makes me wonder if he did it purely to annoy her. There were other things he liked to do just to spite her or cause her some distress. He found it funny. I never did. Nor did she.

He'd strip the bed and leave all the bedding in a heap on the floor so that when she came home from working nights as a petrol station attendant she had to wash and dry it and make the bed before she could go to sleep.

Sometimes he'd push the bolt across both the front and back doors so she couldn't open them when she came home. Then he'd say she nagged him so much about leaving the back door unlocked he thought he'd be more secure.

It was spite.

I knew it. She knew it.

It was the kind of thing the kids at school would do to each other. As though he'd never become an adult. Never grown up. That's what Mum used to say through her tears.

The door is locked now, but I wonder if the spare key is still taped on the underside of the kitchen window.

In the silence and the dark, I run my fingers under the length of the windowsill, bumping them over a smooth bulge. With the tips of my fingers, I investigate the small lump, scraping my nails to lift the brown sticky tape away from the windowsill.

It was still there, after all this time.

I just have to pray they've not changed the lock. I doubt it. The door looks exactly the same and if they can't be bothered to do anything about the gate, fix it up or even just hang it straight again, then I seriously doubt they're going to have changed any locks here.

I slip the key inside the lock and it scrapes and grinds, but it turns.

Sneaking inside, I pause for a long moment, listening for movement, for talking, for breathing.

There is nothing.

No radio, no TV, no people.

I am alone in this house in the dark.

It's not something that scares me. I've lived here for the best part of my life. I know the building inside and out. The only thing I don't know is the position of the furniture which I soon find to my detriment as I stub my foot on something and go crashing into some kind of drawer unit in the hallway and knock my knee sideways.

I bite down on my cry of pain and limp along the hall, hands out in front of me in an act of self-preservation.

As I reach the door to the cellar, I hesitate.

In the dark, I trace my fingers over the wooden surface until I touch the cold protrusion of the old brass doorhandle. I turn it and step onto the first concrete stair.

I thought I wasn't scared until the pitch black was so dense, it became a living, breathing nightmare, determined to swallow me into its depths.

I back up.

I slap my hand on the light switch on the outside of the door, a memory surging in.

That was another thing Dad would do. He'd wait until Mum went down into the cellar, then switch the light off from outside and hold the handle of the cellar door, roaring with laughter as she pleaded to be let out.

I'd sit on the landing upstairs and peer through the rails at the top of Dad's head, tears seeping down my cheeks as Mum's pleas would turn to sobs and then eventually die out as she lost the will to fight for her freedom.

She'd wait in the dark until Dad got bored. It surprised me he never put a bolt on the door. Then again, he was hardly the king of DIY.

As my heart slows from a wild gallop to a gentle canter, I let go of the door handle and make my way to the bottom of the concrete cellar steps. At the bottom I wait.

I listen to my own breathing.

A dark shadow catches my eye as it slinks past and I feel the soft touch of something on my leg, shooting goosebumps all over my skin as a tingling sensation weakens my knees.

I whip my head around just as a large black cat with a white bib does a second pass, shouldering into me so I stroke the length of his body before he pads away and my heartbeat settles back down. I wouldn't classify it as normal as I'm pretty sure I'm about to have a heart attack.

We've never been allowed animals. Dad never liked them. I had one little hamster, but she died really quickly, her belly swollen from the whisky Dad thought she could have. Mum said it was probably best not to have another one. Just to be safe. My mum wasn't stupid. She knew what was best.

I shake away my thoughts and look around.

It's a huge cellar from when the Victorians built massive houses to accommodate servants. Mum had told me. She was so proud of our house. The middle one of three which had been converted from one large property. She loved this house. It wasn't a rental, we owned it. I don't know what happened because Dad never said anything about it, but one of their last arguments was about a repossession. She cried when she told him bailiffs were coming. I didn't know what a bailiff was, but I looked it up when I was at school. It meant Dad drank all the money and had none left to pay the mortgage. The bailiffs were coming to take away everything we owned to pay his debt.

I breathe in, trying not to let memories distract me from my mission.

The smell is so familiar. Of spiders and damp with an underlying taint of something else I don't recognise. Maybe it's from the new people, but it's not pleasant.

Mum had told me the cellar originally sprawled the full length of the three houses underneath but was divided by thin walls. The neighbours couldn't hear much of what went on upstairs, but if they were in the cellar, you could hear them talking, even if you couldn't quite discern their words.

I gaze around at the room, different from when we lived here. The new people's packing cases are stacked up, as though they're getting ready to move on again, or perhaps they've just arrived. Maybe it's only a temporary stay. Maybe they've not bought the house, but are renting it. All these possibilities run through my head as I try not to concentrate on the real reason I am here.

High up in the wall is a small rectangular window which opens outwards onto the front garden. We never used it, but I suppose it was to let in daylight back when the house had servants.

It was too high to reach, but the heavy wooden cases stack a good way up the wall.

My gaze wanders over the room, skipping from item to item, mixing the familiar with the unknown.

I think I know what I'm looking for, but I don't. Not really.

I feel as though I will recognise it when I see it, but for some reason I thought it would jump out at me as soon as I walked down here.

The place is so much cleaner than when we lived here. The

stone floor looks like the heavy brush leaning against the corner of the wall has been used to scrub it until there's barely any evidence of dust left.

There's a chest of drawers and I slide the top drawer open, revealing neatly arranged tools of varying types and sizes. Jeez, who does that? Certainly not my dad. His were all piled into one rusty metal box. I can't recall the last time I saw it. Probably when we moved. Not that he ever used his tools, even though he claimed he was a fully qualified carpenter. I never saw any evidence and not one of his jobs has been in carpentry to my knowledge.

I turn in circles, looking, looking, but nothing jumps out at me.

The room is the same, but so different.

Neat and tidy. Somehow it makes it look smaller. Maybe it's the boxes stacked up. I don't know.

There's nothing here. There's no point. I'm just wasting my time. I don't know what I expected to find, but it wasn't this. It wasn't *nothing*.

Maybe I wanted a hint, some clue as to where Mum has gone. But there is nothing.

I shudder as the cold down here seeps through my damp clothes. My hands are turning blue.

Disappointment lies heavy on my shoulders, so they droop with weariness. I need to go back to our house. I hesitate to call it a home. It's nothing like a home to me. I need to move though, Dad could be waiting.

I turn and place my foot on the bottom step, and noticing my shoelaces are undone, I bend to fasten them.

The ceiling above me creaks.

I freeze.

Shit!

My breath stalls as I listen for another sound from above me. There it is again.

Someone is here, in the house.

What if they notice the light on in the cellar and come down?

I'm going to get caught.

Without giving myself time to think, I slip silently around the bottom corner of the stairs.

The door into the cellar swings open and a deep, bear-like voice yells, 'Who's down there?'

19

PRESENT DAY – FRIDAY, 19
SEPTEMBER 2025, 10.45 P.M. – ALEX

'Who's down there?'

I turn my head just as Phoebe, feet thundering, races down the stairs.

'What are you doing down here?' She's almost growling, spittle forming on lips I swear are thicker than they were the day before. Has she had fillers, or is it an allergic reaction? I swear she's frothing at the mouth and wonder whether I should ask her if she's been bitten by a rabid dog recently.

I'm not sure she would take too kindly to that.

I spread my hands and shrug, trying not to stare too closely.

'I need to put my bedding in the washing machine. This lot's finished so I was about to take it out and put mine in.'

'That's my washing, and you're not fucking touching it.'

She barges past me, elbowing me out of the way. Wow, she is such an animal.

'Hold on, there's no need to be rude!'

She swings around and glares up at me. 'Rude? Rude?' She pokes me hard in the chest with her forefinger. I consider grabbing it, twisting it until it cracks, but then I'd be breaking cover, and I don't want to. Not yet.

'You're the one ripping my clothes out of the washing machine,' she snaps.

I raise an eyebrow and remain silent, which seems to give her pause for thought as the tumble dryer makes its rhythmic whoompf, whoompf, whoompf, because I've not actually touched any of her clothes yet, I'd only opened the door on the machine.

'I don't want you messing with my underwear like a perv.' But the heat has gone out of her voice.

I stay calm. It seems the calmer I am, the more it unnerves her.

'I'm not a perv. If you're looking for one of those, you should look at Saul. He's the reason I'm having to wash my bedding.'

She blinks up at me, I suspect because I just moved fractionally, and the ceiling light skims across her eyes unkindly, showing the crow's feet a woman of her age shouldn't have.

'What are you talking about? What's he done?'

'I caught him having sex in my bed.'

Her mouth drops open. 'You did *what*?'

'Saul was having sex in my bed because he said my room was so much cleaner than his, or something to that effect. So if you're looking for a perv, you're looking the wrong way.'

Phoebe frowns. 'Who was he with?'

I'm not sure it has anything to do with this, but I shake my head. 'No idea.' I put my hand out to indicate the young woman's height. 'Yay high, Chinese, long, shiny black hair.' I add, 'Pretty.' Because she was.

'The shit's going to hit the fan when Alice finds out.'

'Who is Alice?'

Why do I know nothing about these people who I'm living under the same roof with? This is bizarre.

'She's his fiancée.'

'Fiancée?' Now, that is a shocker!

'Yeah.' She turns her back on me and starts hauling the load of washing out, so tightly packed that every item is intertwined with all the other items. She yanks at a bra strap unsuccessfully as the hooks have embedded themselves in what looks like it could have been a fluffy pink fleece. Its sleeve stretches as Phoebe hauls on that too and I have to stop myself from laughing as she turns back to me, her face filled with frustration.

'Saul got engaged last month,' she spits out.

It's my turn to drop my jaw. 'You have to be shitting me. Last month!' My thought is if someone is going to cheat on their fiancée, maybe it's because they've been engaged too long and they're bored. What an arse. He's not changed his lifestyle one bit to accommodate this fiancée.

'I shit you not.'

'How come they don't live together?'

'Her mother is some religious nut, doesn't believe in sex before marriage.'

'Are you saying Saul hasn't had sex with his fiancée?'

Knowing Saul as I do, even in this short period, I can't see that being the truth. I'm aghast. I didn't know it was a thing these days. I thought everyone slept with everyone else until you found a comfortable fit and decided you were getting too old to sleep around any more.

'No!' She looks at me as though I'm stupid. 'Of course they have. She's just not allowed to live with him.' She tugs hard at the washing and something gives with a loud rip. Giving up, she throws it all into a basket with a snort of disgust.

I give her a lopsided smile. 'I'd offer to help, but you might think I'm just trying to cop a feel of your knickers.'

She stares hard at me, and I wonder if she has a sense of

humour at all. She never seems to laugh, she's mainly on the warpath and that path normally leads to me.

'Lighten up.' I push past her and start throwing my washing into the machine.

'I hope you've got your own washing powder because you're not using mine.'

I dig my hand into my joggers' pocket and pull out a single laundry tab. I think it's lavender and chamomile, but don't judge me. They were on offer. Maybe that's why Saul decided to use my fragrant bedding instead of his own. Or maybe he didn't want his fiancée smelling the other girl on his sheets. Sheets he evidently doesn't wash often enough. At the thought, my stomach gives a sharp lurch.

I sniff at the pod to rid myself of the thought before slipping it in with the washing and close the door. As I reach out to set the programme, Phoebe pushes my hand out of the way and spins the dial around.

'What are you doing?'

'You don't want it on the long programme. It costs more and we're all sharing the electric bill. I don't want to pay for your dirty laundry.'

I snort. 'It's not my dirt, it's Saul's.'

She screws up her nose.

'Besides,' I continue. 'You had yours on a long programme.'

'No, I didn't. I just had it on a hard spin because then it costs less to dry if you spin all the water out.'

'But you ended up almost strangling yourself with your own washing.'

She sneers at me. I mean really, this girl has the sneer off to perfection.

'Do as you please. I'm just trying to help.' She seems to be taking the high ground, but there is none to take.

'Of course you are.'

Her phone pings and she takes it from her back pocket of her jeans and reads the message, types a reply and sticks her phone back in her pocket.

Her face has transformed from her normal antsy, don't fuck with me look to stiff with inner fury.

'Wow, I'm surprised there's a signal down here,' I say just to break the heavy silence.

Phoebe glares at me. 'It's intermittent.'

As she turns her back, snaps the door of the tumble dryer open, hauls the laundry out and dumps the contents on top, I sneak a peek at my phone.

'No53-5g1_Ext' shows, which is different from the normal Wi-Fi network upstairs. I tap on it and connect automatically without requesting a password.

Full service down here on the Wi-Fi, which is incredible compared to the signal I get in my own room.

I look up and she's watching me.

I indicate my phone. 'There's full Wi-Fi down here. Better than I get upstairs.'

Her brow crinkles. 'So fucking what?'

I'm looking around, but I can't see an extender anywhere. Nowhere, unless it's behind the washer and dryer, but I can see their plugs are in exposed sockets either side of the white goods.

'What are you doing?'

'Looking for the extender.'

'What? What do you mean?'

'Well, we have the Wi-Fi upstairs which let's be honest isn't the hottest spot—'

'Mine is okay,' she interrupts.

'Mine isn't brilliant.' She opens her mouth again, but I hold up one finger to stop her, which surprisingly works. 'Down here, though, it's a different SSID.'

'I don't know what you're on about. What's an SSID?'

'A service set identifier. It means there's an extender to the original one upstairs. Here, let me show you.'

I reach for her phone, and she snatches it away.

'Wow, Phoebs, do you have a big brother who took all your toys away from you when you were little?'

Her eyes unexpectedly fill and I start to stammer in the face of her tears.

'Jesus, I'm sorry, I never meant to upset you. Forget I said anything. Sorry.'

She blinks up at me, strokes a forefinger under one heavily made-up eye to wipe away the wet and a streak of black eyeliner which she wipes on the leg of her jeans. 'I had a brother. He died when I was twelve. Don't fuck with me, Alex. I don't like it.'

She turns her back, lobs the ball of washing into the dryer, turns the timer, slams the door and stomps upstairs. All without speaking another word.

Guilt makes my chest ache, but how was I supposed to know? It's not as though anyone here really talks to each other. Except for when they think I'm not around, then they break out the booze and have a good time.

It's not that I need to be their bosom buddy, but I would like to know the basics about them.

I scan the cellar. Other than the two sockets for the washer and tumbler, there's no other source of power down here. There's a light switch at both the top and bottom of the stairs, thank God.

With one last look, I turn and head up the stairs, my breathing becoming shallow as I near the top, my back stiffening as I resist the urge to turn and look behind me because despite having the light on, there's an abyss from beyond the grave calling to me. I pause and close my eyes holding on to the stair rail as I compose myself before I reach for the handle and step out of the cellar instead of hurling myself out as I desperately want to.

I pause as a thought occurs to me.

Will the door be open?

Or has Phoebe locked me in?

20

TWENTY-ONE YEARS AGO – MARCH 2004 – ALEX

I leap back behind the stairwell wall, out of sight of whoever that is up there. He didn't sound like an ordinary man; his voice, barked down the stairs, was deeper than any I've heard before. More terrifying than my dad's, but maybe that's because I'm so used to him yelling continually. This guy's voice is like a sonic boom.

'Show yourself now! Don't make me come down there!'

I squint up at the narrow window and back to the stairs. If I go up there and get stuck trying to escape through the window, that bear is going to haul me back down by the ankles and beat the living crap out of me. I know what men are like, especially if they've been drinking.

Panicked, I swing my gaze from side to side. There's nowhere to hide.

Except...

There's a narrow gap between two of the stacks of boxes and I make for it, silent as I can, ripping off my backpack and lowering it into one of the empty boxes on the floor where I hope he won't notice it, before I squeeze myself into the space.

My arms jammed by my sides, I edge back inch by inch and wedge as close as I can behind the one stack of boxes that don't butt straight up against the smooth, cool wall and pray the beast doesn't see me.

He huffs at each step he takes, the expulsion of sound growing louder as he comes closer.

I squeeze my eyes closed, fear spiking so hard, I think I might just wet myself. My feet are cramped at right angles to my ankles like a little kid learning ballet.

He's so loud he must be almost on top of me, his breath coming from above, so close I know he's just about to discover me. I press my lips together, desperate to swallow down any noise that wants to erupt from my throat. My brain is empty of all thought except fear.

My entire body is consumed with a tremor so fine, it probably can't be seen, the dying quiver of a piano being fine-tuned, but I can feel it and it's about to break me open.

'What the fuck are you doing down here?'

My eyes spring open, my mouth doing the same as I prepare to humiliate myself in front of this man. I really am going to pee myself.

But he has his back to me.

'Fucking kids. Did they lock you in again? They're lucky you didn't shit down here, or there would be trouble.'

He bends, letting out a loud fart I think for one mad moment is a gunshot and almost leap out of my hiding spot and confess everything. Instead, as he straightens, his big black cat looks directly at me from the dizzying heights of the huge man's shoulder, glowing green eyes half closed in superior judgement.

'Come on, Demon, lad. Let's get you back upstairs. I hope you've cleared up a few mice while you've been down here.'

I barely breathe as the man stomps one hard step at a time up the stairs, stopping at the top, I assume to catch his breath. It wheezes in and out for a long moment.

The door slams closed.

I am plunged into darkness so thick it almost chokes me.

I sidle from between the boxes, feeling my way with my fingertips, terrified in case I knock something off and that bear comes stomping back down here to investigate further. I literally cannot see my own hand in front of my face. My eyes bug out in a desperate attempt to catch a hint of light.

The small oblong window is paler than the thicket of black all around me and I shuffle towards it, feeling for my backpack along the way. My fingers touch the straps.

Something skitters in the darkness.

It scurries across the back of my hand, and I snatch it away, squeaking with terror.

I dip my hand back into the box and snatch my backpack out, visions of rats and mice scampering from inside the bag where the leftover McDonald's party food is.

I clamber onto the lowest box, envisioning their stacking pattern in my mind's eye. On my hands and knees, I trace the edges of the box, find the next one, scramble up, touch the wall for reassurance that I'm in the right place.

I look above at the pale grey light filtering through the narrow rectangle and hope fills my heart. I stand, stretching until I'm on my tiptoes. I know I can go higher, but once I am on the final box, my head will be against the ceiling, my body flattened. I reach up, grope around for a catch or handle all along the window surrounds.

My breath is coming in short, panicked snatches now as I find a small latch. Blind, I cannot envisage how to undo it. I push, I pull and finally when I lift, something budges.

With relief, I cautiously raise my backpack above my head,

thankful no further furry critters have emerged from the pockets, and place it securely on the final box.

I drag myself up, feeling the box move, tilt.

I drop back down again. Calm myself. I did it for the first two, I can do it this time. Although I am aware this one isn't as sturdy. I'm pretty high up now. If I fall, I could do some serious damage, not to mention attracting the attention of that brute.

I stretch, high as I can, my hands gripping on to the wooden box until something gives. My skin splits and I cry out as a shard of wood pierces through my flesh, but I scramble the last foot of the way and balance precariously on the top, waiting for everything to come crashing down around me.

A huge splinter seems to have skewered the plump base of my thumb, but I daren't try to remove it now, not until I am free. Tears leak from behind eyelids I've squeezed tightly closed while I wait for the wave of pain to pass, hoping the cry that escaped wasn't loud enough to have that beast charging back down here again.

I give myself a long moment before I move.

Almost doubled over between the box and ceiling, I push at the window frame.

It creaks but doesn't give.

I brace my coated arm against it and throw my whole weight against the window, gasping as it punches outwards and a whip of cold air rushes in to leave me breathless.

The window falls back against me, but I catch it, wedging it open with my elbow.

Pushing my backpack through to the other side first, I limbo through the tight gap, holding my breath in as my hood catches, and I am stuck.

There's a moment when I think I'm not going to make it, that I'm going to be wedged here until morning when the sun rises and this family leave the house, seeing me at ground level floundering like a landed fish.

That's not going to happen.

I reverse back through the gap, slide my coat off, shove it through the window and follow, shimmying and writhing until I pop out the other side.

Keeping low, I roll onto my side, check the window and tuck a thin piece of serviette paper from McDonald's between the two edges of the window frame to keep it from closing tight. Just in case. You never know.

A swathe of light washes over me and I duck, hiding my face from view of the car lights sweeping past to pull into the drive next door.

Before the passengers get out of the car, I snatch up my backpack and dash to the nearest tree, hiding behind it as I tug my coat back on, shivering against the cold.

My right hand is throbbing where the splinter has speared through. I investigate with tentative fingers and swallow back the nausea as I feel the swell of my skin around the wood. It's a huge splinter. In the dark, I can't see if there's blood, but I know I have to get it out before it festers and my hand falls off, because somehow, I know Dad won't do anything about it.

I let out a little sob as the memory of Mum cleaning my knees after a fall fills my mind and I know I will never have that again.

I nip the splinter between my fingernails and pull, hopefully in the right direction at the angle it entered – I know about angles, I'm good at maths.

The splinter doesn't budge so I lower my head and grasp it with my teeth.

I smother the howl of pain as I yank the splinter out, the warm rush of blood oozing out behind it to fill my palm.

Gasping, I ferret in my backpack with my left hand, yank out a bundle of cheap serviettes from McDonald's and slap them on my wound. I tip my head back against the tree trunk, squeezing my eyes closed as pain sears through me and bright sparks pop behind my closed lids.

When the rush of nausea eases, I open my eyes.

My bum is frozen against the chilled, damp earth beneath the tree. I have to move. To get home before Dad gets suspicious. What am I going to do? He may not care, but he will want to know how I injured myself.

I glance back at the long, narrow window and wonder how I managed to haul myself through it. It's much narrower than I thought from this angle.

I need to think about when and how I'm going to return.

I'm not done yet.

Because something just occurred to me while my eyes were closed, my body shut down, but my brain still whirring.

I think I know what it is.

I can't do anything about it now, but I do know I'll be coming back.

Flinging my backpack over my shoulder, I stride off along the pathway and through the rusted metal gate until I reach a door with dried, cracked paint and raise a brass knocker. I give it a firm whack, whack, whack and wait a long moment, wondering if I should try again.

As the door creaks open, I plaster on a weak smile. 'Hi, Jean, I'm sorry to bother you. My friend had to leave earlier than I thought, so I didn't see much of him.' My voice is quavering from the first big lie I've ever told. I hold out my hand and crimson stains the wad of serviettes I have held against it and a drop of blood falls onto her dirty doorstep. 'I had an accident as I was leaving. Can you help?'

21

Horror clutches my throat as I lie, tucked into my sleeping bag, in the semi-dark. The rhythmic turn of the tumble dryer a faint and irritating thud adding to the terror of the dream I've just woken from. I'd had no choice but to sneak into the cellar and swap the washing over after I heard Phoebe clunk her way up to her bedroom earlier.

I might get hell from my housemates for putting it on at this time on a Saturday morning, but some bastard took my bedding out of the washing machine and dumped it on the top then filled both the washer and the tumble dryer with their own items. God only knows where this many clothes come from and where did the wet clothes come from that were put in the tumble dryer? Did Phoebe jump the queue with her washing? Does it mean someone else then came down afterwards?

I never heard anyone. It's too bizarre for words. All this sneaking around in the middle of the night.

You'd think after the number of houses I've lived in, I'd be aware of every sound, every movement from someone else. But I never heard a thing. I slept like the dead and now I'm awake but drowsy. I'd like to put it down to jetlag, but I arrived back in the UK a few weeks ago now.

That's how it feels though. Sluggish. Like my body and brain aren't in sync. Like I've picked up a virus.

I wriggle out of my sleeping bag and haul on a T-shirt and a pair of joggers. Slipping bare feet into trainers, I wander over to the patio doors and draw back the curtains. Clouds parting like shredding ribbons, a thin line of pale peach starts to push away the night sky from the bottom upwards.

A quick decision has me sliding the doors open and stepping through. With the door key in hand, I lock up and let myself out of the back gate.

I breathe in the fresh air, pulling it into my lungs so my chest expands.

I start with a walk, legs heavy and leaden, lengthening my stride over the next few minutes, forcing myself to push through this lethargy, then I am running, running, running.

My feet slap on the dry pavement and my knees feel the impact of running on solid ground instead of the grass I'm used to, but I push on, push through, shaking off the tiredness.

I follow a sign and suddenly I'm in a vast park, other runners taking a more leisurely run.

I slow my pace, so I don't panic people into thinking I'm trying to escape a monster. The monster is only in my mind.

'Hey, Alex. It's been a funny old day. I woke up feeling so sluggish I had to drink three cups of coffee before I started to shake off this dreadful feeling. I don't know if I'm coming down with something, but this isn't the first time I've felt like this in the past few days. My limbs feel heavy.

'I asked people at work if they all felt okay and now, they think I have a mystery illness and want me to work from home. No chance.

'I've put my notice in at the house, and I only hope the landlord returns my deposit because this lot seem quite careless. Saul is especially disrespectful. He just doesn't seem to care, and I swear he actually doesn't know how to use a vacuum cleaner, either that, or he believes because he lives with females he doesn't have to clean up after himself. It doesn't matter how many times we nag him to do his bit, he just doesn't.

'He's really started to bug me, and to be honest he's the reason I'm leaving. I don't know what he does for a living, but he seems to be partying all the time, if not here, then he comes bumping in at all sorts of hours of the morning. Now, I'm no prude, but I think it's a different woman every week and the other night, they were smoking weed out in the garden. The stench of it permeated my whole bedroom.

'Perhaps that's why I feel so tired. Maybe they've drugged me.

'Because my room is downstairs, I hear every noise as he gets home, and I swear the other night he was having sex up against my bedroom door. He's loud and very grunty.

'When I complained to him in front of Phoebe, he said I should get a life, have sex more often and take some sleeping tablets if I can't bear him having a good time.

'I think that's the straw that broke the camel's back. Honestly, he's such a troglodyte. I came in the other day and he was sat in the lounge with his shoes and socks off, bare feet propped on the table eating a whole chicken. Like, the entire thing in his paws, ripping it apart like Henry VIII. No plate. And God only knows where he wiped his hands. He is revolting. I think the more repulsed I show I am, the more deliberate he is. Like it's a challenge to make me feel ill.

'I think what shocked me the most though, was how hairy his feet were. Like a bloody hobbit. I wondered for a moment if he'd bought some hairy socks, but no, they were actually his own feet.

'When I opened the fridge and reached in for the milk, which I have labelled with my name, there was grease on it. Chicken grease. I had the most revolting thought that Saul has been drinking directly from my milk carton since the day I moved in.

'I nearly threw up and I haven't kept milk in there since. I'd rather do without.

'I had considered buying one of those desktop fridges. I don't keep anything much in the fridge here because it disappears, even if you label it as Phoebe insists. I would not dream of taking someone else's food. On the odd occasion when I've had no milk, I've asked the others if I could use theirs. Where is the respect?

'I now feel sick because I've used Saul's milk a couple of times and I realise he probably always drinks from the carton.

'Anyhow, I won't be here for much longer.

'Mum will be back from her holiday shortly and I'm taking some days off work to go and visit once I move out. I think there's another place not far away, but the rent is considerably more.

'House shares are so incredibly difficult to get a hold of. Most people already have a group and they all move in together, but if you're a single person on your own, it's not so simple.

'Anyhooo, I'll stop whining. I hope you're keeping well.

'Mum says when she gets home, she'll send you a food parcel. She's never offered to send me a food parcel. You're her favourite child, now.

'Take care, love you loads. Gobbles! Mwah.'

I check my watch and slow to a fast walk. I've been running for almost an hour and I'm now at the opposite end of the park from the house.

Stupidly, I didn't bring water with me and I am gasping, dying of thirst. Not literally dying. I know what that feels like. I was once caught in a sandstorm when on patrol in Afghanistan with two other Army lads. We were so disorientated, it took us two days to return to base after the truck broke down. Never again will I take water for granted.

Sweat is evaporating from my skin as I head towards a small stall selling coffee and bagels.

I gasp in air. I've pushed too hard for too long, and my legs have gone to jelly, my muscles weak. Odd though, this feeling of low-level nausea and tiredness that's struck me a couple of times now in the morning. This is exactly what Nikki was complaining of too. Maybe the house is built on some ancient ley lines or there's radon gas in the ground. Surely, though, it would have been discovered before now. It just seems such a coincidence. Although no one else seems to have complained about it.

I wipe my wrist across a sweaty forehead as I order myself a bacon-filled bagel with brie and cranberry and a large black Americano, both of which remind me of Nikki's mum and our Sunday morning treats.

My stomach clenches as the smell of grease and coffee hits it and I glug down a bottle of water while I wait for the tall, young, tattooed woman to give me my order.

I particularly like the image running across one naked shoulder, up her neck and across her chest, disappearing into the low neckline of her boho dress. I know it's boho, Nikki's mum wears those dresses and has done for almost as long as I remember her.

'Are you always open at this time?' I ask as the woman leans forward for me to wave my Apple Watch over her little square card reader machine.

'Normally eight, but I was a little early this morning.'

'Lucky me.'

'Indeed.'

She has a nice smile and I find myself smiling back as she hands over my food, although I'm not really in the mood for talking. Maybe another day.

I take the coffee and bagel and head for a picnic table no one else is sitting at this time of the morning.

I stare at a huge pond in the distance, birds flocking and taking to the sky in silent murmuration.

Where are you, Nikki? Where the hell are you?

As I wait for my coffee to cool, I scroll through my emails which are few and far between as I never sign up to anything and don't fall for that bullshit 'give us your email address so we can forward your receipt' nonsense from shops, and then they spam you for the rest of your life.

There is one message that catches my attention though.

It's from His Majesty's Prison in London. Belmarsh is where my dad was sent twenty years ago. I've never once visited him, nor replied to his short, demanding letters. I don't want to keep in contact as the social workers advised in the beginning. Why would I want to?

The email is short and to the point.

Dear Mr Whittles,

We are sorry to inform you that your father has recently been diagnosed with stage four pancreatic cancer which has been confirmed to have spread to his lymph nodes. He has declined any treatment and doctors inform us he is not expected to live beyond a few weeks.

He has requested you visit him here in HMP Belmarsh's hospital and expressed he would like your forgiveness in order to give him peace of mind before he passes.

I don't read any further. I delete the message and pick up my coffee, blowing on it so the steam wafts away and dissipates as fast as my thoughts of my dad.

When I finish my bagel, I glance at my phone and there are

no messages from Nikki's mum yet this morning. She's messaged me every day since I arrived back in the country. Sometimes twice a day. I tend to answer even though I have nothing to say.

What is there to say?

Sorry, Julia, no news.

Every day.

There's no hint of her daughter. No evidence she was even in the house, except maybe when I first arrived and I thought I could smell her particular scent as I walked in the door the first time. Like she'd lingered long after her physical being had departed.

I'm not sure she's departed this world though.

Then again, what kind of judge am I?

22

TWENTY-ONE YEARS AGO – MARCH 2004 – ALEX

I sneak downstairs, shivering in the early-morning chill which has frosted the insides of the windows. And I thought nicer weather was on the way and we were no longer in peril of dying of frostbite. Shows what thought did.

Dad is splayed out across the settee, face down, arms and legs wide so his left side dangles, his knuckles grazing the threadbare rug, reminding me of the ape that he is.

The fire has long gone out and I'm not sure how the cold hasn't woken him.

Then, when I check him, I realise why.

The whisky bottle that's rolled under the settee is empty. I can only assume it was full when he nicked it from his employer. It's certainly not one of the cheap brands he'd buy in a supermarket. I know this. I've had too many years of experience to be fooled. He never just started drinking when Mum left, like he tries to fool people. He's always had a drink problem. You could say that was why Mum left. If you didn't know better. But cheap has always been his choice. He'd have bought a mixed blend, not a twenty-five-year-old single malt. Not that I'm some kind of connoisseur, only I like to study the labels on the bottles and I know the difference in price from the receipts I've seen dumped on the kitchen table.

My chest aches.

Does this mean he's out of work again?

I look at the cold ashes in the fire, and over at the stack of logs, wrapping my arms around myself. It's still so cold and the damp has seeped so far into this house it's going to take the whole summer to warm it up. If that's the end of his job, we only have these logs to last us until the weather turns. I don't even want to think as far as next winter. We'll probably have been moved on again by then. They want to do the house up, give it to a family in need. More need, I daresay they mean.

I give his foot a swift kick and get nothing but a grunt from him.

That's him done for the weekend.

I glance out of the window as the sun starts to rise, lighting the sky with brilliant apricots and golds as though nature is totally oblivious to my plight.

Slipping my feet into my trainers, I pull on an extra hoodie over my T-shirt and sweatshirt, then my school coat. I dig my hand in the pocket and pull out my bus pass. At least I have that. It's valid for weekdays only. I was willing to risk the journey last time when it wasn't strictly the route I was supposed to take, but trying to use it at the weekend is blatant misuse and they might take it from me, which will stuff everything.

I lean over Dad and dip my forefinger and middle one into his back pocket and pincer them around what I hope is a bundle of money. Surprisingly, there's quite a lot there and I wonder if he's managed to nick that too. It wouldn't be the first time for that either.

Heat blooms over me as I'm not used to stealing, not even

from my dad, although I have been known to take the occasional pound coin when I've found it down the back of the settee. That's fair game, isn't it? Not stealing, so much as discovering.

This is stealing.

The wad of notes unfolds in my hand and I stare at it as my mouth goes dry.

I sit on the small armchair Dad managed to salvage from the tip and listen as the springs creak and groan under my slight weight.

I count out the money.

There's 380 quid.

My chest squeezes.

I've never seen so much money.

Has he stolen it, along with the whisky? Or did he earn this? Was it a pay-off to get rid of him?

Whatever the case, I'm never going to see any of it. Before we know it, he'll have drunk it all and we'll be back in the same old boat we were before, especially if he's gone on a bender.

I peel off five of the notes, pause for a moment in thought, then take another three and slip them into the inside zipped pocket of my coat.

If nothing else, I can keep some back and make sure the food cupboard is stocked. Dad wouldn't know from one day to the next. I've often shoved milk in the fridge and he drinks it without ever querying where it's come from. As though some secret milk fairy drops by in the middle of the night, just to make sure he's stocked up. I'll do the shopping once I've finalised my first task of the day.

I push up from the collapsing chair and stuff the remaining money back into Dad's jeans pocket, freezing as he grumbles at me, swatting away my hand as if it's a fly. With any luck, he'll either not have counted it, or he's going to think he lost some of it.

I lean back in and tug the wad so it's showing above his pocket, like it's spilling out. That might be more convincing.

Leaving him to sleep it off, I sneak out the front door. I daresay I don't need to be quiet, but there's no point taking the chance of him waking before I've gone.

At least this way I won't be in direct line of his fist when he does wake. He's not going to care if I'm not around. He'd rather I wasn't. In fact, he probably won't even come round for a good few hours anyway.

The bus driver gives me a hard stare as I offer up the twenty. There was nothing smaller in my dad's pocket. His loose change would be in his front jeans pocket, meaning I would have had to root around under him and I'm not willing to do that. I wasn't going to chance him waking before I escape.

'My gran never had anything smaller. She said to say she was sorry, and to bring back the change. She's not very well and she wants me to do an errand for her. I can't be long.' Funny how when you lie once, it becomes easier the next time.

I flash him a smile and try to keep my spine straight. Perhaps the little old lady the other night gave me some kind of confidence. Granny Jean. I almost chuckle. I wish I had a Granny Jean. She was unbelievably gentle, cleaning my wound and giving me hot chocolate. I think she was secretly thrilled that I called in on her, even if she oozed sympathy. I think she enjoyed the companionship and wanted to fuss. I might call on her again one of the weekends, keep from under Dad's feet while making an old lady happy. And besides, she might have some more of those custard creams. I liked those. I've never had them before. She said they were a little old-fashioned with all the chocolate stuff around these days, but I liked them dunked in the hot chocolate while her little coal fire burned and her radiators bounced with heat while she declared she didn't believe in getting cold at her age.

It was worth the clout around the ear I got from Dad when I walked in the door late. The only thing stopping it from being more than that was when I gave him the Maccy D leftovers. I didn't want it anyhow, not once that little mouse tried to get in. I think there was a bit of mouse shit on the paper too, but I flicked it off without him noticing. The cake was further down in my backpack and I wasn't going to share that with him.

The driver huffs loudly and then counts out the change, giving me more coins than he needed to as I can see a fiver in his tray. Rather than risk getting thrown off the bus, I count the change and take a seat halfway up the aisle.

I don't want to attract attention.

By the time we arrive at my destination, the slight hope I had of weather setting in so I'm not seen has been completely annihilated. The sun is blazing and for that, I should be grateful, but I'm roasting in my four layers of clothes and this time, I deliberately didn't bring a backpack.

Although I did bring a couple of tools.

I think one of them is called a chisel.

It's one of the few tools Dad has because he sold them all after Mum moved out. More likely he traded them for a bottle of beer.

Heavy in my trouser pocket is also a hammer which drags my joggers down on one side until I think they're going to slide off. I chose it because it was smaller than the other claw hammer he kept. It fits nicely in his spade-like hand, but I realise now just how weighty it is.

As the bus pulls up at my stop, I get off and wait a moment while the other three passengers disperse before I make my way along the road to my old house.

My heart is throbbing so I gasp in air and tug at the neckline sticking to my sweaty skin.

In the driveway, a large man, belly overhanging his trousers, is bent over, tying the laces of thick black boots.

It has to be the guy who stomped down the stairs the other night. The sheer size of him is so overwhelming that just the sight of him sends terror dashing through me until I need to pee.

I walk past the drive and onwards, entering the small copse of trees where I can quickly relieve myself.

I strip off my coat and hoodie, taking the cash out of the pocket and transferring it into my joggers just in case someone nicks my clothes, which I shove deep into a bush, hoping no one will see them there. There are certain little tricks I've picked up off my dad over time, and this is one of them. We had to when we were sofa surfing as we'd be turned out of one place before we'd found another and you can't tote everything around looking like you're homeless. Even though we were.

I loiter on the edge of the woods, watching as the giant of a man walks flat footed to their open doorway and yells so the whole neighbourhood can hear.

'If you want to go to Nanny's, then move yourselves or I'm leaving you behind.'

A delicate woman, looking older than him, comes out the door followed by two boys who might be twins, possibly younger than me by a year or so. It's not always easy to tell as I am tall for my age. Taller than the rest of the lads in my class.

They load up into the car and a small brown and white spaniel spins in circles, wagging its tail, and I can only think how lucky I was that I didn't encounter it the other day. He surely would have given me away.

As they drive off, I inch forward.

I hope there's no one left at home. A big brother who is going to thrash me, or another dog, which is something I never consid-

ered last time. I know there is a cat, but we're okay. Demon and I
are cool.

I dash to the house, give a quick look around before I unhinge
the cellar window, praying they don't have nosy neighbours who
might see me, and if they do, that they think I'm just one of the
twins getting back into the house after they've been locked out.

I give a brief thought to the key I left in the back door on my
last visit. I wonder if one of the twins got hell for leaving it in the
lock. If they even noticed there was an extra key.

Nothing snags as I squeeze through the gap, and I'm thankful
I left all my layers behind.

Despite being daylight, the cellar is close on pitch black and I
pause for a long moment, getting my bearings. I pull a small torch
from my pocket and place the chisel and hammer on top of one
of the boxes.

I really need more light.

I clamber to the top of the stairs and wait, ear against the door
into the hallway as I listen for movement, sound. There is
nothing.

I shoulder the door into the hall open, reaching around to
switch on the cellar light, before I ease it shut again, not wanting
to risk leaving it wide. Just in case. It would be like waving a red
flag.

Knowing my luck, one of the kids will have forgotten something vital and they're all going to arrive back any second, barging
into the house and tumbling through to the cellar, waggy-tailed
dog in hot pursuit of me. It was bad enough with the cat, but the
thought of a dog leaping all over me doesn't exactly fill me with
confidence. I'd have loved a dog, but the truth is, I think I'm a bit
frightened of them.

I leap down the steep steps as fast as I can and survey the
cellar, my breath heaving in and out of my chest.

Once again in full light, I scan over each part of it. Filled with boxes that were never there when we lived here, does it look smaller than the space I used to play in as a child? Or is it just my imagination?

It does look small, but it brings memories swirling back of a better time, when despite Dad's bad temper, I still had Mum.

That happy space where Mum encouraged me to stay when Dad was on a bender. It protected me from him, I know that now. Even as far back as four or five years old, I can remember playing down here.

The floor had been covered in a threadbare green carpet, keeping the chill from seeping through from the concrete beneath, but Mum had a strange pipe on the wall which sent heat out provided Dad didn't turn it off. There was a large brown beanbag and throws I could wrap around me.

I turn in a slow circle.

This place holds for me a mixture of beautiful memories and dread.

In the far corner there'd been a play kitchen Dad had rescued from someone's garage when he was working for them and I wonder now if he stole it, or if it was given freely. There's no way he would have bought it for me.

Green and white, I spent hours cooking at it after Mum had scrubbed it clean, distracted by all the pots and pans while Mum lay across the beanbag, tears rolling down her cheeks day after day as her black eye turned to purple then yellow.

She taught me to sneak food into the cellar and hide it in the kitchen. Because, hey, why would Dad look in what he called 'a girl's toy'? It strikes me now, why would he bring me a toy he didn't consider suitable for me? Was that an insult? Or had he actually intended cleaning it up and selling it on, but once I took a liking to it, it was too late to do anything about it?

Whatever the case, I didn't see it that way. I saw it as a tool to feed Mum and me, and one day I thought I might run my own restaurant. Which is more than I can say my dad does.

He had no idea we also started to keep a small torch taped to the back of it so when he locked Mum down here all alone, she had a light so it wasn't so scary.

Now, I look at that corner and I am convinced, even with the stacked boxes, the room is a different shape.

My brain likes shapes. It likes maths. So is that how I can see this perspective?

Aware I must leave my escape route open, I manoeuvre the boxes out from the wall to investigate further.

Touching the wall, I skim my fingertips over the flat surface.

This is what I found odd the other night. Pressed tight against it, my memory of this wall was a rough surface, stickled. Mum's face scraped as Dad threw her against it. It was more of a stone fascia rather than this new, smooth surface.

Pressing my face against it, I run my hands over the surface and close my eyes. No, this wasn't here before. This wall doesn't hold the icy coldness of the stone that was here before. It's too smooth and— I step back and gasp. Modern. That's what it is. It's too modern for this old building. It doesn't belong.

I knew it! This is why I brought the tools.

I know the guy here has tools of his own, but I think most of them were power tools and I'm not confident I would know what to do with them.

Without any further thought, I reach for the chisel. I think the hammer would make too much noise, I can't risk the neighbours hearing, especially if they saw the family leave for the day, and besides, it needs something sharp and pointy to pierce through the wall.

It occurs to me I'm about to damage this family's property just before I raise the tool and plunge it into the wall.

23

Tears of frustration trickle down my cheeks as my arm refuses to budge. Not even one more time.

I sit back on my haunches and consider the little I have achieved.

The wall is pock-marked with what looks like hundreds of holes, but the chisel hasn't breached it.

My chest feels as though I've torn it apart and my arm is a lead weight, with no more strength to lift the chisel than it has to wipe my nose.

Plaster dust covers me from head to foot and yet I still have not managed to make a hole in this wall.

The tears drip off my chin and I sniff, opening stiff fingers to let the chisel drop from my hand, allowing it to clatter onto the floor. Defeated. Scattered blisters fill my palm, the worst lodged in the crook of my thumb, little white sacs of fluid that hurt like hell. Dad would say it's because I have skin like a girl's, soft and smooth, not like his work-roughened hands, made for hard work and wife beating.

I blink away the dust and tears and scrub the sleeve of my sweatshirt over my face, leaving a trail of snot up the arm.

I don't know how long I've been down here, but I'm exhausted and my stomach is telling me I should have eaten by now.

As I stand, a wildfire of pins and needles rush into my feet and I can't move. Pain radiates up my legs and I realise the blood hasn't been getting to my feet for ages. I try to step forward but numbness encases my legs until I whimper.

I pat my pocket for the pack of tissues Nikki's mum had passed to me at school with the rest of my survival kit. While I wipe my gritty eyes again and blow my snotty nose, my gaze is drawn to the hammer. I reach for it. Would this do any good now I've weakened the wall?

Dropping the tissue at my feet, I clutch the hammer in my left hand as there is no way I can use my right.

I raise it above my head, claw first, and smash it into the wall with all my pitiful strength.

The claw of it breaks through the small dints I've created in the wall and I rip it back, tearing a hole almost the size of my head. Delirious with success, a spike of energy courses through my body and I suddenly have the strength to carry on.

Gritting my teeth against the pain, I raise the hammer again. This time, ignoring the blisters, I grip it with both hands and slam it into the wall, ripping downwards where the hundreds of chisel marks pitting the wall have weakened it.

An enormous hole opens up and I stagger back, unable to breathe as the stench from inside comes out to greet me, enveloping me in a cloud of the foulest odour, coating the inside of my nose and tongue until it burns, and I know I will never rid myself of the taste of it.

Horror fills me as I stare into the small cavern at the stippled wall of my memory and then my gaze drops down into the dark pit below.

The threadbare rug I used to play on, tassels ragged and stringy, is rolled up and stained with large dark patches, white plasterboard and dust are scattered liberally over the top like snow.

Hand over my mouth and nose, I take one step forward, squinting into the dark hole until the moment I recognise the candyfloss poking out of one end of the rug as Mum's hair.

I back away, swallowing down as saliva bursts out, choking me while my stomach races up to meet my throat.

'What the fuck is going on?'

I spin around, determined to run, only my legs fail me and I stand rooted to the spot.

The huge man in front of me takes a split second before the odour hits him, turning his face from fury to shocked revulsion as his gaze centres on the sight behind me for one long moment. He takes a step forward to get a better look and I know what he will see. I can't think. I can't move. It's as though something in that hole came out and froze every muscle, including my heart.

I know the moment he sees what I have, as he slaps one hand over his mouth, and with the other, he grabs my wrist and hauls me up the stairs.

At the top he slams the door behind us, his eyes wild with fear and confusion, his back against the door as though barring anything from coming out.

'What the hell was that?' He points downwards towards the cellar, but I can tell he's already guessed.

Tears stream down my face and drip onto the back of the hand he is still holding me by.

His sigh puffs out over the top of my head, making my hair flutter.

He bends down so his square head is the same height as mine.

'Listen, son, what were you doing down there?'

The truth bursts out of me.

'We used to live here. It was my house. Dad told me Mum left, but I think he killed her and hid her down there.' I squeeze my eyes shut. 'We left her behind.'

He draws in a swift breath. 'Jesus Christ.' He rubs a hand over the stubble on his face, making it rasp, and then looks over his shoulder at a woman I assume is his wife. 'Fiona, take the kids upstairs, love.' His voice is gentle and hushed, belying the urgency he must feel.

Eyes wide with worry, she is quiet as she rounds the children up and ushers them upstairs.

The man stares at me intently. 'Listen, son. I'm going to call the police. Okay?'

I give one mute nod as numbness settles in, paralysing my brain.

'Come through here.' He leads me into the kitchen and slumps down onto a wooden chair as though the strength in his legs has gone, indicating for me to do the same on the one next to him.

My legs have gone to jelly and there are no words of protest. No words at all.

He digs in his pocket and pulls out a phone. Taps in a number as wrinkles cover his forehead, confusion filling his eyes.

'Yeah, I don't know how to say this, because it's insane, but there's a young boy broken into my house who claims he used to live here and—' He glances at me and a wash of pity fills his eyes. 'He claims his dad killed his mum and left her here in our cellar.'

He wipes away the sweat beading his forehead with the sleeve of his sweatshirt. 'It's insane, I know, but he's busted down a wall and there's something in there. I couldn't see it properly but it's not good. It stinks like he's opened the gates to hell.'

He pauses as someone obviously asks a question.

'Yeah, man.' He blows out a breath. 'The kid's taken down a wall in the cellar and—' He stops again, this time to gag. 'I've never smelt anything like it. You need to get here quick because I have to get my wife and kids out of this house before the stench comes through the cellar door.'

I picture it like a horror movie, a thick yellow cloud edging its way under the door and engulfing us. I lean back in my seat to try and check if it's coming to get us.

Again, he pauses, shaking his head as if the person on the other end of the line can see him.

'No. I don't have a clue who the kid is. I'd say he's about fourteen years old. Yeah. But from the sound of it he's not got a mum to care for him and I'm guessing you'll be looking for his dad.'

I open my mouth to speak but it's as arid as the Sahara Desert.

He looks at me, narrowing his eyes to study me like I'm an amoeba under the lens of a microscope.

'Yeah, you might send an ambulance too. Too late for the woman downstairs, that train has long gone, but I think the kid might be in shock. His name? Yeah, just a minute.'

His voice is soft as he leans forward, but I can still see his whole body tremoring. 'Hey, kid, what's your name?'

This time I manage to say what I need to. 'My name is Alex Whittles. My dad is called Paul. He's at home asleep. He drank too much. We live at number 32 Hillstone Avenue, Malinslee.'

'Did you get everything?' the man asks the person on the other end of the call.

I'm talking now and don't seem to be able to stop.

'We used to live here up till when I was nine and I'm now eleven. My dad used to hit my mum and sometimes strangle her.

We used to hide in the cellar to keep out of his way when he'd been drinking. He said she left us, but I knew she would never leave me. So when he strangled a woman in the new house and was going to put her in the cellar, I knew. I just knew. And I came back. I came back to find my mum because she would never leave me.'

My voice breaks as the man sits opposite, his mouth frozen open and the phone drooping in his hand. But the floodgates have opened, and I can't stop the words spilling from my lips.

'I knew he'd done something bad to her. I just knew. But I didn't realise until a few weeks ago. When that other woman got up and ran away, but I knew what he would have done if she'd stayed dead on the floor. I could see it in his eyes. He said we were in trouble and asked what we should do. But it wasn't us. It was him. Only him. He was the one who did it. Not me. But he wanted me to help him this time.'

I swipe my sleeve across my nose, aware of the dust and snot streaking the material as the bizarre thought crosses my mind that I left the packet of tissues down in the cellar and now I will never get them back.

The man places the phone on the kitchen table, screen up and still connected to the police. He walks over to the sink, strips off a reel of kitchen towel and hands it to me.

I bury my face in the paper towelling and scrub so all the dirt and dust, snot and tears mix together to form a disgusting wet, dirty mess, shredding the paper as I rub too hard. Not hard enough to cleanse the image from my mind.

Nothing will ever do that.

I lower my hands to my lap, my fingers gripping on to the soggy paper.

The man's eyes are now soft with pity and sadness, and I

know it is for me and for my dead mum lying in their cellar, wrapped in my play rug.

My voice catches in my throat as I try to breathe in.

'I don't want to be here any more. Can I go to Jean's house? She said I could go any time I wanted to. She only lives down the road. I can't stay here.' Not for a minute longer do I want to stay in this house.

I think of the safety, the anonymity of her house. Of how she'll let me into sun-filled rooms and allow me to sit in the quiet. Then I think of something else, too.

'Could you please call a teacher for me? She's my friend Nikki's mum. Her name is Mrs Fletcher. Can you ask her to come and get me from Jean's house?'

I wriggle off the seat and dig into my jeans pocket, producing the small piece of paper she'd stuck inside the little bag with my toiletries. The piece of paper I keep on me at all times. It somehow has made me feel safer.

I hiccup as I unravel it, already wrinkled and faded from the number of times I have opened it, tempted to ring. To hear her voice. To ask for help.

'I want my own mum,' I say, a sob in my voice that breaks on my next words. 'But Nikki's mum said she'd look after me when the time came.'

24

I sniff at the milk, thinking it tasted a little weird yesterday, but now there's definitely something wrong. It's well in date and at first I wonder if someone has nicked my milk and replaced it with their own soured one as mine still has a sell-by date of another four days. I wouldn't put it past this lot. Syphon it out of one bottle and into another. They all seem so petty.

There's no one else in the kitchen so I pour it down the drain. It's not gone to yoghurt yet, and I don't even detect that soured milk smell. But there is something.

I rinse the milk away and turn, the carton still in my hand.

'Hey.'

I raise my head and stare at Saul as he leans casually in the doorway, his thumb at his mouth as he picks something from his teeth. There's something about this man I just cannot stand. Maybe I'm influenced by Nikki's words, maybe because he's a dick.

His gaze flickers to the carton in my hand and then back to my face. And I wonder.

'Did you want some?' I raise the empty carton and waggle it at him.

He drops his hand to his side and saunters into the room, opening the fridge to peer in. 'Nah, I'll have some of Phoebe's. It's fresher.'

I walk past him to the bin and drop the carton in with cool deliberation, watching him all the time, curious, because how did he know my milk would be off?

There's a nasty little suspicion stirring in my mind.

He reaches into the fridge and snags Phoebe's milk out. I know it's hers as it has 'PHOEBE'S' written all over it in bright red ink. He unscrews the top and glugs it straight from the carton.

I can't help the distaste crawling across my face. 'Jesus, Saul, you're a fucking animal.' I never even acted like that when I was virtually starved to death as a kid. There are certain basic standards everyone should adhere to. Not drinking from someone else's carton of milk for one. Not having sex in someone else's bed for another.

He smiles as though he's proud of himself, pleased to be classified as an animal, and I'm dying for him to say something, anything to give me an excuse to plough my fist into his face.

'Got out of the wrong side of the bed this morning, mate?'

I open my mouth to reply and then close it again. What does he know about my sleep?

I squint at him, pluck the carton from his fingers and screw on the lid, placing it back in the still open fridge and close the door softly afterwards.

'Do me a favour, pal, get your own food and drink and leave everyone else's the fuck alone. And that goes for my bedroom too.'

He still has that stupid wide grin on his face, perfect teeth I swear he's had whitened gleaming at me and I have the compelling desire to push them down his throat. He raises his fist and gives me a soft push on the shoulder. Nothing to speak of, just another mild insult. Nothing sufficient to warrant a backlash. Not unless that push was a trigger.

Before he's even had chance to pull back his hand, I have him slammed against the fridge door, the rattle of its meagre contents scraping past the white noise in my head to fill my ears.

I may be shorter than his six-foot-four frame he's so proud of, but every muscle in my body is honed for survival.

With my forearm across his neck, I lean in, using my weight to cut off his air supply. Just for a moment. Only so he gets the idea I am not the person he thinks I am. A pushover, a nerd. I know I nurtured that impression in an effort to gain their trust, but no more. I will not stand for it.

'Don't. Fuck. With. Me.'

His eyes are wide and admittedly, they've started to bulge a little from his sockets, but I want to get my point over so I no longer have to deal with this idiot's shit.

'If you ever touch my stuff, or Phoebe's stuff – any of it, including beds, milk, forks, or our fucking mugs, I will splatter you around this room, bury you and clean up the mess before anyone even knows you are missing. I have the knowledge, the ability and the contacts. Got it?'

Under the circumstances, with Nikki missing, this may not be the most appropriate or diplomatic thing to say, but I am beyond caring. According to these housemates I am sharing with, they know nothing.

I realise I'm pressing a bit too much weight on him. My gaze narrows in on him as he tries to gulp, his Adam's apple grinding against my forearm. I ease the pressure before his puce face turns blue and lean out of his space without letting go entirely.

'Do I make myself clear?' My voice is soft, barely above a whisper but there's a deadly edge to it he doesn't ignore.

He gives a quick, desperate nod and I release him, using my hands against his shoulders to push away so he bumps back into the fridge again, his head making a light smacking noise, as I wander over to the kettle.

'Coffee?' I ask in my most pleasant voice and glance over my shoulder to see Saul slumped at the kitchen table, his hand cradling his throat. Wordless, he shakes his head and I can't help the little smile as I turn my back on him to fill the kettle.

'Hey, boys, what's going on?'

I turn, lean my backside against the kitchen surface, giving a casual shrug as Phoebe walks in, heading straight for the fridge.

'Nothing much. How about you, Saul?' There's an evil little stir of pleasure as I note he can't pull himself together enough to bestow one of his blazing grins on Phoebe. She gives him a second, curious look and then pulls her carton of milk from the fridge.

'I've just heard we're getting another girl.'

'Another girl?' For a moment, I don't get her meaning, and then the penny drops.

'A replacement for Jill. She's arriving tomorrow. Someone I know from the nightclub I go to on a Friday night. I recommended her.'

I turn my back and pour boiling water on my cheap instant coffee I only keep because no one else seems to like it, not that it stops them taking any food no matter what it is, and turn towards the kitchen door. 'I've just boiled the kettle, there's enough in if you'd like some.'

Phoebe smiles, but I can see from the quick flick of her gaze to Saul and back to me she knows something has gone on between us. Nothing I care to elaborate on. I'll leave that to him.

She looks at my mug of coffee. 'I thought you took milk.'

I smile. 'I do, but mine is... off.'

'Oh.' Surprise lightens her features, her smooth forehead developing a deep crease between thick black eyebrows I'm sure weren't there yesterday. 'You can have some of mine, if you want.' She holds up her milk carton, gives it a little wiggle like she's trying to tempt me.

I swallow my own spit. That's a first. I wonder what brought on such generosity. She does seem inordinately pleased to have another tenant arriving. Perhaps she prefers having female companionship, which is not surprising when she has that ape to deal with.

She holds the carton out and I can't help the eye slide over to Saul. There's no way I'm subjecting myself to his backwash. I know what he's been up to.

I flash her a quick, apologetic grin. 'No, thanks all the same. I caught Saul drinking straight from that carton earlier.' I point at it with my mug, fully aware he might get more shit from Phoebe than he did from me. I give a little head jerk. 'I'll give it a miss. Nice of you to offer, though.'

I don't look back as I walk out the kitchen, but Phoebe's voice has already hit a crescendo as I slip into my room and shut the door behind me.

25

PRESENT DAY – SUNDAY, 21
SEPTEMBER 2025, 5.10 A.M. – ALEX

Blackness envelopes me. Not the comforting hug of a velvet blanket, but a cruel claustrophobia that wraps around my neck, tightening its grip until I can barely breathe.

Taking in sips of air, I move one cautious step at a time down, down, down into the dank, dark cellar, one hand grasping the stair rail, the other touching the cold stone wall on the other side.

I pause at the bottom, blinking to clear my vision, but there is nothing in the darkness, not even a glimmer of light, not even that greyed-out rectangle of window.

With my hands in front of me, I shuffle my way to the far wall, fingertips tingling with anticipation.

My naked toes find the play kitchen first as they crack into the hard plastic base. I cry out as I fall into it, as the small kitchen topples over and I tumble across it, arms and legs flailing and I roll off the other side, plunging further into the abyss.

I lie for a moment, the only noise in the pitch black my harsh breathing as I struggle to my hands and knees.

My fingers skim something, and recognising this is what I was after, I grasp it, my heart tripping over itself with relief as I scrabble to find the little button I thought was on the side, but it turns out to be on the end.

Light blazes into my face and I screw my eyes closed, but the inside of my head is already lit up with a fireworks display, pain lancing through my brain.

I fumble to turn the torch in the opposite direction and slowly open my eyes.

Fear is a fist clutching at my heart, squeezing until it might just stop it from beating.

I step forward. Silence is a crashing wave coming towards me, threatening to engulf me. I shine the light into the dark cavern in front of me and lower myself to my knees.

Hope fills my heart as I see Mum, fast asleep and snuggly, wrapped in my play rug.

I tug at the edges, and it rolls towards me, coming to rest against my knees. Its iciness seeps into my skin.

A blackened, desiccated hand flops out from the sleeve of my mum's once soft grey cardigan, now stiff and soaked with thick brown fluids, the fingers gnarled and frozen, reaching for me in a desperate clutch.

With trembling fingers of my own, I stretch out to touch the swathe of thick golden locks.

Terror crawls over me like a thousand birds pecking at my skin as I stare at thin straggles of hair coming away in my hand, threading through my fingers like steel wool so it's impossible to shake free of them.

A cry chokes in my throat then dislodges as Mum's head makes a slow turn. Empty eye sockets meet mine while her mouth gapes, paralysed by the distant memory of a scream.

My eyes fly open to be met by a pale grey filtering through the edges of the curtains. Tangled in a heap of choking bedding, I leap from my bed, sweat sticking to the sheet as I charge to the window, desperate for air.

My foot tangles in the bedding and I slam headfirst into the floor, cutting my desperate sobs off mid-cry.

I lower my forehead to the cold wooden floor and squeeze my eyes shut against the tears streaming down my cheeks.

Jesus, I've not had that dream for years.

I let out a long, soft sigh and push up from the floor, taking my time to untangle my foot from the sheet now strewn across the floor as the slick of sweat dries on my naked skin, sending goosebumps to pebble their way from my neck downward.

I throw the sheet onto my bed and reach for my joggers, tugging them on before wandering back over to the patio doors, ripping the curtains open so I can simply see the outside world.

With my hand raised and resting on the cool of the window, I stare into the garden, watching as blackbirds run across the small patch of lawn, gathering morsels to take back to what must be their second hatch this year, my mind closed down for the moment in an act of self-preservation.

As it slowly awakens, a half-formed thought lodges there, questioning why I would have that dream. Why here? Why now?

I already know why.

My subconscious has been working overtime to protect me from the thought that Nikki is gone. Just as my mum has gone. How could this possibly happen twice to one person?

What kind of cruelty is this? As a child, it never crossed my mind Mum had suffered such a cruel fate. Now, I know evil is a possibility and it makes me worry for Nikki.

The memory of the smell curdles in my stomach as a stark reminder it will never leave me.

In my line of work people get killed. I am accustomed to death, although no one gets used to it. You'd be a monster if you did. Never have I come across such a putrid stench as I did that fateful day, but the scent of it lingers in my nostrils.

As my heart slows to its normal rhythm, I think of phoning Nikki's mum. Julia. My new mum, as I used to call her. Still call her. Even though I'm a grown man who moved away ten years ago or more now.

I may have moved, but I never left.

My heart is still there. For more than one reason.

I push away from the window and turn, reaching for my T-shirt so I can go out on a run again.

It's too early to call Julia. Even if it wasn't, what could I say to her?

Still no news, Julia.

Your daughter is missing. Presumed dead.

26

TWENTY-ONE YEARS AGO – MARCH 2004 – ALEX

I awake screaming, and screaming, and screaming.

'Hush, Alex. It's okay, I've got you. I've got you. Everything is going to be okay.'

For a second, I want to fight, to scratch and kick and bite my way out of these arms until the soft soothe of Julia's voice hurtles me back from the precipice to the here and now.

I'm gulping down air, only able to breathe in, not out, until my chest fills, ready to burst open.

Julia rubs a gentle hand over my back and rocks me, like I'm a baby. Or an innocent child. But I am no longer innocent. Not since that day when I discovered my mum's ravaged body in the cellar. My innocence was ripped away in one fell swoop.

Every dream I ever had of her returning to take me away from him was sucked down into a pit of mire. Every hope I had of seeing her again trampled in the dust of that dark cellar.

Julia strokes my hair, and I pull away from her, searching her eyes. It's all there, the pity, the sadness, the devastation. Nothing near to what I feel. She never knew Mum, but she knows me and she's taking care of me at the moment.

She'd promised she would, and that's exactly what she is doing.

Little did she know the circumstances by which I would come into her care, but she'd set everything up ready with the social workers, knowing Dad would let me down in one way or another.

She's my official foster carer.

Of all the circumstances, she'd never dreamed it would be because he'd murdered my mum.

I might say in my innocence I never dreamed it, either. But I did. I knew in my heart Mum would never leave me. She would have taken me with her if she'd left of her own free will. Protected me.

Once Mum was gone and this woman came into my life, I knew there would be a time when we, the three of us, would become a kind of family.

Uncle Alan was asked if he could care for me, but he's a single male and said he's not got a clue how to look after a kid and besides, he works really long hours. He had loads of excuses, but the upshot was, he didn't want me, despite what he'd said to Dad that day.

My grandparents on my mum's side said they were too old, and in any case, if Dad got out of prison they weren't sure they wanted to get involved. They want nothing to do with him. Nor me. They seem to think I'll turn out the same way. As though that kind of thing rubs off on people like an infectious disease.

So Nikki's mum had applied to be a foster carer some time before anything actually happened. She'd wanted to help after she'd witnessed what Dad was like and the social worker had advised her the best route to take.

She pulls away now to stare into my face. 'Are you okay, now, Alex?'

I nod, even though I'm not, because what's the point? I can't keep hashing over old news. It's been months. That's what my counsellor is for. I don't need to burden Julia with my dark thoughts and painful memories.

She sweeps the hair back from my forehead. 'Would you like me to read you a story?'

Sometimes she does, but tonight I need more involvement. Something to concentrate on so I can't think of anything else. More of a challenge than simply just listening.

'Can I read something to you?'

A little flash of amusement crosses her face.

'Of course. What would you like to read?'

I shuffle down so her arms fall away from me and I reach for my backpack I always keep on the end of my bed. I'm not sure why, but there's a small comfort in knowing I can make a quick escape if I want to. Julia knows this, but she never mentions it, never confronts me on any level.

At first it was because I felt so unsafe. Not because anything Nikki or her mum have done to make me uncomfortable; quite the contrary. But I do feel like a cuckoo in the nest.

I pull out *Frankenstein* by Mary Shelley and place it on my knee.

A flash of surprise crosses Nikki's mum's face. 'Well,' she says as she leans over to touch the beautifully crafted book.

'Mrs Bruce said I could have it,' I say quickly in case Nikki's mum thinks I've stolen it from the English teacher because it's quite distinctive, this small hardback leather-bound book with gilded page edges and dark green and gold-embossed pattern, both back and front of the book. 'She said she's finished it. Her daughter is taking GCSE English and it had been a while since she read it so she bought the book for herself too but then she said I could keep it, once she finished,' I rush on. 'You can ask her if you want, Mrs Fletcher.'

Nikki's mum gives me a smile, but it's laced with sadness as she raises a hand to cup my cheek. 'I don't need to ask Mrs Bruce if you say that's what happened. I believe you, Alex.'

I look into her eyes and see the truth of her trust. Dad never trusted me. He was proud to admit he never trusted a soul. That seems sad to me, not being able to trust anyone ever. I think I trust Nikki's mum.

'Also, I think it's about time you started to call me Julia when we're at home, don't you? You can't keep calling me Mrs Fletcher every time you speak to me, except at school, and "Nikki's mum" isn't right either. If you're going to be staying with us, we all have to feel comfortable.'

'How long do you think I will stay with you?'

Julia sighs. 'I think it's safe to say for the foreseeable future, don't you?'

I have no idea what that means, but I nod enthusiastically because it's all I can do. All I can hope for. My family don't want me, but Nikki and Julia do.

Julia is silent for a long while, then she takes in a breath as though she's about to say something. She pauses.

Then she starts again. 'Alex. I want you to remember something, for me, for you. It's important you realise that just because your father is a bad man, that doesn't mean you are, or that you will become one. It doesn't rub off. Everything you've done so far has been honourable and thoughtful. Don't let yourself be dragged down by your father's image. Be your own man. His heinous crimes do not need to carve your future. Think what your mum would want you to be.'

She reaches for my hands and holds them in hers. Mine are

almost as big as hers now. She's a fine, delicate woman, her fingers cool as they link with mine.

Her eyes meet mine and although she's not crying, they are bright with unshed tears.

'You are the better person, and we love you, Alex, for who you are.'

27

I'm staring up at the house, a stir of unease in my chest.

Could it simply be because it reminds me so much of my childhood home?

The memory of it is so distant I'm not sure if I'm creating a juxtaposition of then and now as I see the buildings side by side in my mind.

There's no little window from the cellar. Other than that, though, it feels so familiar. A small judder ripples through me. Maybe it's the same style of architecture; after all, I think it was probably built in the same era. It's difficult to know, the memories of my childhood have merged with the present. I never returned. Never wanted to.

I can't help thinking something dreadful has happened to Nikki. She's not the type to swan off as Saul and Phoebe and the landlord seem to want Julia to believe. Even the police don't seem to have taken it very seriously. She's not been gone long. A few weeks. She's an adult. Her mum was away, she has every right to take off with a new boyfriend. All the excuses and most of them sound reasonable. Only they aren't reasonable, and they're not right. Because I know this woman. I know Nikki so well and this is not what her messages were saying to me.

As far as I am concerned, there is no boyfriend, no reason. Which is part of my guilt as that's the real reason she moved here. To get away from the man she should never have said 'yes' to in the first place. And there was no one else. Not to my knowledge, and not to Julia's.

She would have told me. The police found nothing suspicious about Nikki's voice notes. How could they not? I found them odd. Which is precisely why I am here carrying out my own investigations.

From experience, I know better.

Or am I letting my past experience taint my present imagination?

As I cruise my gaze over the house, a shadow flits past the window and then pauses, returns, staying just far enough into the shadows. Watching me as I am watching the house.

It's the bedroom Jill was renting. There's no reason for anyone to be in the now empty room. Is there? I didn't think the new girl would be there yet. If so, they've moved bloody fast. This house is a revolving door; as one goes out another comes in. There's barely time to breathe. It does make me wonder how many have 'disappeared', seemingly under perfectly normal circumstances. Have the police pulled together any information on previous missing persons from here? Have they connected the dots, or do they need a little nudge? Because I do think there's something odd going on here.

I walk towards the house and the shadow retreats, dissolving like ink in water, leaving the stain on my mind's eye.

I wonder, if I barge through the front door and race up the stairs, will I catch the interloper midway along the landing or will they have retreated to one of the bedrooms? Is it Phoebe in there, or Saul? There's nothing left to take, no reason for them to be in there.

I unlock the front door and walk in. There's music playing, the sound coming from the kitchen as I make my way towards it. Happy voices chirp in excited fashion.

I pause beside my bedroom door and consider going inside and locking it, just staying the hell away from them all.

If Saul has brought a posse of girls around, claiming to be some sort of movie mogul instead of what he is, which is a loser, then I don't want to get involved in his party.

Then again, I'm curious.

I step inside the kitchen and a tall redhead turns brilliant blue eyes on me, almost knocking me off my feet with the power of her gaze.

Saul, the prick, is leaning against the fridge, arms crossed over his chest like he's posing for a male model magazine. He sickens me. The longer I am with him, the less I like him. He was obviously expecting her because he's wearing knee-length denim shorts and a white linen shirt open almost to his belly button, like he's been stranded on a desert island, but with a can of hairspray and a bottle of Tom Ford Oud Wood eau de parfum. He has that look some men can perfect of continual day-old growth. Personally, I shave every day, otherwise my day-old growth becomes a beard on day two.

Phoebe has the cheap Prosecco out and looks at me with surprise.

'Oh, hi, Alex. I thought you'd be at work.'

I glance at the three of them, all staring at me, suspicion narrowing Phoebe's eyes. They don't know I don't work. Well, I don't work here. Not in this country. You see, I worked for the Army for twelve years and then slid nicely into a civilian role advising foreign governments on high-risk issues using my mathematical skills. It's not high risk but it is top secret and it certainly isn't as dangerous as being in the Army. It's more civilised now. I'm a number cruncher on a grand scale with deadly friends who I joined the Army with. I'm the brains, but I still keep in contact with the boys in Special Forces.

My lips twitch as I imagine them raiding this place. It might be worth seeing Saul shit himself. Perhaps if I don't get some satisfaction from the police, I might get hold of a couple of my old cronies. See if they can dig up some information.

I am on leave right now, and time is running out because my next assignment is coming soon and will be based in South Africa. Not that I can tell Julia and Nikki, my family, where I am at any given moment. Mostly, I keep my head down, do the work and pretend I don't exist. Another few years of this and I'll be able to come back to England, buy a house outright with my earnings and look at settling down. Not that I have anyone to settle down with, but that's not my concern at the moment.

Right now, I just want to know what this lot are up to.

'Hi, what's going on?'

'This is Eleanor. She's moving in today, so we're just having a little celebration.'

I swallow back words I might regret. Like 'what happened to Jill, the last woman?', and 'I hope you fare better than the last three tenants'. Is it fair of me to scare her off? Is she wiser to walk away from this place?

I hold out my hand and she's quick to put her cold fingers in mine for a good, firm shake. 'My friends call me Elle.' Her voice is a soft seduction and when the smile spreads, it's wide and open.

'Alex,' I introduce myself. 'And my friends call me Alex.' I'm just trying to make light of this situation.

The other two laugh awkwardly and Phoebe shuffles around. 'Oh, Alex thinks he's a comedian, he's always making us laugh.'

I turn my attention to her without cracking so much as a smile and the laughter dies from her eyes. She scrabbles quickly for a glass and quickly fills it with shaky hands so it's mostly bubbles as she offers it to me. 'Join us to celebrate.'

I'm not sure what there is to celebrate, but I'm pretty sure there's another young woman whose safety is in peril.

I take the glass and raise it. 'Nice to meet you, Elle. I hope you enjoy your time here.'

Elle looks a little uncertain, as though she's sensed the atmosphere immediately and is on her guard. I hope she keeps that guard up.

Funny how I felt exactly the same when I arrived. An over-abundance of enthusiasm so you can taste the lies.

'Have they explained the cleaning and washer-dryer rules to you?' I slant Saul and Phoebe a sideways glance.

'Oh, Alex, stop teasing,' Phoebe laughs as she pours herself another glass and slugs it down so I know I've got her rattled. I take a sip of mine and place the glass on the table, wandering over to the bench where something has attracted my attention.

I reach for the book lying on the side next to an empty dish, but Phoebe is there first, snatching it away from me.

With a frown, I turn and hold out my hand. 'What's that? Let me see.' Heat races up my neck.

'It's mine!'

My lips twitch up in a crooked smile. 'I'm aware it's yours. I just want to look at it.'

'No. You're not having it.'

'I don't want it.' Although I do. I desperately do. I'm still holding my hand out and it's becoming awkward. I'm aware of Elle looking from one to the other of us and then glancing at Saul, who has pushed away from the fridge and is watching us intently.

'Let me have a look, Phoebs. I just want to see it.'

She puts it behind her back as if by doing so, I can't tell she still has it and raises her chin. 'You're not looking at it, so fuck off.'

Now I know there's something off. There's no reason for her to refuse to let me see it. Not unless she has something to hide.

I step into her space, reach around and snatch the book from her hands. She doesn't stand a chance.

She screeches at me, arms flapping in the air trying to snatch it back, but I step away.

'Give it to me, you fucking bastard. Give me my book back. It's mine. It was a gift!'

I put my hand on her forehead as she flails at me for a minute until she runs out of steam and glares at me as I drop my hand back down to my side.

Elle is frozen, glass halfway to her lips, and I look down at the contract she's yet to sign and raise a brow.

She lowers the glass and places it on the table. 'Look, guys, I think I've made a mistake. I'll be asking for my deposit straight back. I'm not living here with you. You're all raving mad.' Her quick gaze around seems to include Saul, making me wonder if he's already made a pass at her, before she dashes for the front door.

I'd love to grin, because I think I may have just saved this woman from some kind of ill fate, whatever it was both Nikki and Jill suffered, and very possibly Michelle and the woman before her, but I have something more important to think about.

The book I hold in my hand is *Frankenstein* by Mary Shelley. Not any version, but a green leather-bound hardback with gold-embossed page edges I gifted to Nikki on her last birthday. The first and last time I ever kissed her.

28

I'm not going to lie. I'm not frightened of big, burly men beating me up down a back alley. No, they're not the thoughts that keep me awake at night. What keeps me awake at night is the thought of sliding into nightmares where I'm caught in the dark with nowhere to escape and the body of my mum is lying in a rolled-up carpet, rotting. Her matted hair wound around my fingers, and bodily fluids seeping from the rug.

As a child, that horror was no nightmare. It was a reality. A true-life horror. As I wake, the stench of that find is still in my nostrils.

I swing my legs over the side of the bed and cup my face in my hands.

All that time, all those counselling sessions.

Maybe they kept me safe and sane for the best part of my life. Being in the Army never rocked the foundations of my counselling, but now, with the thought of the person I love most in the world missing, every night terror I ever had has combined, rolled into one and come rushing at me.

There's an eerie quietness to the house as I sit contemplating the situation.

What the hell am I doing here?

Is there any point to this?

No one seems to know or care about the revolving door of girls coming through this place.

Perhaps I did Elle a favour when I frightened her out of signing her contract. Maybe I'm going insane. Neither Saul nor Phoebe have spoken to me since, but quite honestly, I don't care.

The temperature hasn't dropped since the sun went down and I slide open the patio doors, trying my best to be as quiet as possible as I breathe in the night air heavy with the scent of jasmine that's gone wild, clawing its way over the fence from the garden next door.

I pick up the book I took from Phoebe and run my fingers over the embossed covering. She'd wanted it back and I simply held it above her head and waggled it when Elle had gone and the situation had been defused.

'This isn't yours.'

I met her eyes and something flickered in hers, some recognition that I was right.

'You're a thief.'

She'd gasped and stepped back, letting me simply walk away.

I haven't told Julia yet, because I'm not exactly sure what I am supposed to tell her. But I have the book and I'm going to the police tomorrow, fully armed with all the evidence and intelligence I've gathered here. There's nothing of note to point us in the direction of the lost girls, but I'm fairly sure presenting the police with this book has to escalate matters. It's just too suspicious. Too much of a coincidence.

Then again, we know Phoebe is a kleptomaniac and won't she just argue that Nikki left it behind? Nikki already told me in her voice notes about Phoebe's penchant for taking things. Maybe that's all it was. Did Phoebe sneak into Nikki's room and steal the book from her?

I drop the book into my lap.

But if that was the case, why didn't Nikki mention it on one of her many voice notes?

The last one was the strangest.

'Oh, hey, Alex. It's me again. It's been a really odd time at work, and I've barely been able to concentrate. Mum is home on Sunday, and maybe it's the excitement of seeing her again that's causing me all this distraction. I'm going to pack up and travel down so I can get the house ready for her, do some shopping, maybe get a meal on. I'm so excited she's coming back. I've not mentioned it to this lot. I'm considering not coming back, not living here for the whole of my notice period, so I'll take my essentials with me and they can keep anything I leave behind.

'They're not nice people and I don't know why but I feel less and less comfortable around them. I guess I'm homesick.'

She lets out a long sigh.

'When are you coming home, Alex? I think we need to talk.'

I echo the sigh I hear in my mind. Picking up the book, I trace the embossing on the front once again, closing my eyes to get a better sense of it and I'm catapulted back to the last time I saw her.

* * *

'He's not good enough for her,' I murmur to Julia, who is sitting next to me in the Italian restaurant where we're having dinner with Oscar and his parents.

She leans back, that haughty look she gets from time to time sneaking over her face. 'And just who do you think would be good enough, Alex?'

In the face of that question, I fall silent, taking a sip of my wine. She has me over a barrel there. As far as I am concerned, Nikki has never brought anyone home who is good enough for her.

Julia slides her hand over the top of mine and looks deep into my eyes. 'You do know she's given you every opportunity?'

Shock slithers through me. What does Julia know? What has Nikki told her?

I'm frozen in place, and I can barely swallow. 'I'm her brother.'

Julia leans back in her chair, a trace of bitterness in her crooked smile. 'She's never seen you as that since she hit puberty.'

We're both silent for a moment until she leans in again and speaks just above a whisper. 'You are not blood related, Alex. There is nothing wrong with you having feelings for my daughter. You need to let that guilt go.'

'But, what if—?' What if I fail her, what if it doesn't work out, what if I lose my family because of all of this?

As though she heard my thoughts, she squeezes my hand. 'But what if you don't?'

Oscar comes to his feet and taps his glass with the back of a spoon in that officious way I've never admired and Julia and I both sigh, relaxing back in our chairs, our stomachs full of pasta and pizza.

'I want to thank you all for coming tonight.'

He makes it sound like he has an audience at the Royal Albert Hall, and weirdly I think it was Julia who arranged for this meal, not him. Although I guess it was him who unexpectedly expanded the guest list to include his parents and sister.

I look around the table and catch Nikki's eyes which are unnaturally bright. Is that fear flickering in them?

'I'm so pleased to gather both our families together for this special occasion, not only is it Nikki's birthday but the six-month anniversary of Nikki first allowing me to take her out.'

Her eyes grow wider and from the other end of the table, I can tell she never realised it was their six-month anniversary. I dip my head so no one notices my wry smile.

'I'm so delighted we could gather both families together as I knew we would all get along so well.' He smiles, encompassing all of us. He raises his glass to me and I respond in kind, only I take a sip of my wine whereas he slugs his back with a slight shake of his hand, placing the glass down with a decisive click.

I blink as my heart stutters. Shit. I know what this is about.

My gaze shoots to Nikki and there's a frozen smile plastered on her face as I suspect she's also realised.

Julia's nails dig into my skin as she grips my hand. 'Oh, no.' It's barely a whisper and I think no one else but me hears it.

With a suddenness which takes everyone by surprise, Oscar drops to one knee in front of Nikki and takes her hand in his. I notice a slight struggle as she tries to remove it from his grasp, but he holds on, turning her slender fingers white.

'Nikki.' His voice is impassioned and all I want to do is lurch to my feet and get the hell out of here. But Julia places a hand on my arm, not to restrain me so much as to calm me.

'Would you do me the honour of becoming my wife?' With a slight fumble, Oscar produces a box, springing the lid open to reveal a rock that almost takes my eye out with the power of its sparkle.

Nikki forces a laugh as everyone including those at surrounding tables sigh and aww. I say nothing. I can't because my heart has just shrivelled and died.

Nikki places a hand on her chest and nods wordlessly, but it doesn't matter because he's already sliding the ring on her finger as though he can't even wait for her answer. Clapping breaks out and the spell is broken.

No one notices me as I slip from the table and make for the men's room.

My heart is shredded. All I gave her was my special edition novel, *Frankenstein* by Mary Shelley, the most valuable thing I have in the world – and she knows that. Knows how precious it is. How much it means to me.

She's waiting for me in the hallway, her eyes dark and unfathomable.

She holds out her hand and the rock gleams. 'What do you think?'

I take her trembling fingers in mine and know this is my moment to reassure her that all is well, that I approve of her choice. But I find I can't be so gracious, not when I'm dying inside.

My mouth has turned dry and I find I can't swallow. 'I think if you marry him, you'll be making a mistake.'

She stares at me. There's no shock in her expression, just a look of resignation. 'What would you suggest I do? Do you have a better idea?' She raises her chin.

She's challenging me, but I don't know where to go with this. So sue me, I'm a man.

I shrug and she drops her fingers from mine.

'Are you still leaving tomorrow?' There's a slight wobble to her voice and my chest tightens.

I nod. 'My contract is signed. I'll be back in a year.'

'In time for my wedding?'

I incline my head. 'If that's what you wish,' I say, when what I want to do is scream at her that she's made the wrong decision.

'Oscar wants you to be his best man.'

I snort and pace away from her, both hands in my hair. When I turn, she's right behind me.

'Cheeses, Alex. Say something. Anything.' There's something in her eyes that I can't fathom, but they're glittering with... hope?

I drop my hands from my head and reach for her, drawing her in so my mouth hovers over hers. There is only one thing I can say to her.

'Don't marry him.'

I lean in and kiss her.

* * *

My table lamp flickers and blows out, plunging me into the dark and silence and ripping me from my memories.

I sigh.

The bloody electrics have gone again. This is ridiculous.

Phoebe's probably left the tumble dryer on too long again. I'm positive that's what trips it. God knows what she's put in there this time. I'm starting to think it could be a fire hazard.

I push up from the bed and walk barefoot towards the open patio doors. Stepping outside, I let my head clear of half-remembered memories as I stare up at an ink-black sky peppered with tiny dots of stars and the red and green taillights of aircraft so high up, they appear to drift silently.

I can't do this any more. I'm going to leave this place soon, just as soon as I speak with the police tomorrow. I don't think I can stand being here any longer in the company of these two despicable people.

I slide the door closed then open my bedroom door to saunter along the hall to my bathroom. Automatically hitting the light switch, I sigh as I remain in the dark. I brushed my teeth earlier, but my skin feels clammy, so after I pee and wash my hands, I swish cool water over my face, patting it dry with a hand towel smelling strangely of female perfume or hand cream. Probably that git, Saul, letting one of his girls use my bathroom, even though he knows they're not supposed to.

I open the bathroom door and step into the hallway. As I pass the cellar steps, I hesitate.

Instead of ignoring the electrics, I guess I should go down there and switch them back on. It's a bit rude to leave it to someone else to do. They won't understand my hesitation. They'll think I am a coward, and perhaps I am, when it comes to this.

I open the door, peer down into the blackness.

My heart speeds up. Sweat pops out all over my skin.

A rolled-up rug. Black stains. Blonde hair.

I take a step back and then another.

I turn and walk to my bedroom, scoop up my phone and tap the torch. I have to return, even though every nerve ending is screaming for me not to.

As I take the first step, something in the darkness shuffles, then bumps.

'Hello?'

I take another step.

'Hello? Who's down there?' I punch power into my voice as the memory of that bear-like man coming down the cellar steps invades my mind and I remember his bellow scaring the living daylights out of me at the time. If there's someone down these steps, I want to have the same effect.

'Who's there?' I bellow, despite terror clawing its way up my throat.

We may be having a heatwave, but the chill of the cellar steps seeps into my bare feet and as I step off the bottom stair, the rough flooring digs into the soft skin of my soles.

I pan the torch around and catch movement in the shadows. A paleness emerges from the dark.

I narrow my eyes at the figure moving towards me. 'What the hell are you doing down here?'

29

THREE WEEKS EARLIER – 2.05 A.M. – NIKKI

Nausea clutches at my stomach and I sit up in bed, hugging myself as I rock against the pain. It hurts so much I might even pass out.

I need painkillers.

I wonder briefly if I should go to hospital. Is there something really wrong with me?

Should I get help?

This is the type of thing I would normally pick up my phone and speak to Mum about. Not that I would call her at this time of night, but knowing she's there would be a comfort. She'd reassure me in no time.

Her ship is due to dock in Southampton in the morning, then she should be home around lunchtime.

I've taken the day off and I was going to drive home in the morning, do a shop on the way and get something ready for dinner as a surprise. I've not told her I'm going to be there. It might make her worry that something is wrong.

Something is.

I groan as I double over, tears springing to my eyes.

Nothing good has happened in this place since I've been here. I really don't like it. I know my stomach pains have nothing to do with the house, but somehow nothing has gone right. I've felt nothing but ill since I got here. Is that entirely fair? Not necessarily ill, but constantly off kilter and simply dreary. With each day that passes, I'm becoming more and more miserable.

Once I get home, I'll talk to Mum and see what she thinks of me moving back in with her for a short time until I get my feet back under me. This has been a horrendous experience and all I want is to be back home. I really miss Mum.

I won't be coming back either. I know I will probably lose some of my deposit for not giving the correct notice, but at this point I don't care.

Bloody Saul and Phoebe are horrible and it looks like they're setting up to have another new housemate. How come they got to meet her, and I didn't? It's almost like there's a hierarchy here that I've not been told about, as if I didn't read the small print so I'm not in on their little clique, their in-crowd.

Weirdly, though, I swear I could smell Saul's aftershave on my bedding. What the hell was that all about? Has he been in my bedroom, lain on my bed? Worse still has he been *in* my bed, maybe with one of his girlfriends?

My stomach pitches and I'm not sure it has anything to do with the pain, more the idea of Saul in my bed making me feel sick.

What a pervert.

I couldn't bring myself to use it, so I stripped the bed and took the bedding downstairs earlier in the evening, only to find both the machines were full. I had to sneak down later and shove them in the washing machine, finding – much to my irritation when I checked an hour later – someone had taken the bedding out and left it on the top of the dryer so they could fill the washing machine again. Inconsiderate or what?

Initially, I thought it had finished its wash, but when I picked it up, it was barely damp. Whoever did it must have been down there like a shot after I came up, switched the machine off and removed my bedding before the programme had a chance to get going properly. They didn't even have the decency to put it in the small laundry basket I'd put down there.

What sense of entitlement would make a person do that? To consider their washing holds any more value than mine.

I don't want to challenge these people. They're too vile. Both of them. I know I'm being whiney, but I wouldn't put it past Phoebe to get physical if I was too pushy. I've seen her punch Saul and it didn't seem too friendly to me, even though he kind of laughed it off.

I'm currently wrapped in my quilt, no cover, and I'm miserable.

Is it stress that's giving me stomach cramps?

If I didn't know better, I'd think it was food poisoning. Chance would be a fine thing. Bloody Saul ate the pizza I'd put in the fridge for my dinner tonight. I'd even written my name in big, fat black lettering on the front and back. He's an ignorant pig. Never even showed any remorse.

So I had to settle for Weetabix and warm milk. Hardly a fair substitute and there was only Weetabix left because I had a box I kept in my wardrobe. I think he'd had half my milk as well as there was only a small amount in the bottom of the carton.

Maybe that's what's given me stomach cramps.

I swing my legs off the bed and stand up.

Perhaps the milk was off. It didn't taste sour, but I wasn't sure at the time if there was a slight taint to it.

I hope Saul's feeling worse than me if that's the case.

All I want is something to comfort me, remind me of home. I lean against the wall for a moment while I stare at the top of my chest of drawers. Shit! It's not there. I blink away unshed tears, hoping my vision improves enough to see what I'm looking for. It's gone! Someone has taken my copy of *Frankenstein*. It's not my imagination. I know they have because I had it last night. I stroked my fingers over the cover and held it to my breast as I contemplated what I might say to Alex the next time I see him. The next time we meet. Because this can't go on. He needs to know.

I have to tell him I love him. Whether that drives him further away or not, I have to take the risk.

My head spins as I turn away.

First, I must find out who has taken my book. My precious bloody book that Alex gave me for my birthday.

With a slight weave and a stagger, I reach my bedroom door and slide across the small bolt that the landlord fitted. My head swims as I lurch down the hallway, almost bouncing off the walls like I've been on a night out and well and truly overdone it. I'm not sure if I'm going to be sick.

The hallway elongates in my blurred vision and just as I approach my bathroom there seems to be a dark figure loitering outside. I try to blink the image away but it stays, immovable.

I hesitate and then stumble onward.

I need help.

There's something terribly, terribly wrong.

I lurch forward and then crumple to my knees in front of the dark figure.

'Help. Please help me.'

I crawl, reaching out, trying to blink that person into view, but they've stepped back and are standing watching me while I heave, my back arching, my stomach in spasm.

'It's you. Thank God, it's you. Help me. Please.'

I look up as the figure bends over me. There is a cold hatred in their eyes and I know the moment I look into them that help isn't going to come. I am all alone with this monster and I have no idea what my fate will be, but I know it's not going to be good.

30

PRESENT DAY – MONDAY, 22
SEPTEMBER 2025, 12.40 A.M. – ALEX

Saul walks towards me, his eyes trained on my face.

'It's you!' I say.

I fucking knew he was up to no good. I bet he's not down here to turn the electric on, but for some odd reason he's powered it off himself.

As I stare, his lips part as though he's about to say something, but instead of words, a trickle of bright red blood seeps from the corner of his mouth to drizzle down his chin, and I stall.

Confusion washes over his face as his brow furrows, his eyes stare unblinking as I lower the light from his face to his chest so as not to blind him.

He staggers, then stumbles forward another step.

Fuck! What's going on?

'Saul?'

He reaches out with both hands and for a moment I wonder if he's going to grab me, but it's all a bit slow motion as his body crumples into mine. He's a heavy guy and as I drop the phone to catch him it smashes against the hard floor, slivers of glass twinkling in the illumination of the torch which flickers for a moment, threatening to die, and then holds steady.

I stare at the body in my arms. The handle of a knife sticking out from between Saul's shoulders, the blade buried deep in his back.

He curls into a foetal position as I lower him gently the rest of the way to the floor, hunkering down so I can get a better look. He seems to have fainted, which may not be a bad thing.

There's surprisingly little blood from what I can tell in this limited lighting.

I don't touch the knife embedded in his back. With my field training, I know the worst thing I can do at this point is to try and pull the blade out. That's a job for the experts, the medics. I press two fingers against his neck, just under his jawline as I feel for his carotid artery. His pulse is thin and thready, but it's there so I'm hoping the knife has missed his vital organs. It doesn't bode well that a thin drizzle of blood oozes from between his lips though, now puddling like liquid rubies, sparkling in the spotlight of the phone torch.

I pat Saul's body down, looking for his phone so I can call for help, but there's nothing in his jogger pockets and he's wearing a T-shirt. I briefly wonder why he came down here in the pitch black without his torch, but it's something I'll think about later, once I have this sorted. Maybe he came down to turn the electric back on before I did. Lucky me!

What I need to do now is throw the switch on the electrics to get some light down here and call the paramedics as well as the police and let them do their jobs.

Whoever stabbed Saul has to be nearby. Because in spite of everything, it makes no sense that he might have wandered down here after he'd been stabbed. It would be pure madness.

There's no one down here, though, which is really peculiar. No sense of any presence.

No one passed me as I came down the cellar steps, and I'm damned sure when I spotted Saul he was the only other person here.

Unless...

I push up from the cold stone flooring and beat back the image of Mum, wrapped in my play rug, her candyfloss hair sticking out of the end, wispy tufts of it coming away in my fingers.

I reach for my phone. The screen is smashed and there's no illumination to it. It's completely blank. There's no way I can use it to call for help. I'm going to have to go upstairs, check on Phoebe's bedroom and get her to help.

As I straighten, the light from my phone tracking around, I realise that instead of a wall, there's a black void in front of me.

Is that where Saul came from? What was he doing down here?

Like me, had he just come down to turn on the power?

Or was there a more sinister reason?

I train the phone light on the dark cavern and take a step forward just as the beam flickers and threatens to die.

I need to throw the switches on the fuse box first, then I can investigate.

As I turn, I swing the torchlight around and suck in a horrified gasp.

Phoebe descends the last of the cellar steps into the pool of light from my phone, eyes wide with fear.

'Alex, is that you?'

I grunt an acknowledgement, because what the hell is she doing down here, lurking in the dark?

'What's happened?' She steps forward and then freezes, her

gaze dropping to the body at my feet. She slaps a hand over her mouth and edges back. 'Shit, Alex, what have you done? Why would you do that?' She flicks a hand out, her fingers trembling in the torchlight. 'I know you don't like each other, but did you need to knock him out?'

Evidently, Phoebe can't see the massive knife handle poking out of Saul's back, otherwise she'd be off like hot shit off a shovel, as my old man used to say.

'I didn't,' I say. 'I found him like this.'

She narrows her eyes at me, suspicion leaching through.

'Maybe you can turn on the electricity?' I suggest, as she is standing the closest to the box.

'That's what I came down for but I always struggle to reach properly to flick the switches up.'

'Okay. Just leave it, I'll do it.'

I take a step forward and she lets out a yelp, jumping back.

'Don't come near me.' Fear trembles through her voice.

I hold my hands up, the torchlight wavering erratically in the dark.

'Look, I'm not going to harm you. I came down to turn the electricity back on and found Saul. My phone's broken, Phoebe. You need to call the police and an ambulance.'

She shakes her head. 'Your phone looks like it's working to me.' Which is probably true from her viewpoint as the torch is working, but she's just going to have to trust me on this.

Irritation sparks a little in my stomach. She has no idea of the urgency. 'Phoebe, Saul isn't just out cold – someone in this house has stabbed him in the back. Only the torch works on my phone, so *you* need to call for help. Now!'

Her hand goes to her chest and her lips open and close like she can't get the words out.

'My phone is dead.' Her voice is thin and wobbly. 'I don't

know when the power went off, but it didn't charge, that's why I'm here in the dark.'

'Okay, you need to go upstairs and find Saul's phone. He's not got his with him, either. He's been stabbed, damn it. Do you understand? Run, Phoebe, run!'

Christ's sake! I'm not used to this. As a major in the Army, I was used to people taking orders without question. Now she's fannying around, putting Saul at more risk with her delay. I just need her to do one job.

She turns and then stops, her hand on the stair rail and I grind my teeth at yet another delay. 'What if he's up there, waiting for me?'

I almost snap out that it might be a relief if he was, but that's just cruel. Phoebe might have a lot of foibles, but she doesn't deserve to die. Neither does Saul.

'You'll be all right.' I step towards the fuse box. 'The likelihood is they've taken off. After all, what person in their right mind would hang around after they've stabbed someone?' I'm starting to wonder if it might be the husband or boyfriend of one of his many fleeting flings.

She hesitates again. Christ, it's like the Spanish Inquisition.

'Phoebe!' I bark. 'Go!'

Fear flashes in her eyes before she whirls and races up the stairs.

I touch Saul's neck once more. Is it my imagination or is his pulse getting weaker? Blood from the wound is starting to pool around him, the trickle of it slowed down by the knife wedged in between his shoulders, but I don't know how long he's got. I can only hope Phoebe hurries.

I straighten and make my way through the darkness, one small beam of light leading the way.

I reach for the fuse box, open the cover and then slam the

heel of my hand upwards against all the switches so they immediately turn on.

It's still pitch black down here but I hear the comforting buzz of power going through to the washing machine and tumble dryer, which means if I just reach for the light switch at the bottom of the stairs we'll have full illumination.

Saul lets out a low groan and I bend down to touch his shoulder, hoping it brings him some comfort that I'm here. There's a light tremble shuddering through him and I pray Phoebe is quick and the paramedics are soon here.

As I said to her, whoever the hell stabbed Saul in the back must be long gone. There'd be no sense in hanging around. Would there?

My mind is buzzing with possibilities.

Could it be one of his many one-night stands? Or possibly his fiancée? Maybe the boyfriend of one of those ladies, because quite honestly, to wedge the knife in so deep would take a pretty powerful person with a strong stomach. Let's face it, hand-to-hand combat is no easy feat. The bollocks they show on TV is nothing in comparison to taking another person's life. It's not something any of us want to do.

I stare at the knife handle. You don't stab your enemy in the back. Surely this has to be something far more sinister.

What was he involved in?

Has he got something to do with the disappearance of Nikki and the other girls? For a moment, when I came down the cellar stairs, I thought it was him, that I'd caught him out. Have I? Does he have something to do with all of this and a partner has turned on him?

It doesn't seem feasible. He may be full of ego and good looks, but the man is really not terribly bright. I certainly can't see him as the mastermind of some major criminal activity.

Whatever the reason he's down here, he doesn't deserve to die and he needs help immediately.

I give his shoulder a light squeeze once more and come to my feet, about to locate the light switch, when there's a soft scraping sound from behind me.

I whirl around and stare at the chasm of darkness along the left wall. Someone is in there. What are they doing? Can they see me? I open my mouth to speak and my phone torch gives up, plunging me into darkness.

31

PRESENT DAY – 2.05 A.M. – NIKKI

Regret is a sharp pain in my stomach, making me curl into a tight ball.

Have I been poisoned?

My head is spinning like a top and I can't focus my eyes on anything as they seem to bounce around the room, never settling. I squeeze them closed and feel the dried tears stretch across the skin of my cheeks, turning it itchy. I've shed so many, I never seem to have stopped crying.

Wherever I am, it is as black as night and there's a fusty smell of old dust and dead spiders. At least, I hope they're dead. There are other creatures too. I hear them scuttling and close my eyes tight to the possibility that there may be mice, or worse still, rats down here.

I don't know how long I've been here, but just when the fog seems to lift from the sludge in my brain, I'm given something to make it roll in thick clouds so I'm never quite compos mentis. I tried to refuse the food, but it sat there congealing until my stomach screamed for nourishment. The bottle of water was what contained the drug though. At least, that's what I assume as I'd declined everything else.

It's cold here and I feel I'm underground as it would be much hotter if I was in a house. I tuck the duvet cover around me, my teeth chattering as whatever drug they gave me starts to wear off. This is normally when the shadow appears to take me for a toilet break. I think at some point I'm going to be able to escape, but I'm simply too weak each time the opportunity arises. I guess that's the idea. Keep me quiet, keep me compliant. The shadow never makes any noise, except for an occasional grunt. I wish it would. I've asked time and again what I am doing here, but there is nothing. No answer. Apart from guiding me by the arm to a bucket where I can relieve myself behind a thin curtain, there is no communication, no humanity.

There's nothing for me to do here but live through the regrets I have. Mostly what I didn't do, as opposed to what I did do.

The biggest of those was not telling Alex how much I love him, allowing him to believe that I was still engaged to Oscar before he left.

Another regret. The memory of that day swims in.

* * *

'Mum says she can't wait to choose your wedding dress with you.'

I look up in surprise and Oscar is grinning. 'She's so excited. She can't wait for me to get married.'

Me, as opposed to us?

I feel as though I've been sidelined for the big day. That his mother's wishes are far more important than mine.

I know I've made a mistake. I knew it the moment his proposal was out of his mouth and I agreed to it. What else was I supposed to do? In front of everyone, it was the last thing I expected and we'd not even talked about getting married. We'd only been seeing each other for six months. Is that time enough to know if you want to spend the rest of your life with someone? It was time enough for me to know I didn't want to spend it with him. Only, what are you supposed to say when a man drops to one knee in front of both families?

Awkward!

And yet, despite not loving Oscar, I wouldn't dream of humiliating him in front of everyone. The refusal could wait until later. It had all happened so fast, I'm sure he would understand once I explained it to him.

I never even had time to think, but once Alex kissed me, I knew I'd made a mistake. More than one.

Gasping, I pushed him away. 'What the hell do you think you're doing, Alex?'

He stepped back. There was no shock or remorse in his face, just resignation as he held both hands, palm outwards to me and gave a slow nod. 'You shouldn't marry that man. He's not right for you. He's not good enough.'

I spluttered. Quite honestly, I was in shock, both from the proposal and then being kissed by Alex. Mostly the second, because I've wanted Alex to kiss me for the past ten years and now he has, it's under the worst circumstances and not for the right reason.

I wiped the kiss from my lips with the back of my hand and watched the twitch of hurt cross his face at the deliberate insult, but how was I supposed to react?

'So, who is good enough for me, Alex?' I was hurt and angry and I wanted to slap back at him for saying exactly what I know. What I wasn't brave enough to do. It's not that Oscar isn't good enough for me, but he's not right. I don't want to marry him, but there's no need for Alex to humiliate me. To make me feel stupid for agreeing to the proposal because I was in effect railroaded. Can't he see that?

I narrowed my eyes at him. 'Who is good enough?' I repeated, stepping right up into his face. 'You?' I poked him in the chest with one sharp fingernail.

Shock streaked across his face and I wanted to cry as he took a hurried step back, but I stayed tough. He wouldn't be getting off so lightly.

'No. I thought not.' Bitterness curdled in my stomach.

I turned and walked away and he didn't try to stop me. He would be gone in the morning and until then, I would stay the hell away from him.

And now the task ahead is almost as bad. Distasteful, as Oscar and I sit side by side on his sofa the following morning.

'Oscar.' I bend my head, the ring I have slipped from my finger clutched in the palm of my hand. 'I know you'll be disappointed, but I've given this considerable thought, and I can't marry you.'

'What?' A deep line creases the middle of his brow and I can't help thinking that if we get married the furrow is going to be a permanent fixture. We're not right for each other.

'I'm sorry.' I take the ring with the fingers of my left hand and hold it out to him. 'I should never have said yes.'

I can see confusion giving way to fury building in his eyes, but it's not within my control to make him feel better about it. 'I...'

He surges to his feet, so I bounce on the sofa, snatching at the ring in case it falls. Oscar is staring down at me, his arms wide. 'Why did you say yes? What am I supposed to tell my mum now? She's expecting a wedding.'

A wedding. Any wedding. Not necessarily to me.

'Oscar.' I try to placate him by using his name, but he's

towering over me, hands on hips. I feel if I stand, I'll be nose to nose with him and that seems like an aggressive move.

Instead, I raise my hand, opening my fingers so the ring balances on my palm.

'I'm sorry. I was put in a difficult situation and I didn't think you'd appreciate me turning you down in front of both our families.' My words are strong, but there's a definite wobble to my voice.

He runs his tongue over his teeth as he breathes out as though he's trying to control his temper. 'Look. Let's just stop this now.'

Relief starts to burgeon, only to be slapped down with his next words.

'Keep the ring, and I'll have a word with Mum. We'll make it all low-key until you're more comfortable with the idea.'

I don't drop my hand. I'm giving him a chance to take the ring back. 'I don't want to marry you. Not now and not later. Especially not low-key.' I could make a dig about his mum here, but I'm not that petty. She's obviously extremely excited about the wedding, so much so that she would probably take over given half the chance. That convinces me even more about marrying him being the wrong thing. For both of us. He doesn't love me. He loves his mum, and she wants him to get married. I just happen to be the sweet girl she considers suitable for her son.

'I'm sorry if this isn't what you want, but we never even discussed the matter of marriage before you sprang it on me.'

'Sprang it on you? What the fuck did you think we were doing with both families invited to dinner?'

I frown. 'It was my birthday. I thought...' Well, honestly, in my naivete, I thought we were having a bit of a birthday party. For me.

He snatches the ring and steps back, his eyes glittering with fury.

'You never even thought it was a probability that we would get married, did you?'

'Sorry...?'

'You!' He pokes a finger at me, pocketing the ring as though it's meaningless. And perhaps it is. Maybe this whole thing was to keep his mum happy. I certainly don't feel as though his love is undying.

Mine certainly isn't. I can't actually recall telling him I love him. We've not even moved in together. We occasionally stay at each other's at the weekend when his mum is away and she doesn't need him. There's a sliver of guilt sliding in that somehow I've led him on, made him believe there was so much more to our relationship. Guilt or not, I can't allow myself to be manoeuvred into something I know I don't want.

He paces away and I take the opportunity to get to my feet, slipping on my trainers so I can make a quick exit because I don't need to stay here and take this. It was not of my making and I'm pretty sure we can't 'still be friends'.

His anger is vibrating and before it escalates, I need to get out of here. If there is one thing Alex's upbringing has taught me, it's to get out of the room before the angry ape escapes.

I glance towards the bathroom. I never leave much here, just a toothbrush on the shelf, but my make-up and moisturiser I keep in my handbag.

I edge towards the dining room table and reach for my handbag just as he swings around.

His eyes are red-rimmed and there's a stirring of pity in me.

I don't like to hurt people. I don't want him to be sad.

I blink away the memories of a devastated Alex when we were younger. Me, six years younger than him, rocking him in my arms like he was a baby. At the time, I never knew the complexities of his story, that came later when I was in my teens. What I did know was he needed me to comfort him, to make him feel better because I was the next most important person in his life other than his mum.

My heart squeezes in my chest.

I've let him down too, and now it's too late. He's gone.

Oscar turns as I loop the handbag handles over my arm.

'I'm sorry,' I whisper.

'Is that it?'

I nod slowly. There's really nothing more to say.

His mouth twists in bitter disappointment, but I'm not as concerned at the upset I caused him as I am about tearing Alex's feelings apart. Alex who kissed me last night with everyone in the room down the hall with more passion than I've ever known from anyone. As though to let me go would rip his heart to shreds. And yet I let him go. The biggest mistake of my life, because he's gone, and life will have changed by the time he returns in a year's time.

As I reach for the door, Oscar steps up behind me. 'You know, you're never going to be able to keep any relationship while that brother of yours is around.'

I don't even turn as I open the door and step through. I know he's right. But there's just one thing.

'He's not my brother.'

I close the door and walk away.

32

Rather than staring wide-eyed and blind, I close my eyes and calm myself enough to use my other senses. Allowing them to guide me.

I tilt my head, almost doglike, to pick up the vaguest of sounds. Soft material brushing against itself to my right.

The musty scent of garlic and BO causes my nose to twitch. I recognise the smell. It definitely isn't Phoebe.

Instinct has me softening my knees, anticipating a blow at the soft footstep approaching. I am ready.

A bright white light flares in front of me and I blink open my eyes, just to snap them closed again as something rushes towards me.

I raise my arm as the light flashes off and something hits me, vibrating through from wrist to shoulder.

I let out a grunt and then duck so the next whack catches my back, sending shockwaves through my body with the power of the blow. I throw myself forward into blank space and pant as I lie face down, spreadeagled on the floor. The lights blaze on and I roll over onto my back, hoping to defend myself.

My head snaps up and I stare up at the long, skinny cadaver of a man in front of me. Confusion ripples through me.

'You?'

The landlord steps forward, a bitter twist to his lips. A long cricket bat held two-handed, pulled back to give him full swing.

What the hell is going on? Is he crazy? Have I got a serial killer on my hands?

After all, this is the man who must have stabbed Saul in the back. What the hell did he think he was going to do with the body?

'When will you kids stop interfering and just let me get on with my job? You're forever bleating on about things, getting in my way. I don't know why I tolerate you.'

'I don't understand.' I come up, warily propping myself against my elbows, trying to transfer my weight as my shoulder protests with a whining creak. If that bat comes down on my head, I may not survive the next whack. Phoebe's going to have two dead bodies on her hands if that ambulance crew doesn't arrive shortly.

'You were never supposed to understand, you foolish young man.' He spits out the last word as though it was poison. 'It was bad enough Saul coming to live here with his girlfriend but when she left, he was supposed to go too. It wasn't meant to be this way. It was supposed to be all girls. And you had the gall to scare the latest one away.'

Warily, I push up a little more so I'm now resting on my hands, my mind whirling in different directions.

'What do you mean?' Can I keep him talking until Phoebe gets the police here? She's no idea this man is down here with me, and I hope to God she doesn't come back down to check on us without bringing the police with her, because I can just imagine the body count rising. 'I didn't know Saul moved in with his girl-friend. I thought he was engaged.'

The landlord stares at me as though I am shit on the bottom of his shoe.

'Saul only wheedled his way in because his girlfriend came to live here. Next thing we know, he's living here, she's left him, and there's virtually nothing I could do about it, but then it's had its advantages, him bringing in all these women. Some of them stay a night, others a few more. He certainly doesn't seem to be able to hang on to women and he's never bothered if he doesn't see them again.'

He lets out a wheezy little laugh. 'And believe me, there are quite a few of them that haven't been seen again.'

I can't disagree with him there. Easy come, easy go. But I still don't understand what he means.

'If it was supposed to be all girls, why did you let me move in?'

He snorts, letting go of the bat with one hand while he does a quick pick of his nose as though it's irritating him, wiping his finger against his trouser leg before taking up the two-handed stance again.

My muscles bunch in readiness. If I can only catch him off guard.

'There was a mistake. We thought you were a girl. Alex, you see. Could have been Alexandra. We were sloppy, got a little care-less, but it looks like we can kill two birds with one stone here.' He makes a strange cackling noise. 'Then we can get back to having an all-female household again. They are so much less trouble than you young men.'

We? I don't ask the question because I'm not sure how he'll respond. Is this a Gollum-type 'we'? Has the guy lost his marbles?

I shuffle until I'm sitting upright, my arms wrapped around my knees. I just need to buy more time, for me, for Saul. It doesn't matter what sort of prick he is, he doesn't deserve to die. And nor do I.

'Look—' I move my hand to appeal to him, but his fingers grip the handle of the bat even tighter, raising it while his knuckles turn white, making me wonder just what the trigger will be, because it's not a matter of whether he will swing that bat again, more, when he will. I just need to keep him talking. 'I don't even know your name.'

He sneers at me. 'No one does. Nobody bothers to find out. You're all the same, you lot. Don't give a damn.'

'I'm sorry.' I don't care what I say to him, how grovelling I appear, as long as I say something, keep him talking. 'What should I call you?'

He shrugs and makes a small swaying motion as though he's stepping up to the plate, having a small practice before the true swing. I know how hard he can hit. My arm hurts and I wouldn't be surprised to find it's fractured. My shoulder fared better but it burns like a bitch.

'You don't need to call me anything. There's no point.'

I nod in acknowledgement and shuffle again.

The moment those police burst through the cellar door, I'm going to launch myself at his knees and take him down. The most important thing, other than saving my life, is to get help for Saul and every minute we delay is a minute closer to his death.

I let my gaze drift past the landlord and terror sends icicles shooting through my veins. The dark chasm I thought I saw before is real. I knew there was something wrong with this room, just as I knew it about that other cellar all those years ago.

Funny how fear comes in different forms. There's no fear of this man standing over me. I know I have the physical ability to take him, just give me the opportunity. Unlike Saul, who never stood a chance, wouldn't have even seen his aggressor coming as he stabbed him in the back. A cowardly attack in anyone's eyes.

No, my deepest fear is what lies beyond the darkened doorway which seems to have slid open to reveal a room beyond.

I squeeze my eyes closed for a moment, determined not to allow the image to creep in, but it's no good. She's there, in the inky blackness, rolled up with her fine blonde hair poking from one end of the bodily fluid-soaked play rug, waiting for me to discover her.

'Alex.' Her soft voice whispers through my mind.

I swallow down my nausea and open my eyes.

'Why girls?'

He might as well tell me. There's no point in him keeping his secret. The game is up. I may be his prisoner, but I suspect he knows I have the upper hand. His skinny, emaciated body isn't up to taking on a full-grown man, unless he strikes from behind, like he did with Saul. But this time, he doesn't have a knife, and I'm facing him.

He shrugs, changes his grip on the bat as I make a minute move. Perhaps I shouldn't underestimate him. I narrow my eyes and wait. Does he think he has me?

'Girls?' I prompt when he gives no indication he's about to engage again.

'Girls.' He does that strange snort again, taking one hand off the bat to stick a finger up his nose. He wipes his hand on grubby trousers and changes his grip. 'Girls. They come here, then they leave. Never to be seen again.' He lets out a dark chuckle.

I glance past him to the opening. A doorway to hell. My worst nightmare come true. I can barely stand the thought of it, but I know at some point, I'll have to look in there. Unless the police arrive first. In which case I will happily walk away and leave them to their job.

Where the fuck are they?

I hold my breath for a moment, listening for movement upstairs. I never even heard Phoebe. She was silent in the dark. Where is she? Did she run from the house screaming, or is she sitting on the stairs listening in to our conversation as a witness, waiting for the emergency services to arrive?

'What do you do with them? These girls.'

I don't actually want to know, I just don't want him to stop talking either, because once he does, we're going to have to go to battle and I could do with another moment to centre myself.

I shuffle around onto my hip, make an overexaggerated groan as I raise one hand to the opposite shoulder. 'Fuck. That hurts.'

'I sell them.'

We speak almost at the same time so I'm not sure I've heard him right through the cloud of pain engulfing me. 'Sell them?'

'Yeah. You know, there's no money in property any more. Not if you're an honest landlord just trying to make a living. Thirty years ago, I bought this entire row of houses.' He swings the bat side to side as though indicating the row. 'One after the other. I did them up. They were almost derelict when I got hold of them, and look at them now. I poured every penny of my money into them.' He stabs the cricket bat at me, so close I dodge my head back and take a moment to wriggle around. This time he takes no notice. He's too wrapped up in his own life story.

'Do you know how much each one of these houses costs to maintain?'

I open my mouth and close it again as he takes one hand from the bat and lunges at me like it's a sword, barely missing my face as I scrabble back again.

'A fucking fortune, that's what. And then the Government, in their innate wisdom, decided we had to make safe these places we'd poured our money into. Mine were all safe, but I still had to change all the boilers because they were too old and no longer safe, according to the jobsworth inspector who called around after a complaint, at two and a half grand a pop. Twelve houses. Thirty grand. I couldn't afford it, so I had to sell four of them, but I got a pittance because the boilers weren't fucking compliant. That's what happens when the Government gets greedy. They take money from hard-working folk and make us suffer for their privileges.'

A soft groan comes from Saul and all I can think is, hang on in there, buddy. They won't be long. Surely they won't be long. Because I'm not sure how much longer I can listen to this pathetic little man whining about the cost of the upkeep of houses as an excuse for trafficking women. What planet is he on? No wonder Saul is groaning.

Lost in his own reverie, the landlord witters on. 'So then most of the money was taken in tax. I didn't know they were going to tax me on the profit from the sale of the houses. All I wanted was to use the money to invest in improving the remaining properties, but no. They fucking took damned near quarter of what was mine. That doesn't even take into account the money it cost to dispose of the sitting tenants who refused to move. They caused me more hassle than I can ever recover from, together with the price of those dickhead solicitors.'

His speech is getting faster, his tone more frenetic. He's crazy. Just off his head.

I don't care what his problems are with all his properties. He must be rolling in money, despite the rough, homeless look he sports, I assume for effect, so no one suspects him of anything.

Or perhaps his lack of personal hygiene is the root of all his issues.

I move closer to Saul, stretch out a hand and slip my fingers down his neck again. His pulse is getting weaker. It's not my imagination. His skin is cooling too, the colour leaching from it. He needs help. I can't wait much longer. I hope to God Phoebe has called the police. How long do they take?

'Then, just when you think you have everything straight, the Government goes and changes the rules again and add yet more legislation through the Renters' Rights Bill which has just come in, stopping me from raising the rent when I need to, and the fucking solicitors cost a small fortune just to enable me to keep my houses. The robbing bastards. The income from which barely covers the expenses these days, never mind earning me a living. Everyone wants so much more from me. Well, I need to take back.'

There are so many things I could say to him, because in general, he's talking garbage. He's a landlord, yes, and they have responsibilities, but not so many that he would be that broke. He's off his rocker.

He holds the bat and swings with both arms like he's just hit the cricket ball and is watching it fly into the distance.

'So, when I was made an offer, I couldn't refuse, could I?'

Something in the back of my mind sends out an alert. He's no longer prattling on about his houses. This is now the stuff I want to hear.

'What was the offer?' I drop my hand from Saul's neck and shuffle away.

'To supply girls.'

'To supply them? To whom? For what?' But I have a sickening feeling I already know.

He snorts and does his finger up his nose thing again.

'I don't ask questions. I don't want to know. All I know is I get them the girls, and they pay me the dosh. Cash in hand. No questions asked. No money for the Government to whip off me.'

'Are we talking people trafficking?' I'm not shocked. I'd already reached that conclusion.

He screws up his face, his wrinkles deepening until his skin resembles old leather, cracked and worn.

'If you want to call it that. It doesn't sound very nice, though. I'd prefer to call it supply and demand.' He lets out a short cackle in appreciation of his own dark humour.

'So, you take on new tenants, females, and then you entrap them. Sell them. Only I wasn't a girl and nor was Saul so it must have scuppered you in some ways.' I think of the other houses in the row. How many girls does he have in those?

'In many ways. As I say, Saul wasn't so much of a problem as he brought a number of girls here. No one even knew half of them had crossed the doorstep. Saul doesn't care, he simply wakes from a deep, satisfying sleep in the morning to find the girls gone. It never crossed his mind to question it. He's all too full of his own ego. Of course, we didn't take them all. We couldn't allow him to become a person of interest to the police. For him to be connected to their disappearances and thereby leading anyone to us. We left a few to return another day.'

My mind clings to the thought of Saul's deep sleep and I realise what he's saying.

'You drugged us?' I'm both stunned and somehow unsurprised. I knew there was something. It suddenly makes sense, my feeling of exhaustion and nausea, trying to shake off the sluggishness on a Saturday morning after the Friday night Saul parties.

The old boy's laughter is short and bitter. 'Of course. It had to be done. Not so much with you, but a few times when you couldn't be trusted to sleep through while the girls were moved.'

I think of Jill. Her sudden disappearance. Is that what happened to Michelle? To Nikki?

'How did you do it?' I ask, in a tone of wonderment I feel he's enjoying.

'Gas. When you were already asleep it was easy to pump just a little bit into your room through the air vent. It didn't take much and then I could check on you. You're a big guy, so is Saul. I've given him a little ketamine in the past. He'd never noticed the injection site in his armpit, but I considered you would. So we drugged your milk.' He shrugs, adjusting his grip again. 'It didn't work so well. You knew.'

I did know. I thought it was off even though it was well within date.

'So you pumped what through my air vent?'

'Isoflurane. It's more effective if you administer it through a mask, but it suited our purposes. It made you sufficiently unaware of what was going on around you.'

And gave me nightmares. But I'm not going to admit that to him.

'How many girls have you taken?'

He snorts and my muscles instinctively bunch, but his hands remain firmly on the cricket bat handle.

'More than ten?' I prompt.

He shrugs. 'I've lost count. Maybe five from this house. More from the others.'

'What do you do with them?' I want to know where Nikki has been shipped off to because I know I will never give up looking for her and once the police are aware, I'll expect their full back-up.

A small flash of irritation crosses his face to make me wonder what I've stumbled upon. Something he's evidently not happy with.

'Someone collects them.'

'Where do you keep them until they're collected?'

Now, it's pure annoyance creasing his brow and deepening the hollows in his cheeks. His dark eyes flash with aggression and he raises the bat. I tense, readying myself for the onslaught. He might be older than me, but those muscles are like finely honed elastic, and I think he's stronger than I've given him credit for. After all, he moves inert bodies around and from experience in the field, I know that's no mean feat.

'It's none of your business.'

But his head moves, and his eyes slide towards the dark chasm behind him as a flicker of interest dashes through me. Nikki said she'd heard tapping on the pipes one night. The washing machine and tumble dryer have been going so much. Is that to disguise noises?

I touch Saul and his body gives a soft tremor. I don't think he's even aware of my presence.

'Look, we need an ambulance. Saul's going to die if he's not seen to soon, and then you'll be imprisoned not just for people trafficking, but murder. That's got to be a much steeper sentence.'

Where the hell is the ambulance, the police? What is Phoebe doing?

Upstairs is silent and yet I know those floorboards creak whenever someone is on the move.

The guy spreads his feet and shrugs. 'I haven't killed Saul. And they're not going to catch me.'

'You bet your sweet life they are. The police are on their way right now.'

This time, instead of answering, the landlord lets out a raucous snort, raises his hand to his nose and I twist, throwing the whole weight of my body at his knees. The cricket bat comes down on my head and white sparks burst behind my eyes.

33

I'm half his age and twice his size, but fuck, that hurt! So did the next couple of thwacks. He certainly got the jump on me. My arm is numb from my shoulder to the tip of my fingers from where he walloped his bat against my collarbone. I swear I heard something crack.

My advantage is, he's on the floor and I scrabble up the length of his body like a freaking ninja spider, terrified he's going to land another blow and take my ear off. My head is spinning like a whirling dervish as I draw back and throw a punch at his jaw.

No longer numb, my hand vibrates as pain shoots from my knuckles.

'Fuck!'

The landlord's head hits the floor with a sickening thud and his grip on the bat slackens. I snatch it from his limp hand, come to my knees above him and, like him, take a double-handed grip on it, but I swing it like a golf club.

It smashes into the side of his face, blood, spit and snot spewing across the floor and up the wall in a wild spatter pattern that yields a certain satisfaction. There will be no covering this scene up.

Yellowed teeth which were possibly loose anyway scatter next to his ear while the other ear explodes from the impact of the bat. It takes a second to swell into a cauliflower as a trickle of blood makes its way down into his grubby shirt collar.

It's not like on TV, there's no glory in battering another person. I grunt as I stagger to my feet, using the bat to brace against. Every bone grinding, every muscle screaming.

I'm getting too old for this shit.

I stumble to the cellar stairs and yell up. 'Phoebe, have you called the police?'

'They're on their way. There's been a pile-up so they're having to go the long route. They've asked me to wait and let them in. Just in case—'

Her voice is clear as crystal, as though she's perched on the top step, but I see nothing through eyes blurred with pain.

'Okay. Tell them to hurry. I've got this bastard of a landlord down here. He's on the floor.'

There's a long pause.

'They're on their way.' Her voice is a quiet murmur.

There's no distant sound of sirens, but then again, perhaps down here it would be muffled anyhow.

I can barely speak as I raise my hand to my head and stumble back to where Saul has curled into a tighter ball. Shit, if they don't get here soon, I'm not sure he'll make it. There's nothing I can do for him, except maybe make him more comfortable.

I look in the tumble dryer and there's something in there. I grab the door and pull, reaching in to find a cosy throw, still warm, which will help stave off hypothermia. Phoebe might just kill me when she finds out, especially as it's about to be covered in blood. I stretch it out over Saul and reach in for a second one which I fold and place under his head. What else can I do? For the first time I feel genuinely helpless. What he needs is medical attention. Now. I don't have sufficient knowledge to even attempt anything.

Glancing over at the landlord, I decide there's nothing I can do for him either. It looks like a bloodbath in here and I'm pretty sure if this guy dies, the police are going to believe I've murdered both of them.

He's out cold and unlikely to move.

I don't even have Phoebe as a witness. She's seen none of it. I can only hope she heard it.

Straightening, I shuffle over to the gaping hole in the wall, my heart pounding, only now seeing it's a sliding door that covers what? A room? A corridor into the next house? There are no notches or handles so I wonder for a moment how it works. Then I realise it's electronic and it must have a remote somewhere.

I know I should leave this to the police and I'm probably spreading my DNA all over the place, but there's a draw to that cavern I can't resist. The image of a roll of carpet, fine hair flashes into my mind. I have to take a look.

I scrabble around in the old boy's pockets, and he doesn't make a move. Maybe I hit him too hard, but what is too hard when there's a man lying on the floor near to death and you're about to be next? I hope the police see it that way and side with me.

A small fob is in his front jeans pocket, almost like those ones for electric garage doors, which is essentially what this is.

I know the door is open now, but what I don't want is to accidentally get caught on the other side. In the pitch black. I don't know where this leads, but I'm going in.

Inky blackness beckons to me, and I have to stop momentarily, just to catch my breath. It's okay, the police are on their way, I reassure myself. Though God only knows how long they're going to be. It must have been twenty minutes or more since I sent Phoebe upstairs. Maybe she couldn't find Saul's phone and had to wait for her phone to charge a little now the power is back on before she could ring them. Whatever the reason, I'm not exactly pleased about this.

The bad man is poleaxed. I close my eyes and they spring open again immediately, just to dispel the image in my mind. Mum rolled in my play rug, dark patches staining it, her blonde hair sticking out of one end.

The image is still imprinted on my mind as I step forward.

This is not what I'm going to find. It can't happen again. Nikki must have had a better fate than that.

The moment I walk through, the atmosphere hits me in its claustrophobic confines and I freeze. There's something in here with me. Nothing I can put my finger on, just a presence I sense pressing the darkness down like a wet woollen blanket. My breathing becomes shallow as I touch the wall without turning my back on the dark.

There has to be a light in here. Surely with all this high technology for the sliding door, there must be a light. I let out a soft hum and step back into the cellar to stare at the fob. The image of a light bulb is on one tiny button and I press it.

Flickering comes from within the cave and I step inside, instantly consumed by the strange feeling that I'm not alone.

The light has a pale dullness to it, casting shadows around, but I can see now. Clear enough that my heart lurches as I clasp at my chest.

'Oh, dear God in heaven. What has he done?'

Rows of what looks like oversized dog crates line the small room, most of them empty, but in four of them, dark figures appear to be curled in the foetal position on their sides. Not dogs but humans, bedded down on what looks like the quilt cover sets I've seen in the washing machine. My stomach lurches.

In the fifth crate, the furthest away, something stirs.

A light scraping, a soft mewl followed by a voice constrained and scratchy.

'Cheeses, you took your time.'

I rush past the crates containing comatose bodies and crash to my knees in front of the dog crate.

'Nikki. Oh God, Nikki!'

Her forehead is pressed against the crate, huge eyes sunken into deep sockets staring at me. Pleading without words as though she can't believe I'm here. I'm real.

'It's me, Nikki. I've come for you.'

Relief floods her eyes a second before they close, tears squeezing from behind the lids to track down dirty cheeks and drip off her chin.

Her fingers wrap around the bars, clutching, dirt thick under nails that have grown long and jagged. Six weeks she's been here, by my calculations.

Her small face is filthy and ravaged, eyes dull. But there's hope lurking behind the sadness as though she wants to believe I'm real but can't quite convince herself.

I raise both hands and gently rest my fingers on hers, press my forehead to hers with only the bars between us.

'You're safe. I've got you now. Phoebe has called the police and ambulance and they are on their way. All I need to do is get you out of here.'

I pull back, ready to break her free of this crate, and she gasps, clutching for my fingers. 'No!' Her voice drops to a frantic whisper as though she's desperate for me to listen.

'She's behind you!'

34

I freeze. Every muscle bunching.

In a split second, every suppressed thought I've had in the last few minutes rush in.

How stupid am I?

The landlord kept saying 'we'. I thought in his madness he had developed a Gollum syndrome, was using the royal 'we'. It seems I was wrong.

Now I know who it is.

There is no ambulance on its way. No police. I am alone, except for Nikki and these other poor souls.

The space between my shoulders flexes in anticipation of a blade plunging deep into my back as I stare into Nikki's eyes. I can't fail her. I can't fail Julia. My whole life has led to this moment. There was nothing I could do to protect my mum. I was too small, too weak against too big a foe, but that's not the case now, and I'm not going to let it happen again. These women deserve more from me.

I push upright, whirling to face her at the same time, keeping low in expectation of the attack.

With a hideous, ear-splitting banshee wail, Phoebe rushes towards me, arm raised, hand grasped around a knife, the blade long and thin.

I barely have time to acknowledge the wildfire in her eyes as she launches herself, knife slashing, at me. There's no room to dodge back, so I leap to the side, but not quick enough as the blade slices down my left arm, ripping through the sleeve from shoulder to wrist, leaving a long gash in my flesh. Blood blooms in a rivulet of hot agony.

My howl of pain matches her one of fury as inertia carries her forward and she stumbles, falling against the top of the crate Nikki is imprisoned in. The blade slips through the bars and Nikki screeches as she flings herself on her back away from it.

I take that brief window of opportunity and throw myself on top of Phoebe, grasping her hand in one fist and jerking her head back with the other. Her shriek almost bursts my eardrums as she twists towards me, teeth gnashing as though she's going to rip my cheek off. Given half the chance, I wouldn't put it past her.

Her knife hand jams in the bars and then she hauls on it again just as Nikki reaches for the blade from inside the crate.

'No!' I bellow, imagining her hand being ripped to shreds.

I throw my whole weight against Phoebe again, slamming the side of her head against the crate. She's like a wildcat caught in a snare as she wriggles in my clutch, bucking to try and throw me off, her legs thrashing against mine, her arse thrusting back as she surges against me, narrowly missing my balls and catching the top of my thigh instead. It hurts like hell, but I'm not letting go. My fist is wrapped in her faded green hair and I yank her head back again, pause momentarily. It's instinct.

I've never so much as raised my fist to a woman in my life. Having witnessed my dad smack women around, it's something I've promised myself I would never do. This is no woman, though

– this is a monster, a parasite who has been feeding off other women, throwing them to the wolves for God only knows what reason. Surely, it can't just be for the money.

This time, when I smash her face-first into the crate, I hear the crack of her nose, and she lets out a feral snarl. I slam her wrist against the bars and she drops the knife. Nikki throws herself to one side as it clatters through, missing her leg by a millimetre.

Phoebe kicks out backwards at me. Her foot slams into my knee and I grunt with pain, doubling over. She's like a slippery eel as she flips over and wriggles from my grasp. She grabs my hair, virtually ripping it from my scalp, all the time her screams blaring like a warning siren until I think my ears might bleed.

I've underestimated this woman from the word go. She may not be big, but she's wild and feisty and what I mistook for plumpness seems to be pure muscle. The size of her makes it difficult to pin her down. She's a street fighter, and that's not what I do.

Tears course down my face as she rips a handful of hair from my head and then goes for my eyes, her fingers gouging as she wraps her legs around my waist. The shock of it is, she's not trying to escape, she's going full out, determined to kill me.

I whirl around on the spot as she clings like an octopus, trying to throw her off, but there's no escaping her.

I fling her onto her back on the top of the crate, desperate for her to let go. I grab her by the shoulders and ram her down, just trying to free myself from the grip her legs have around my waist, squeezing the air from my lungs. There seems to be no end to her strength as she almost climbs up me like a monkey, going for my eyes again.

There's no offence going on in my actions, it's all defence.

With a determination born of sheer panic, I throw her back down on top of the crate again.

There's a strange ripping noise and Phoebe grunts.

Then everything goes still.

There's an uncanny silence.

Phoebe's body freezes and she stares into my eyes, hers shot through with tiny spider veins. The fury in her face drops away and she opens her mouth to speak.

A thin line of blood trickles from the corner of her mouth and she stutters in a small breath as though anything more would be too much.

Confused, I slowly peel myself away from the woman, my own breath wheezing from my chest.

I skim my gaze over her and only when I see a short, sharp piece of material and blood-covered metal protruding from her chest does the penny drop. I unravel her arms from around me and gently place them by her sides as her legs loosen their grip and flop down to dangle off the side of the crate. Her unnaturally slack limbs make her look like an abandoned ragdoll.

Her eyes are wide and staring and one tear rolls from the corner to run down her temple into her garish hair. She draws in a crackling breath and judders it out again.

I step away. Numb.

Nikki is sitting cross-legged in the crate, both hands still gripping the shaft of the knife, which is embedded deep into Phoebe's back, the steady drip of blood streaking down her left cheek from the body lying across the bars above her. She blinks at me, offering up a watery smile. 'You came. I knew you would. You saved me.'

I move to one side and crouch down so I'm face to face with her.

'It was you who saved me, this time,' I whisper. Our fingers loop through each other's around the bars for a moment, both streaked with blood from each of our attackers. There are no more words to be spoken.

I pull myself upright, shock slowing me down, making me stiff, but there is so much more to do.

There's a stirring from the next crate along and it takes me a moment to recognise her.

'Jill.'

Tears streak her filthy face and she offers up a wordless, wobbly smile and a slow nod as though anything more would be too much.

I glance around, but the other three are sleeping. I assume they've been given some kind of drug to knock them out.

Phoebe's phone lies face down on the floor where it must have dropped when she launched herself at me. I pick it up, relieved to see the case has protected it and hold it over her face to unlock the screen before her lifeforce seeps from her.

I look at the signal, but it's weak here in this cavern. I know if I step out into the cellar there's a full signal.

As if anticipating my move, Nikki reaches up, her fingers curling around the bars of the crate as she crouches in the near corner, as far away from Phoebe as possible, knees pulled up to her chest. 'Don't leave me.' Her voice is rusty and hoarse with fear.

There's a hollow in the pit of my stomach.

I don't want to leave her, but getting help is more important than freeing her right now.

'I'll be back. I need to call for help and find something to break you free.'

'Her dad—'

I turn back to her, narrowing my eyes. 'What? Whose dad?'

'Phoebe's dad keeps the keys.'

I do a slow turn towards the doorway, my mouth dropping open. You've got to be shitting me. 'He's her dad? The old man?' Surely to God he's too old.

I twist my head to look at Nikki again. 'The landlord? Are you sure?'

She nods. 'I heard them talking.'

'Okay. He's through there.' I point with the phone.

She shies away, eyes wide with horror.

'It's okay. I knocked him out.' Felled him, more like. I offer up a quick, bitter smile which I hope is reassuring but know really that it falls far from that. 'I'll get the keys and be back.'

She looks at the open doorway and back to me, giving a small nod of acquiescence.

As I dash through, the old guy is just staggering to his feet, one hand held to his bloodied head as he turns in a circle as though looking for something on the floor. Without hesitation or further thought, I pick up the cricket bat, weigh it in my hand and slug him once more.

He doesn't even see the hit coming as his body almost somersaults backwards and he lands flat out, eyes closed.

'Bastard.' There's not an iota of sympathy in my heart.

I dig in his pocket and find the bunch of keys, barely taking any notice as a grunt of pain comes from him.

I dial 999 and wait. When they answer, the best I can manage as an introduction is, 'You're not going to believe this.'

35

I thought it would be noisy in the middle of the night on a hospital ward, but it's surprisingly quiet. Each one of the night angels who come in to take obs glide by, making barely a sound. There's just the low-level buzz of dim lighting as they check on one or other of the patients, the soft expulsion of air from the blood pressure machines.

I'm sitting in a chair next to Nikki's bed, considered well enough to be discharged from hospital, but reluctant to leave her side. I told them we were related. That I'm her brother. There's something inside of me though calling bullshit on that statement. I don't feel like her brother. I haven't felt that way for some time.

That's the reason I left home. The reason I barely come back.

Because what I feel for Nikki is not brotherly love.

I move my arm and wince at the stiffness. They've bandaged me from shoulder to wrist, having first stitched the deepest section of my wound at the fleshiest part of my arm and plied me with enough painkillers to floor an ox. Still, here I am, unable to leave her side, knowing Julia will be another forty minutes before she arrives.

Her voice trembled with fear and doubt when I let her know I'd found Nikki, and she was almost in the car before I'd finished telling her. The details are something she'll hear once she arrives. She needs to see her daughter is safe first, hold her in her arms, before she hears the sordid story.

I tip my head back against the chair and close my eyes, drifting in and out of consciousness, the painkillers making me woozy, although I'm reluctant to sleep in case the nightmares close in on me.

I blink and look around me, knowing I did sleep, but not for how long.

The ward is dedicated to those who survived their ordeal. Barely able to walk from being kept so long in those cramped dog crates, each one of these victims has a different version of the same event. All of them from my house share except one. The police were searching the cellar for further captives, but I have a feeling that was all. It was certainly enough. Even one was one too many.

There's a police officer stationed outside the ward door. If I lean to one side, I can see the top of his balding head through the small window.

Mostly, these young women were unable to answer questions posed by the police officers. Partly because they were in shock, but mostly because they had all been drugged. It's going to be an uphill struggle for each of them to be weaned off whatever drug it was they gave them. Nikki has been on it for six weeks, ever since she was taken. Two of the other girls, Michelle and Daisy, for even longer. They'd been kept in the dark, their crates covered in throws or bedlinen so they weren't aware of each other's presence for some time.

This is what I heard as I held Nikki's hand while the police questioned her. Exhaustion had taken her down before we heard it all, but I feel sure she has more to tell.

My gaze flickers to the door as I see movement there. I come to my feet, tears filling my eyes as Julia flows into the room, anxiety pulsing from her as she rushes to my side, her arms wrapping around me, holding me gently as though I might break and truthfully, I possibly could. Silent sobs are muffled by her neck as my whole body is racked with grief, horror and relief.

Nikki could well have been dead, but in my heart, I knew it wasn't possible.

Whether you believe in the paranormal or not, when I was a boy, instinct told me my mum was dead. It was just a matter of finding her body.

In Nikki's case, it was more a race against time because I knew with every fibre of my being she was still alive.

Julia releases me from her embrace, stroking away the tears from my cheeks with shaking fingers before her gaze roams over her daughter.

She sinks into the chair I've vacated as though her bones have melted. She reaches out to take Nikki's hand I was holding until a moment ago.

I stand for a moment, undecided whether to give them some privacy.

'Sit down, Alex,' Julia tells me, waving vaguely in the direction of another chair by the side of one of the sleeping girls' beds.

There are no other visitors. There won't be until the police question these women, find out who they are and track down their relatives, because mostly they weren't in a fit state to speak. One woman appears catatonic, and my heart breaks for the family she will have looking for her.

I drag a chair over one-handed and sink into it. Exhaustion and codeine are taking their toll and I close my eyes, slipping into a light doze where I'm aware of the movement of the night nurse, the slow, deep breathing of Nikki, and the tears Julia sheds when she thinks no one is listening.

Funny, I never give the others a thought until the police arrive the next morning. Not truly. They are just there, in the same room, sleeping.

Sergeant Billie O'Connelly, which I thought was a joke at first, sits in a chair opposite me in a quiet corner of the hospital canteen. I daresay it's not always quiet, but this is shift changeover and we've struck lucky.

I realise it's been almost twenty-four hours since I've eaten and I devour my sausage sandwich, despite the bread being plastic, the sausage rubber and the whole thing reheated in a microwave. It doesn't matter because I've disguised it all in, would you believe, Daddy's Sauce which smothers any taste and drips out the end onto my plastic recycled plate.

'Alex.'

I realise I've barely taken notice of the sergeant's words as I lean back and pick up my coffee, taking a slurp before transferring my attention to her. Under any other circumstances I would say she was pretty, bordering on beautiful, with large hazel eyes gazing at me with soft empathy.

But I'm not interested. Not any longer. Not in anyone else.

'Sorry, what did you say?'

'Your sister—'

'She's not my sister.'

The officer looks confused as she glances down at her notes.

'Not really. I was fostered by her mum, Julia, when I was eleven, almost twelve, but we're not related. Not by blood.'

I don't know why I feel the need to stress this point.

Who am I kidding? Of course I do!

'Nikki, then,' the police officer compromises. 'She said she'd overheard, hmmm—' She checks her notes. 'She'd overheard Phoebe and her dad—'

'The landlord,' I verify, in case there is any doubt.

'The landlord.' She nods. 'Nikki said she'd heard them panicking the other day. Do you know anything about this?'

I shake my head. 'No. I never even knew Phoebe was related to the landlord until Nikki told me last night. They looked nothing alike, acted nothing alike.'

Sergeant O'Connelly nods. She's already questioned Nikki while I returned to the house to collect my clothes from an officer who wouldn't let me enter as it was a crime scene, but who bagged me a pair of underpants, some joggers and a sweatshirt to keep me going. I had to settle for a quick shower in the hospital using a sachet of shampoo and a disposable toothbrush with toothpaste that tasted like sick, but was kindly donated by one of the lovely nurses who took pity on me.

Julia hasn't left Nikki's side yet, except for a loo visit and that was only once. She must have a bladder of steel. Or the determination of a mother in need.

Just as I think that, Julia herself walks through the door and heads straight for us. I stand as she approaches and pull out a chair, but she doesn't sit down as I sink back into mine.

'Is everything okay?' The dark rumble of concern churns in my stomach.

'Nikki wants you.'

I look to the officer and back at Julia, my mum. There's no contest. I swipe a thin, cheap napkin over my chin to remove any grease and sauce, gently patting around the split in my lip and come to my feet, grunting as the stretch of my arm sends a spike of pain shooting through me.

Sergeant O'Connelly follows suit. 'We can talk up there.'

I shrug. 'I can only tell the story from my side of the wall.' I blink.

A rolled-up rug, dark stains, blonde hair.

My breath shudders in.

Julia's gaze slides to meet mine, hers filled with horror at the knowledge of what is going through my mind as though she's only just made the connection. She reaches out a hand, touches the back of mine with fingers that are icy.

With a fleeting glance at the exchange between us, Sergeant O'Connelly pulls out her force radio. 'I'll be with you shortly. You go on up.'

Julia twines her fingers in mine and we track our way through straight corridors and up long flights of stairs, back down the corridor in the opposite direction, along another wing.

Nikki is propped up in bed, eyes dull until she sees us. Her smile is bright, but pain loiters behind it.

'You look better.' I'm not lying. Compared to yesterday, she looks a million times better.

'I had a shower. Washed my hair. Brushed my teeth.' Her smile wavers. 'I feel almost human again.'

I nod. Exhaustion hits me and I slump into the nearest chair. It's big, high-backed and makes a whooshing noise as my backside hits it.

Nikki reaches out for me to take her hand. 'You saved me.'

My heart is exploding.

There are tears in Julia's eyes and I'm not sure I can bear this collective pain.

I lean back, my head flopping against the chair, my arm stretched so I don't lose contact. We sit in silence, Julia in the next chair.

When Sergeant O'Connelly returns, Nikki drops my hand

and shuffles up in the bed, tugging at the neckline of the hospital gown to loosen it from her neck.

There are marks of concern on the officer's face that weren't there a moment ago.

'Is something wrong? What's happened?' I can't help the worry in my voice as I skim my gaze around at the rest of the women in the ward, most of them sleeping again after, it appears, like Nikki, they've had showers as they all have damp hair wisping around clean faces.

Sergeant O'Connelly glances around and then grabs a small plastic chair for herself and sits on the opposite side of the bed from Julia and me.

'I need to inform you that Phoebe Reynolds died an hour ago due to injuries sustained in the fight. It seems the knife pierced her heart and despite their best efforts, there was nothing the surgeons could do for her. I am very sorry.'

I lower my head because of all the feelings rioting inside of me, sorrow is not one of them. Pain pulses through my face where she gouged at my eyes, scratched my skin, punched me, kicked me, and I lift my hand to the bald spot above my ear. I raise my head and look the officer in the eye.

'She was a madwoman. Feral.'

'Tell me.'

'I don't know where to start.'

'From the beginning.'

36

PRESENT DAY – THURSDAY, 25
SEPTEMBER 2025, 4.20 P.M. – ALEX

Saul's normally healthy glow has been replaced by a sickly pallor. Purple bruising circles his eyes and his lips are chalky white. There are a multitude of wires plumbed into him and connected to a machine making faint beeping noises, and he's been in intensive care for the past three days, but he's survived. He's alive.

'Mate,' he whispers, his voice old and raspy, as I slide into the chair at his bedside. 'You saved my life.'

I want to say it was nothing. I did nothing. The truth of it is I didn't save his life – the doctors and nurses did that – but I did stop him from dying.

Instead of arguing the toss, I incline my head in acknowledgement.

'The police told me Phoebe's dead.' His eyes fill with tears and as he blinks, one slides down his cheek. His hands lie limp by his sides and I suspect he doesn't even have the energy to wipe away his tear. 'Crazy fuck.' He shakes his head. 'I can't live with myself, mate. All those girls. She used to encourage me, you know. Make out that it was a bit of fun for her, a laugh to see how many women I could bring home. Two of those girls down there were ones I'd dated. Jesus Christ.' He does lift one hand now and pinches his nose between thumb and forefinger as he squeezes his eyes closed against the pain. 'I had no idea.' His voice breaks on a sob. 'The damage I've done. Those girls they might still be searching for. I feel responsible. I'd lived there a year.'

I find I can't offer up any reassurances because he was a prick. Maybe this lesson in life will turn him around, but it's not my business. We were never friends, but it doesn't mean I don't care what happens to him.

Despite everything, he did not kidnap these women. It's not his fault. His crime was simply his ego. How was he to know what was to become of those girls?

'Did you know the landlord was her dad?'

His hand flops back down to his side and he lets out a pained grunt. 'No. I had no idea. They never once mentioned any connection. I told the police. The only thing I found a bit odd was that all the communication was done between those two. Light bulb changes, broken fridge, blocked toilets. I didn't care, because Phoebe saw to it all. I thought it was just one of her little quirks. That she wanted to be in charge. I was happy for her to be, it meant less aggro for me. But the amount of times I called that old man a twat in front of her and never once did she admit to their relationship.' He looks at me. 'How is he? The old twat?'

I nod. 'He's alive. I gave him a bit of a headache though and apparently, he has swelling on the brain, but he's awake and aware.'

Saul snorts and for the first time his face flushes with a little colour.

'The police are just preparing to arrest him,' I say to reassure him.

'Arrest him? Didn't they do that straight away?'

I shake my head and explain it the way they told me. 'There's no point in arresting someone who is comatose as the moment you do, the clock is ticking and you have to get all your ducks in line before the klaxon goes off and you either have to release them after twenty-four hours, charge them, or apply to court for an extension. So they wait until he's fully compos mentis and in the meantime he's been under twenty-four-hour guard.'

'Have they told him Phoebe is dead?'

I shake my head. 'I don't know.' It doesn't really interest me. The landlord's pain is definitely not my concern.

'How are you feeling?' I change the subject.

Saul gives me a weak smile. 'Like shit.' He raises the hand with the catheter attached. 'I needed a blood transfusion, and they still have me on a drip. I was bloody lucky, though. Another inch lower and a longer knife, I would have suffered the same fate as Phoebe.'

I shudder and he nods, affirming the situation. 'No major organs damaged, but I was in surgery for almost eight hours while they extracted that bloody knife and tied off veins and shit. Thanks, mate. I could have bled out on the cellar floor if it wasn't for you. They tell me you did a sterling job saving me from hypothermia as well.'

We're silent for a moment and when his voice comes again, it's weaker this time. 'I don't remember much. The electrics tripped again, I thought because of all the bloody washing and drying Phoebe kept doing, which the police presume was to disguise any noises coming from the hidden room. Anyway, I went down into the cellar, flipped the switches and went to walk away. I heard a scraping noise, turned and saw that bloody door sliding open, the power outed again, and it was the last thing I remember. Piecing it together, the police think Phoebe came down behind me, not realising I was there, triggering the remote-control door. The police suggested it could have been that door that tripped the power. She was armed with the knife and just went for me. According to what the landlord told the police, they'd been operating under a huge burden of stress waiting for someone to come and take the girls away. Something had happened further up the chain of command and communications had broken down. They were supposed to have collected the girls four weeks before, never any more than two girls at a time. The crates were loaded and they were starting to panic. They weren't averse to trafficking the girls, but they wanted nothing to do with keeping them so long and risking their demise, according to what the police have ascertained. It appears all they wanted was to get rid of the girls.'

As the thought strikes me, I stare at him in horror. 'Maybe that's why Phoebe had the knife... to kill the girls?'

He nods. 'The police have suggested that, but her dad is adamant she wouldn't hurt a fly.'

It's my turn to snort as I raise my hand to my face where the bruising is in full burgundy flush four days after the event. 'Having been on the receiving end of her ire, I can confirm she was mad as a box of frogs, and if she could have killed me with her bare hands, she would have.'

My eye sockets throb like she has her fingers inside them again.

I look at Saul and he seems to have wilted.

I come to my feet and touch his shoulder.

'Good luck, mate. I'll see you around.'

He gives a weak nod, his eyes sliding closed. 'I don't know where, neither of us has anywhere to live. My fiancée dumped me the moment I told her the truth.' He bows his head. 'I thought she would have stuck by me, but her mum insisted she have nothing to do with me.'

I have no words. What did he expect? Although I can't help the stir of pity for him.

I pat him on the back of the hand, turn my back and walk away. I don't like to tell him I'll be going back with my family. Back home with the two women I love most in this world. The two women who are packed and ready to leave just as soon as I say my goodbyes to all the women I helped to save.

Jill, in particular, was very grateful. I know because she sent me an email to tell me as much.

37

PRESENT DAY – SIXTEEN MONTHS LATER – ALEX

Weak winter sunshine filters through the tall floor-to-ceiling windows of the old Mansion House which is bedecked in white chrysanthemum and swathes of vast greenery. Simplistic, I am told, but to me it is everything a man could wish for.

My heart overflows with happiness as I stare out over the vine-yard rolling away from me down the side of the hill that the mansion is perched on, the vines resting in their shallow beds of snow, hiber-nating until spring arrives to encourage them to bloom. Just as my Nikki will bloom with all the tender care and love we bestow on her.

I turn, looking at candlelight flickering along the aisle, the guiding lights leading her to me.

It's a small affair.

Nikki is still getting her strength back from her ordeal and so are the other four young women who have come along for the celebration. There's a bond between them that formed in that soulless pit, and they will forever be tied by it as survivors. That's going to help when the court case comes up as the landlord decided to plead not guilty, placing the blame firmly on his dead daughter. What human would do that? A true monster, through and through.

We still have a way to go, but I'm here waiting for Nikki to join me. To stand by my side. She's undergoing therapy, but more than anything, she needs her family to strengthen her.

Saul messaged me to say he's taken a new job closer to his family. He wants to leave the past behind him and swears he's a reformed character. Personally, I have my doubts because he's already talking about dating one of his many childhood sweethearts. But that's his life and is no concern of ours now.

His Majesty's Prison Belmarsh wrote to let me know Dad had died. There was no sense of loss, and I didn't feel the need to attend his funeral.

They say blood is thicker than water, but they are wrong. So wrong. This is my family, right here. It is all I need.

The irony of it is, if Dad hadn't murdered my mum and left her all alone in the dark cavern in the cellar, would the possibility ever have occurred to me that just to be in the same house Nikki disappeared from would lead me to her? Somehow, I knew that was where I needed to be.

In the end, I didn't save Nikki, we saved each other.

Julia catches my eye from the other end of the aisle and I stand tall, shoulders back, as haunting music swells, the guests come to their feet and turn. I remember last night in the dining room when she made her way across the room to join me. I'd wrapped her into my embrace, this small, delicate woman who is now about to truly become my mum through marriage.

She leaned out of the hug and touched my face with cool fingers and a wide smile.

'I always knew you were meant for each other.'

I knew it too. From the first moment I met Nikki. If you

believe in fate, in love at first sight, we were destined for each other.

I can't help the wide smile that breaks out on my face as Nikki, resplendent in a sleek white silk wedding dress, enough to take my breath away, steps into the aisle. She links her arm through her mum's and they set off together towards me. Each of them elegant and proud, heads held high.

We are, all of us, survivors of the most horrific ordeals, and yet it has led us to this.

We are family.

* * *

MORE FROM DIANE SAXON

Another book from Diane Saxon, *A Stranger in the Family*, is available to order now here:

https://mybook.to/AStrangerBackAd

ACKNOWLEDGEMENTS

It's been a tough year or so for our family. Not only have we lost my mother-in-law, Betty Parkes, but also our handsome black Labrador, Beau to cancer, our regal cat, Sam (Salmon) at the age of twenty-one and most recently our incredible and beautiful Skye at the age of fifteen. Her death was particularly hard as it has left our usually busy home empty of the tippity-tap of nails on the tiled floors.

Those of you who have read my DS Jenna Morgan series will also know that Skye was my inspiration for Jenna's very important sidekick, Domino. A stunning Dalmatian who played a huge role in my series. The name and sex was changed to protect the not so innocent Skye.

I've never known a dog with such a big personality. From the day we picked her up at nine weeks old when the breeder told us she'd escaped the night before and gone partying with her mum, and did we really want her?

Well, of course we did.

She was so special, and maybe without her, I would not have come over to the dark side to write psychological thrillers. We often said she was the reason I had a desire to kill.

We had fifteen years of pure love and entertainment.

She has left an enormous hole in our lives and so it also appears in the lives of so many of my followers on Facebook who were devastated by her loss. Strange how one dog could have such a wonderful and positive effect on so many lives.

As always, I have a list of people I'd like to thank. There are so many these days to whom I am so grateful, for their support in all manner of ways. If I've missed anyone, I apologise.

For some time now, I have gathered names of real people who attend my talks, and my book release parties, both on Zoom and in person. I hold competitions for them and pick out a name or two on the understanding that the character I create can be anything from murderer to murdered, dog-walker to police officer. Good, or bad.

It's never easy to choose names for characters, so, to these wonderful people who throw themselves at my mercy, I am exceedingly grateful. Not everyone immediately gets their name in my next book, because I sometimes have something much more in mind for them...

A special 'thank you' to Alex Whittles who I pressurised into allowing me to use his name as I find decent men's names hard to come by. My audience are predominantly women. His is a good, strong name.

A big thank you to Nikki Fletcher who won the competition on this occasion to be featured in my book, but also a mention to the lovely Nikki Swallow who so desperately wanted her name included – so here's a mention in any case.

One of my other fun facts is introducing 'items' that are picked by my audiences.

So, thanks to the imagination of these people:

A camper van – Sarah Oakes

Shoelaces – Keith Roberts

I write these items down on my whiteboard and give them very little thought until my subconscious drags them out of my mind and plants them appropriately inside my manuscript.

I also have the following to thank, as always:

For the wonderful support of Andi Miller and her Facebook group, Books with Friends.

To my amazing family, Andy, Laura and Meghan, Stephen and Matthew.

To my sister Margaret, as always, for reading through my manuscripts and loving every story I write.

Thank you to Francesca Best, my editor at Boldwood Books, who is massively supportive and has just renewed my contract for another four psychological thrillers. She had a great many suggestions and tales of living in shared accommodation, of which I used some, and others made me laugh.

A thank you also to Gary Jukes, who smooths out any remaining wrinkles in my manuscript and whom I have found to be so observant that I requested him to proofread my last four novels. Long may that continue, as I have already flagged him for my next book.

And lastly, thank you to all my readers. Without you, I would be writing solely for myself.

ABOUT THE AUTHOR

Diane Saxon is the author of bestselling psychological thrillers including *My Mother's Lies*, and a bestselling crime series featuring recurring heroine DS Jenna Morgan. She is married to a retired policeman and lives in Shropshire.

Download your exclusive bonus content from Diane Saxon here:

Visit Diane's website: www.dianesaxon.com

Follow Diane on social media:

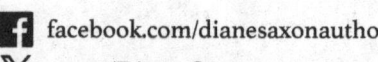 facebook.com/dianesaxonauthor

x.com/Diane_Saxon

instagram.com/DianeSaxonAuthor

ALSO BY DIANE SAXON

DS Jenna Morgan Series

Find Her Alive

Someone's There

What She Saw

The Ex

Standalone Novels

My Little Brother

My Sister's Secret

The Stepson

The Good Twin

My Mother's Lies

The Quiet Wife

My Missing Sister

A Stranger in the Family

THE *Murder* LIST

**THE MURDER LIST IS A NEWSLETTER
DEDICATED TO SPINE-CHILLING
FICTION AND GRIPPING
PAGE-TURNERS!**

**SIGN UP TO MAKE SURE YOU'RE ON
OUR HIT LIST FOR EXCLUSIVE DEALS,
AUTHOR CONTENT, AND
COMPETITIONS.**

**SIGN UP TO OUR
NEWSLETTER**

BIT.LY/THEMURDERLISTNEWS

Boldwood

Boldwood Books is an award-winning fiction publishing company seeking out the best stories from around the world.

Find out more at www.boldwoodbooks.com

Join our reader community for brilliant books, competitions and offers!

Follow us
@BoldwoodBooks
@TheBoldBookClub

Sign up to our weekly deals newsletter

https://bit.ly/BoldwoodBNewsletter